Dear Reader,

On December 22, 2020, I received an unexpected gift for Christmas—I tested positive for COVID-19. To be honest, I was pretty shocked! I didn't feel terrible. I only had a little cough and a slight headache. I probably wouldn't have even thought about getting tested if our daughter wasn't pregnant. In any case, twelve hours after getting tested, I received a text with the news. Of course, that meant my husband, Tom, had to get a test, too . . . and we had to tell our kids we might have transmitted the virus to them.

Over the next two days, Tom awaited his results (he also tested positive), the kids got tested (they were negative), and I learned how to get groceries delivered to the house. Then reality set in. We were going to be quarantined for Christmas. I'm usually a pretty positive person, and I kept reminding myself that our children were okay, that neither Tom nor I were in the hospital, and that we had exchanged gifts with the kids a week before. I had even turned in my last manuscript that was due for the year (this very book!) a month previously. There were many things to be thankful for!

But I must admit that it was a hard holiday to get through. I was tired, I missed going to church, and I pouted when our neighbors left us Christmas goodies on our front porch but I didn't have anything to give in return.

My husband made the best of things by watching movies and a couple of series on Netflix. I read. Oh my word, did I read a lot of books! I read hardcover books I'd bought but never started, Kindle books that looked fun and would hopefully provide three or four hours of escape, but most of all, I read books I had already read before. I probably have about thirty favorite books that I reread again and again. Their happy endings and uplifting messages never fail to provide me with comfort. Reading those treasured books felt like being reunited with good friends.

My love for books is the reason I enjoyed writing the Berlin Bookmobile series so much. I've always been grateful for the gift of reading. I've also been so thankful to the librarians and booksellers who make sure books get into readers' hands.

I have a feeling I'll one day look back on our COVID Christmas with a bit of fondness. Unlike some other Christmases, the day wasn't hectic or exhausting. Instead, it was filled with gratitude, appreciation for our family and friends, and quiet moments spent in prayer. I'll always remember the daily emails and texts from my siblings, the kind words of our neighbors and friends back in Ohio, and how content I was to simply sit on the couch with Tom and a dog or two.

Only the Lord knows what next year's Christmas will bring. All I know is that no matter what new "unexpected gift" I receive, I'm going to remember to give thanks and treasure the memories.

Thank you for picking up this book. I hope you enjoy it, and I wish you the happiest of holidays.

Merry Christmas,
Shelley Shepard Gray

"Shelley has another winner with *A Perfect Amish Romance*. I loved getting to know these well-written characters and reading about their romance and faith journeys. Shelley's fans will be pleased with this sweet story, and without a doubt she will win over new readers, too!"

—Kathleen Fuller, bestselling author of
The Innkeeper's Bride

"Enjoyable . . . Readers will be delighted by Sarah Anne's gentle matchmaking . . . Each of the main characters undergoes realistic personal evolutions as they are shaped by transformative powers of love, hope, and faith. Gray's fans will love this quiet, endearing tale."

—*Publishers Weekly*

AN AMISH SURPRISE

"Shelley Shepard Gray never shies away from tackling hard subjects in her novels, yet she does so with a winsome touch. In *An Amish Surprise*, Gray shows the effect of infertility on a young couple, adds in the strain of raising foster children, and finishes it off with a charming late-in-life romance. Don't miss this gem of a book—it's a story to remind us that happily ever afters can and do happen, at any age."

—Suzanne Woods Fisher, bestselling author of
Mending Fences

THE WALNUT CREEK SERIES
THE PATIENT ONE

"Gray tells a beautiful story of friendship, love, and truth born out of pain and grief. This story reminds us to hold those we love close."

—Rachel Hauck, *New York Times* bestselling author of *The Wedding Dress*

"Gray has created an endearing cast of characters . . . that both delights and surprises—and kept me thinking about the story long after I turned the last page. Bravo!"

—Leslie Gould, #1 bestselling and Christy Award–winning author

"A pleasing story about recovering from grief and a solid beginning for a new series."

—*Publishers Weekly*

"Like sunshine breaking through clouds . . . readers who love Amish stories and/or Christian fiction are sure to take pleasure in following the saga of this wonderful group of friends [who] learn to support each other and follow their hearts as they attempt to discern God's will in their lives."

—*Fresh Fiction*

THE PROTECTIVE ONE

"A slow-burning, enjoyable romance . . . Embedded in this quaint story is a poignant message about the importance of community, compassion, and doing what's right rather than what's easy."

—*Publishers Weekly*

"Gray deftly weaves the threads of abuse, friendship, love, and faith into a thought-provoking, emotional story."

—Patricia Davids, *USA Today* bestselling author of *The Wish*

"Filled with heartbreaking and uplifting moments, this love story stars Elizabeth Anne, or 'E.A.,' as she reevaluates her life . . . Now, E.A. must go on a heart-opening journey that may lead her to everything she's been searching for."

—*Woman's World*

THE TRUSTWORTHY ONE

"Gray's biblical themes are nuanced and well integrated into the narrative."

—*Publishers Weekly*

"Hope is found in unexpected places as this sweet Amish love story unfolds."

—*Woman's World*

SHELLEY SHEPARD GRAY

A CHRISTMAS COURTSHIP

POCKET BOOKS

New York   London   Toronto   Sydney   New Delhi

Pocket Books
An Imprint of Simon & Schuster, Inc.
1230 Avenue of the Americas
New York, NY 10020

This book is a work of fiction. Any references to historical events, real people, or real places are used fictitiously. Other names, characters, places, and events are products of the author's imagination, and any resemblance to actual events or places or persons, living or dead, is entirely coincidental.

First Pocket Books paperback edition October 2022

POCKET and colophon are registered trademarks of Simon & Schuster, Inc.

For information about special discounts for bulk purchases, please contact Simon & Schuster Special Sales at 1-866-506-1949 or business@simonandschuster.com.

The Simon & Schuster Speakers Bureau can bring authors to your live event. For more information or to book an event, contact the Simon & Schuster Speakers Bureau at 1-866-248-3049 or visit our website at www.simonspeakers.com.

Interior design by Erika R. Genova

Manufactured in the United States of America

10 9 8 7 6 5 4 3 2 1

ISBN 978-1-9821-4850-8
ISBN 978-1-9821-4851-5 (ebook)

Fear not: for, behold, I bring you good tidings of great joy.
—Luke 2:10

The smallest deed is better than the greatest intention.
—Amish Proverb

A CHRISTMAS
COURTSHIP

one

If Sarah Anne Miller Canon ever decided to write down a list of things she thought would never happen, being a newlywed at age sixty-two would be at the top. Of course, after a twenty-eight-year career at a major accounting firm, she never would have imagined that she'd have a whole new career as a bookmobile driver, either.

It seemed the Lord was giving her surprises when she least expected them.

After she and Pete had had their small ceremony, they'd gone to Niagara Falls for their honeymoon. Pete's daughter had been appalled and had even come up with other options for them. But while both Paris and Mackinac Island did sound lovely, Sarah Anne and Pete had decided months ago to stop listening to everyone's well-intentioned advice and make their choice based on what they wanted. Sixty years of living meant they'd earned that right.

Their honeymoon had been wonderful, and they were settling into married life. To Sarah Anne's surprise, they'd also experienced a few bumps along the way. It turned out that when two independent people decided to move in together, a period of adjustment had to take place. She hadn't known that her new husband loved to watch so much football, and Pete hadn't known that she was such a messy cook. She was slowly learning that marriage the second time around meant even more compromises than it had with the first.

When the door of the bookmobile clicked open for the first time since she'd parked on Mill Street forty minutes ago, all thoughts of her life evaporated.

Because Atle Petersheim had just arrived, bringing in a burst of cold air with him.

Pleased to see the shy, stalwart, handsome man for the second time in two weeks, Sarah Anne walked over to greet him.

"*Gut meiyah*, Atle. How are you on this chilly morning?"

As it often happened, his cheeks turned pink when he turned to face her. "I'm all right. And you, Miss Miller?"

That reply was typical Atle. His voice was always controlled, and he always spoke to her in a formal way. She'd given up attempting to make their conversations more personal. But she couldn't resist teasing him a little bit, either. "I'm all right as well. Though I am Mrs. Canon now, remember?"

"Ack!" He rubbed a hand across his scruffy jaw. "*Jah*. Forgive me. I don't know why I keep forgetting you got married."

"You know I'm just joking. Is there anything I may help you with?"

"*Nee*. I just came in to look around for a spell."

"That sounds like a nice plan. Would you care for a cup of coffee?" She pointed to her trusty Keurig machine. "It is a bit chilly out this morning, you know."

It was now near the end of November, and the brisk mornings never failed to make her yearn for a second or third cup of coffee.

Atle gazed at the coffee maker for a long moment before nodding. "*Danke*. I will take you up on your offer this morning."

"You will?" She tried to cover up her shock, since this was truly a first. "I'm so glad. Do you take it black or with cream and sugar?"

"Black, with one cube of sugar, please."

"I'll bring it to you as soon as it's ready."

"That's kind of you."

"It's no bother," she said as she watched Atle wander around the bookmobile, every so often running a finger along the title of one of the books. She wondered what was on his mind. Atle seemed to be thinking really hard today, which was saying a lot, given that he wasn't the type of man to say much about anything.

When the machine clicked off and she had added his cube of sugar, she handed the cup to him. "Here you go."

"Hmm?"

"Your cup of coffee. Remember?" she asked.

"Oh. *Jah*. Forgive me." He smiled sheepishly. "I'm afraid my mind was out walking."

"Atle, is there something you'd like to talk about?" She tried to smile in an encouraging way. "Anything at all?"

He blew on his cup, then took a tentative sip. "*Nee*. I am finding the state of the bookmobile to be in good shape and the selection of books to be . . . adequate."

Adequate? She was a little miffed by the descriptor but shrugged it off for the moment. "I'm glad you're pleased with the bookmobile, but I wasn't actually talking about books and the condition of the vehicle. I was wondering if there is something you'd like to get off your chest. People say I'm a really good listener."

Atle sputtered a bit on the sip of coffee he'd just taken. "*Nee*. I mean, I have no worries to share."

"Oh. Of course not." She backed up a step. "I'm sorry if I offended you."

"I only came in here for books."

"I understand. I'll go sit down and leave you to your browsing."

This time, he didn't even bless her with a reply. Instead, he kind of harrumphed before turning away.

Sarah Anne felt like harrumphing herself. She usually got along with all of her patrons. She was chatty by nature and found most of the folks who stopped by enjoyed visiting with her or discussing books. Atle was a bit different, however. He was continually guarded and pensive. Oh well; she should have been prepared for that. After all, one couldn't expect to win over every patron.

Sitting back down at her desk, she checked her phone, then pulled up the library's database. With Christmas coming, she was going to need to order lots of holiday-themed picture books, cookbooks, novels . . . and even some DVDs for her English patrons. Immediately her spirits brightened. It really was going to be such a fun Christmas season this year. She had so much to celebrate with Pete.

Humming to herself, she started writing down lists of materials to order, all while envisioning Pete's expression when she presented him with her special gift—a trip to see his daughter's family. They'd recently moved to Colorado, and Pete missed them terribly. Now they could plan a Colorado Christmas vacation. Snow, sleds, and lots of fun family time. She couldn't wait.

"Hmph."

Glancing up, she realized Atle was standing in front of her. His hands were empty, and he had a disgruntled look on his face. "I'm sorry, Atle. Have you been standing there very long?"

"Only a minute or two." He was gazing intently at her list. "What is that?"

"I'm making a list of Christmas and Hanukkah books and materials to order."

He pointed to one of the titles she'd just jotted down. *Love's Christmas Courtship*. "What is that?"

"That one? Oh. Well, it's a romance novel. Some of my patrons really enjoy them." She did, too.

He narrowed his eyes. "What are they about?"

She would have thought that was obvious. She shrugged. "Usually boy meets girl, there is an attraction, then a reason the couple can't get together, so they have to work through it."

"Then what happens?"

"There's a happy ending. The couple resolves their problems, gets engaged or married, and lives happily ever after." She braced herself for another grunt or maybe a derisive comment. Some folks, especially some of her male patrons, just didn't understand the appeal of romance novels.

"Do any of those books take place at other times of the year?"

She pointed to a row of short paperback romances from a popular publisher. "Oh, sure. We've got lots of them here."

Atle stared at the novels for a long time. At the title written on her notepad. At her. Then, at long last, he seemed to come to a decision. "I think I might be needing one of those books to help me with my courting."

"Pardon?" It was taking everything she had not to gape at him.

Looking even more serious, he nodded. "I've decided it's time I took a wife, Sarah Anne."

"Do you have a special lady in mind?"

"*Jah*. She's . . . she's someone special." He frowned. "The problem is that I don't know much about courting. I don't know much at all." He paused before lowering his voice. "I think I need to figure out how to add romance into my life."

"Add romance."

"*Jah*. I mean, women like flowery things. Ain't so?"

Sarah Anne found herself nodding before she thought the better of it.

"I started thinking that it ain't like one can take lessons on wooing and such." He looked at her intently. "Have you heard of men going to courting classes or the like?"

Atle might as well have just asked if she believed in UFOs. She really was that caught off guard. It took a minute, but she found her voice. "No, no, I have not ever heard of classes like that."

"Well, then." He rolled back on his heels. "A book is what I need. A courting book for middle-aged men. Can you find me something like that?"

"Yes— I mean, I'll do my best to find you a suitable book." When his eyebrows rose, she fumbled through another explanation. "I mean, I'll do my best to select a book that you might find helpful."

Breathing a sigh of relief, Atle nodded. "*Gut*. I'll be in next week, if that suits you?"

"It suits me just fine."

He finished his coffee, carefully disposed of the paper cup, then, with a nod, exited the vehicle.

Only then did Sarah Anne realize she'd been standing there with her mouth wide open. It was a wonder she hadn't let in flies!

She had been driving the bookmobile for a while now and she'd thought she'd seen and heard everything.

It turned out she had been very wrong.

Returning to her desk, she leaned back in her chair and started thinking about self-help books that focused on relationships. None of them seemed like the right fit for Atle, though.

Just as she was about to fire up the search engine, she remembered a different sort of book altogether. It was an older novel, originally published in the mid-1970s, featuring a dashing businessman and his lovely secretary. It was all before cell phones and computers, definitely old-fashioned compared to today's dating apps. But, though everything was rather over the top, the hero was truly romantic, and the heroine did give him a run for his money.

Making a sudden decision, she clicked through the library's database and ordered *Finding Love's Fortune* to be sent to her right away. Now all she had to do was figure out how to get a man like Atle to open up an old romance novel.

She had a week to figure that one out.

two

There was something about Jane Cousins that intrigued Carson Marks. She was nothing like all the other women he'd dated. But maybe that was the exact reason he couldn't stop thinking about her.

—*Finding Love's Fortune*, page 32

It was the kind of morning that made a person exhausted before noon. Standing in her kitchen in front of the stove, Sadie wished she could simply go back to bed and pull the covers over her head.

Especially when her fourteen-year-old daughter, Viola, was in a mood. And lately, she was always in a mood.

"Mamm, I don't understand why we have to pick up Samuel every morning. It takes so long."

"I've told ya. Samuel is too young to walk to school on his own. Neighbors help each other."

"He whines a lot," Jason said. "I mean, all the time."

"He's only six."

"He turned seven last week, Mamm," Viola said, as if that made all the difference in the world. "Yet, he still whines."

"Well, I guess he's your cross to bear, then. Now eat your porridge before it gets cold or you run out of time."

"Why can't we ever have pancakes? Samuel gets them all the time," Jason said. Her youngest was eleven and already acting like a teenager. "Half the time Samuel still has sticky syrup on his face when we pick him up." He shuddered. "Last time he got syrup on my new shirt, and I smelled like it all day."

"I know why Samuel eats pancakes and we don't," Viola answered. "It's because Samuel doesn't have to leave the house ten minutes early in order to pick up a little boy."

"He never even thanks us for our trouble, either," Jason grumbled.

Taking advantage of the fact that she was standing in front of the stove, Sadie rolled her eyes. She'd learned to ignore her children's grumpy mornings, but hearing them complain about not being thanked was stretching her patience thin. She would like to be thanked from time to time for anything she did for her children. But, as her mother used to say, one's children having children is a grandmother's revenge. Perhaps one day Sadie would get her revenge at last.

Of course, since she was not even forty yet, and her oldest only sixteen, she hoped that grandmother part was still a while away. For now, all Sadie knew was that there were moments when she felt completely outnumbered.

"Mamm? Mamm, did you hear me?" Jason asked.

"Hmm? *Nee*, son. What did you ask?"

"What time is it?"

"Jason, there's a clock on the wall."

"I know, but you are right there. I would have to get up."

And that was the straw that broke the camel's back. Glancing at the clock above the range, she turned to both of her cantankerous children. "I'll tell you what time it is. It's time you two stopped complaining, rinsed off your dishes, and left for Samuel's house. You're going to be late otherwise."

Both chairs slid back, and to her relief, they went to the sink and started rinsing their bowls and gathering their lunches from the refrigerator.

Turning off the stove, she hurried to the mudroom to help them pack their lunches in backpacks and collect their boots, coats, hats, and mittens.

"Where is Cale?" Viola asked.

"He went to work at the Overholts' *haus* like always. You know that."

"I didn't hear him get up this morning," Jason said. "He must have been really quiet."

"You didn't hear him because he slept on the couch last night."

"How come he did that?"

"I didn't think to ask." Sadie shrugged. "He told me he likes sleeping on the couch from time to time."

"And you let him?" Viola frowned. "He gets to do everything."

Sadie very much doubted that Cale would call sleeping on an old, lumpy couch "everything," but she saved that thought for another day. "You may tell Cale that when you see him tonight, Viola," Sadie said as she helped Viola put on her mittens. "I'm sure he'll have lots to say about that."

Looking embarrassed, Viola averted her eyes. "Never mind. Jason, are you ready?"

After Sadie buttoned his coat and handed him his backpack, he nodded. "*Jah*. We better go get Samuel."

"Try to be nice to him. It's not his fault he's the oldest of four *kinner*. You two had Cale to walk you to school when you were small, remember?"

"I remember. I just hope he's not covered in syrup again," Jason mumbled as he hurried out the door.

"Bye, Mamm. I love you," Viola said.

And that, Sadie reflected, was why mothers had children. There was nothing like a child's love. "I love you, too, dear." Raising her voice, she said, "I love you as well, Jason!"

Jason waved, showing he acknowledged her but was now far too old to be shouting his love across the yard. After watching them trudge down the cleared path that Cale had shoveled three hours earlier, Sadie closed the door.

They'd made it through another hectic morning. Her children had been fed and were off with their lunches and homework in tow.

Now she had seven blessed hours to herself before the noise returned. Even better, since her small business was doing so well, she'd recently quit her part-time job at the clinic. Now that she didn't have to worry about that, she'd be able to continue making her caramel corn and granola today. She adored whipping up tasty snacks, putting them in pretty jars and tins, and sending them out into the world.

They did rather well, too. So well, in fact, that Mrs. Anderson at the Berlin Junction had offered to pay her in advance for as many jars of her granola and corn as she could deliver. It seemed they were selling like hotcakes. And that money was surely going to come in handy, since she intended to get a queen-size bed for Cale this Christmas.

Though he hadn't complained about his sleeping arrangements, she knew it was bothering him something awful. Her eldest was now several inches taller than she was and would likely be even taller than his father had been. His feet were literally hanging off the end of his twin bed now. That was why Cale was sleeping on the couch. That, and the fact that he desperately needed a break from his little brother at times.

Sadie didn't fault him for that. Cale was sixteen now, which was in many ways a world apart from eleven-year-old Jason. Those five years created a gap in experiences and responsibilities that Jason wouldn't fully understand for years to come.

She, on the other hand, well remembered her life at sixteen. Marcus had just started taking notice of her. He'd been so handsome and strong and confident. She'd considered herself the luckiest girl of all her friends. It was only later, after they were married and she'd given him three children, that his eye started straying and she'd realized Marcus was as full of faults as anyone else.

Sometimes, maybe even more so.

He'd died of sepsis of all things. A bad cut that he'd ignored and refused to get help for had let an infection seep into his bloodstream. By the time he allowed her to take him to the clinic—he'd refused to go to the hospital—it had been too late. He died soon after.

Shaking her head in the hope of forgetting the memory, Sadie pulled out a large plastic container of popped corn and heated up the caramel again.

She had one hour before Atle Petersheim came over to give her a quote for fixing up the storage room in the barn for Cale. Atle was known to be very fair, and she hoped the price would be something she could afford.

Hopefully, by Christmas Day, her boy would have both a bed and a room of his own. Neither would be fancy, but they would give him his own space and privacy. It was the least she could do for her hardworking son.

three

Carson Marks, Jane's debonair, millionaire boss, was starting to act very strangely. Even though he was always busy, on Monday he spent five whole minutes standing in front of her desk, talking about the weather.

—*Finding Love's Fortune,* page 41

Cale was fairly sure there was no dumber animal on the Lord's earth than sheep. Coaxing them into the large pen outside was both a test of his patience and his cunning. Sheep didn't follow his directions too good and they really didn't enjoy standing around in the snow and cold for a few hours every day.

He'd soon learned that his only hope was to convince Prudence, their designated leader, to go out to the corral. If she decided to go, then the rest would follow.

"Come on, Pru," he said, pulling on her lead. "It's sunny out. You won't hate it."

Prudence bleated and tried to move away.

"Prudence, get on with ya now. There's feed out there and plenty of it."

At the mention of feed, old Prudence stopped fighting him, and her beady black eyes sharpened. Then, as if it had been her idea all along, she walked outside.

The other twenty sheep looked at him. "See? She thinks it's a fine idea." He waved a hand, shooing them onward. "Follow her, if you please."

Ten minutes later, they were out of their barn and contentedly milling about.

"I need a shepherd," he said with a sigh. At this point, he didn't even care if it was a shepherd from the Bible or a dog. He was eager for any and all help with those silly, aggravating sheep.

"Come now, Cale. If you had a shepherd do all the work, you'd spoil my fun," Hope called out.

Great. His boss's daughter had been watching him talk to the sheep. And complain about his job. He didn't know which he was more embarrassed about.

"How long have you been standing there?"

She stepped out of the small hallway that led to the tack room. "Only long enough to hear you grumble about your lack of canine support."

Which meant she'd been there long enough for him to wish he'd acted at least a little more on the ball.

As Hope daintily made her way to his side, her rubber boots stepping lightly over the packed dirt ground, he took a moment to appreciate just how pretty she was.

To him, at least.

Hope wasn't exactly what a lot of his friends would call pretty. She was a little on the heavy side, but she wasn't fat or anything. She just wasn't as thin as a lot of the other girls their age. He didn't mind the weight, though. He'd always thought it suited her. She was the type of girl who was full of life and fun. He'd always thought she was real pretty just the way she was.

She also had really pretty cheeks and blue eyes. And even prettier dark brown hair. He'd seen it down once when she'd been sitting in front of the fireplace one morning drying it, and he'd thought there was nothing more beautiful. It was thick, wavy, and almost reached the middle of her back.

"What are you doing out here?" he asked. "I thought you had plans today."

"I did. I was going to volunteer at the nursing home. But I guess the flu is going around, so they aren't going to be making art projects today."

"That's too bad."

"It is. I really like Miss Emma, but I don't want to get the flu." She sighed. "Mamm had me help with the cooking, then sent me out here to see if you needed a hand with anything."

"I'm going to be cleaning the pen. You can't do that."

"I don't know why not."

"I do. You'll get all dirty."

"I know, but my mother said it would be good exercise."

Her expression was a little bleak, which was hard to see. It was moments like this when Cale wished he could actually say what was on his mind. He knew there was nothing wrong with Hope and a whole lot that was right. Why her mother constantly brought up her weight confounded him.

However, he worked for her family and needed the money it brought to his house. Thinking quickly, he said, "After I clean up the straw, you can fill the troughs with fresh water."

She frowned. "That isn't helping you too much."

"Sure it is," he said. "I hate having to go fish out the hose, unravel it, and fill the troughs only to wind it up again."

She popped a hand on her hip. "*Jah*, I can see how that would be mighty difficult." Every word practically oozed sarcasm.

"It might not be a difficult chore, but I don't care for it none." Unable to keep a straight face, his lips twitched.

"I don't know about that, but I'll choose to believe it." She sighed. "I don't know what's wrong with me. I don't think I eat any more than Anna, but I'm twice her size."

"Your sister might be smaller, but she's not half your size. It wouldn't matter to me if she was anyway. I think you're real pretty, Hope. I always have." When she still looked doubtful, he continued, "I've never seen a girl with prettier hair. Not ever. Plus, you're really nice, too. *Got* just made you different than Anna, that's all."

Her blue eyes widened. "Cale, you sound so sincere, I almost believe you."

"You should believe me because I'm telling you the truth." He winked. "This time."

"'This time'?" Looking triumphant, she pointed a finger at him. "Ha! I caught you in your lie."

"You better be careful, or I'm going to make you help me round up the sheep."

She lifted her chin. "Believe it or not, I've rounded up my fair share before."

"I don't know how. Prudence is as ornery as any critter I've ever met."

"Now that, I fear, is a lie."

"It isn't. She never listens to me."

"There's a reason for that."

"Which is?"

Hope stepped a little closer, her bright blue eyes shining almost as much as her smile. "Cale, your problem is that Prudence doesn't like you."

He could smell the faint scent of her shampoo or lotion or whatever it was. It smelled like honey and oranges. He tried hard not to notice it. Instead, he reached for her hand, then swung their clasped hands. "You ain't lying about that," he said. "If Prudence liked me, my life would be a whole lot easier."

She giggled. "I guess it's good I like you, then, Cale Mast." She pulled her hand from his and turned away.

Which was a good thing, since he was pretty sure his cheeks were bright red. Not sure what was going on between them, he picked up the rake and started scooping up the soiled straw.

It was a relief when she walked around the corner to take care of the hose.

four

"I hate to be mean," Jane's best friend, Gretchen, said, "but your gorgeous boss is never going to give you the time of day, Jane. Mr. Marks only dates models. No offense, but that isn't you."

Jane would usually agree, but she couldn't forget how he'd seemed to touch her hand a little longer than necessary when he handed her a pile of paperwork that morning.

—*Finding Love's Fortune*, page 53

Once again, Sadie's black front door held a fresh green wreath adorned with red velvet ribbons. Even though it wasn't necessarily in keeping with most Amish homes—Christmas wreaths weren't exactly encouraged—Atle liked it.

He liked a lot of things about Sadie Mast. Especially her cheery disposition. Being around her made his world seem a little brighter.

"Thank you so much for coming over this morning," Sadie told him mere seconds after he knocked on the door. "Come in and get warm!"

"*Danke*. We do have a bit of snow today, ain't so?" he asked as he toed off his boots.

"More than a bit, I'd say. It's already snowed three inches."

He chuckled. "That's December for ya."

"I suppose, though I wouldn't mind a bit of sun for a change." She shrugged. "Well, at least I have company today."

She meant him.

That was the thing about Sadie. She was always welcoming and had a smile for him. She'd been that way even when Marcus had been alive, which he'd privately thought had been a minor miracle, as he'd been a rather dour sort.

Belatedly, Atle realized she was holding out her hands for his heavy black coat. "No need for you to take it, Sadie. It's heavy and now soaking wet. I'll take care of it."

"Want to set it over by the fire to dry off?"

"*Jah.*" Walking over to the hearth in wool socks, he felt self-conscious, like he was in her house half dressed. Shaking off his foolishness, he laid the coat on the blue-and-gray woven rug in front of the fire. "Is this okay?"

"You could put it on the arm of the sofa if you want. It might get dirty on the floor."

"It already is dirty, or at least not all that clean. I haven't taken it to the laundry since last March."

"I could wash it for you. The laundry costs a fortune."

"Not so much." He opened his mouth again, trying to think of something witty or interesting to say, but nothing came to mind.

So he elected to get right into his reason for being there instead. "Should we go look at the storage room in the barn?"

"Maybe we could wait a moment, at least until your coat isn't soaking. You could catch a chill. Would you like some coffee? Or coffee cake?"

He wasn't sure if that was permissible or not. Was it better to say no and be respectful . . . or to say yes? This was the problem with being a bachelor. Things that should come easily to him didn't. "Um, well . . ."

Slowly her happy smile faded. "I'm sorry. Of course. You are busy, and here I am, making you feel bad about saying no. We can go right out to the barn if you'd like."

Now he'd made a mess of things. "I have the time. It's just that I'm not sure if it is proper."

She blinked, then her expression turned even more distant. "I understand," she said in a far cooler voice. "I wouldn't want you to do anything you would feel uncomfortable about."

Feeling like his stomach had just plummeted, Atle watched Sadie turn away and walk to her mudroom to get a coat. His mouth opened, his heart wishing his brain had something to say that was meaningful, but it was inconveniently blank.

He was beyond hopeless.

Before he could make a bigger mess of the situation, he padded back to the living room, slipped on his damp coat, and then shoved his feet into his boots.

Sadie opened the front door. "After you," she said.

He gritted his teeth as he strode through the door she held open for him. Even he knew he should've been the one doing that.

As snowflakes pelted their faces, he walked by her side to the barn. Finding it unlocked, he pulled it to the side and followed her in.

The animals in their stalls looked up at the two of them in annoyance. When they did things like that, it always amused him—it was as if they were unhappy to have their territory disturbed. If he wasn't so sure he'd say the wrong thing yet again, he would have made a joke about them.

Instead, he ignored the mare who poked her head out of the stall, obviously hoping for an apple or at least a rub behind her ears.

"The storage room is over here, to the right," Sadie said as she walked to the room.

He reckoned it was as good a room as any for a teenage boy, though it was a long way from being livable. By his estimation, at least. There was no insulation, and the wood that Marcus had used wasn't the best quality. There were gaps between the boards and even some knotholes in the slats themselves. On a day like they were having today, it would be nearly as cold inside this room as it was outside. "Hmm," he murmured.

Her eyebrows rose. "What does that mean?"

"Not a thing."

She waved a hand around the room in an impatient way. "Atle, will it be possible to make this into a bedroom for Cale?"

"*Jah*, but it's going to cost some. Some of the boards need to be replaced, and then I'll have to put in insulation. I'll need to patch the ceiling, too." Looking around the room, he scratched his chin. "And you'll want a good lock for the door."

"I understand. Would you have time to do that?"

The room wasn't all that big. Maybe eight-by-ten or -eleven feet. It also had a large bench taking up much of one side. "What do ya want to do with all that?"

"Move it, of course."

"*Jah*, but to where?" He hadn't noticed anything else in the barn besides the horse stalls.

Walking back out into the main part of the barn, Sadie frowned. "I don't know." She looked around the vast area, then pointed to where all the tack was kept. "Perhaps in the back?"

He led the way, but it was obvious there wasn't any space for the workbench. "You might have to use one of the stalls, but I'm not sure how that would work."

Looking more agitated, Sadie sighed. "I know you think it's a lot of work and maybe not even the best use of my money, but I really want Cale to have a place of his own. And a decent bed. He's already done so much and put up with so much . . . He needs this, I think." Looking at him intently, she whispered, "Do you understand?"

Gazing into her eyes, he found himself nodding. "I suppose I do."

"You suppose?" She frowned at him. "Atle, if you don't believe I should make my son a room out here, then please just say it."

"I haven't thought that at all," he said quickly. "I'm sorry. I . . . Well, you know I was an only child and then have been living on my own for years. I've never had a room anywhere other than in a house, you see. But that doesn't mean I think you're wrong."

"So . . . will you be able to fix it up for him? And have time to make a bed . . . by Christmas?"

Making a cold storage room into a place a teenage boy could be proud of was going to take a lot of work. Finishing the room enough to feel good about it was going to take even more work. But making a place good enough for a mother like Sadie to give her son? That could take months.

He had just a little more than five weeks—and a half dozen other jobs he'd already promised to do.

But as he looked into her blue eyes and saw the hope reflected in them, he knew there was only one answer he was willing to give.

"I'll be happy to do it, Sadie."

She bit her bottom lip. "And the price? Do you have a rough idea?"

Oh yes, he did. It would cost several thousand dollars, given the current price of lumber. And he was a master carpenter for whom a lot of people in the area paid top dollar. His time, along with all the extras, like using top-of-the-line insulation and trim work, would hike the price up even more. And that wasn't even taking into account the bed he needed to make.

Six thousand would be reasonable, especially for the rush job.

"Does fifteen hundred sound about right?" he asked instead.

She swallowed. "One thousand five hundred dollars?"

"*Jah.*"

She breathed a sigh of relief. "Oh, Atle, yes." Tears suddenly filled her eyes. "*Danke.* That's . . . that's *wunderbaar!* I feared you were going to tell me a number far higher, like at least three thousand. I can do fifteen hundred."

"We're settled, then."

"Would you like a deposit? I think I have four hundred in the cookie jar in the kitchen."

He was a lot of things, but he wasn't the type of man to take money from a hardworking widow's cookie jar. "*Nee.* There's no need for a deposit," he said. "You can pay me when it's done."

"Are you sure? I mean, I bet you have to pay for nails and some such." Looking even more unsure, she gripped the edge of her apron.

It was hard not to smile. "I do have to pay for nails, but they don't cost much. I'll make do."

"All right, then." Sadie smiled at him.

The relief in her eyes warmed his heart and made him wish yet again that he was as confident around her as he was around hammers and nails. But . . . his mind went blank.

When the silence between them lingered a little longer, he said, "Sadie, I don't know how you're going to keep the project a secret. I *canna* transform it in just a day or two."

"Oh, I realize that. I'm going to tell Cale tonight." She smiled again. "Maybe he'll even be able to help you."

"*Jah*. That would be real good. Now, um, I should get busy. I better take some measurements and such."

"Would you like my help?"

"Nah, I'll be all right. You go in where it's warm, Sadie. When I'm done, I'll be on my way, but expect me to start in a day or two. Do you mind if I just come over whenever I can?"

"Not at all." She clasped her hands together. "Oh, Atle, I'm so excited. And grateful! I'd hug you if I could. Thank you again."

It was on the tip of his tongue to say she absolutely *could* hug him. He wouldn't mind that one bit.

But he had no experience in hugging women—or with relationships at all.

So instead, he just waved off her offer with a laugh. "Go get warm now. I'd hate for ya to catch your death. I'll be back real soon."

She smiled as she walked back to the house, leaving him in the empty barn.

Just then, Sadie's mare popped her head out and whickered. Unable to help himself, Atle walked over to her, wrapped an arm around her neck, and hugged her close. She whickered again, sounding pleased with the attention.

"I know how you feel, girl. I feel the same way," he murmured.

five

Carson couldn't figure out what he was doing wrong. Jane used to stop everything she was doing every time he stopped by her desk to chat. But now? Well, she would hardly give him the time of day. It was confounding.

—*Finding Love's Fortune,* page 81

Sadie had waited as long as she could. After she served Jason, Viola, and Cale a hearty supper of chicken and noodles with roasted Brussels sprouts, cauliflower, and carrots and helped Jason with a homework project and braided Viola's hair, she was fairly quivering with excitement. It was time to tell Cale about his Christmas gift. At last!

When he came into the kitchen to get a handful of oatmeal cookies and hot chocolate, she motioned for him to sit near the fire. "May I speak with you for a moment, Cale?"

He hesitated, then nodded. Looking concerned, he stood directly in front of her. "What's wrong, Mamm?" As always, he seemed determined to help her carry her load, no matter how heavy it might be.

"Nothing's wrong at all!" Hardly unable to keep the grin from her cheeks, she said, "You see . . . I just wanted to talk to you about something. A good thing. It won't take long."

As Cale padded over to the sofa, she noticed one of his thick socks had a hole in it and that the flannel pajama bottoms he was wearing were about an inch too short. Her eldest needed some new clothes and soon.

When he sat down, he popped a whole cookie in his mouth.

She'd long given up on chastising him over things like that. Boys were always hungry, and that was that. At least, that was always what her mother had been fond of saying.

"Cale, I asked Atle Petersheim over this morning to work on a special project for you."

"What kind of project?"

At last it was time to give him the good news. "Cale, I'm hiring Atle to fix up the storage room in the barn for you."

He put the three other cookies on the coffee table. "What do you mean by fixing up? And why?"

"He's going to make it into a warm, insulated room," she said. "He's going to put up sheetrock, paint the walls, lay down a better floor, add baseboards." She took a deep breath. "And make you a queen-size bed."

Cale's eyes were wide. "Why, Mamm?"

Discouraged by his reaction, she started talking faster. "It's your Christmas present. I thought you'd like some space for yourself. Even I know sixteen-year-old boys need some privacy. And, as for the bed . . . Well, the one you've got is just too short for you. Dear, we both know the true reason you've been sleeping on the couch."

"I can't believe you're going to do all this just because I've been sleeping on the couch."

"That isn't the only reason, of course." When her boy continued to stare, she cleared her throat. "You know what? I think Atle was excited about this project, too." Remembering how awkward yet kind he had been that morning, she added, "He's such a nice man. He said he could get it done by Christmas, but he'd have to work on it a little bit at a time." She leaned forward and reached for Cale's hand. She was so excited to do something for her son who always took on too much. "Just think, Cale, on Christmas morning you'll be able to wake up in your new bed in your cozy new room. Won't that be wonderful?"

But instead of finally looking pleased, Cale looked even more upset. "It would be nice, Mamm," he said in a halting voice. "But it ain't necessary."

Little by little, her enthusiasm faded. Cale wasn't just surprised; he wasn't excited about the room. Not at all. Struggling to contain her dismay, she swallowed hard. "Of course it's necessary, Cale. I thought you'd be so pleased."

"It's going to cost a lot of money. Too much, especially now that I'm sixteen."

Now that he was sixteen? What in the world did that mean? "Do you have plans I don't know about?" she teased.

"*Nee*, but I'm sure I'll be moving out one day in a couple of years. I mean, I will as soon as you don't need me."

As soon as you don't need me. "Cale, I hope you will live at home at least until you're eighteen or twenty." When she noticed a muscle in his jaw twitch, she realized that he most definitely did not want to live at home another four years.

How did she not know that?

"Do you have plans for your future, Cale?"

He shrugged.

She grasped at straws. "This is your *rumspringa* time. Are you, perhaps, thinking about your options?" And that was as close as she was going to be able to get to asking if he was thinking about jumping the fence.

He looked more agitated. "Mamm, I worked all day and I've got to get up early to do it all again tomorrow. I don't want to discuss my future right now."

"I understand, but can't you just tell me what you're thinking? You must realize that I feel shocked and confused right now. I really thought this would make you happy."

Cale closed his eyes, just as his father used to do when he tried to control his temper. He would never know it, but that felt like a slap to her face.

Before Sadie realized she was doing it, her hands clenched

in tight fists. Her short nails dug into her palms, stinging slightly. She used to do that when Marcus would get really mad at her.

Cale stood up and walked a few feet away, almost as if he needed the breathing room.

"Mother, I love you, but you are asking too much of me. I've done everything I'm supposed to do. I kept Jason and Viola out of the way when Daed got angry. I helped you deal with his funeral. I got a job over at the Overholts' farm practically the day I turned fourteen, and every time I've gotten paid, I've given you half of the money. Don't you think I deserve some privacy right now to make choices about my future?"

Guilt and regret, her old and trusted friends, returned with a vengeance. Suddenly, Sadie felt embarrassed and silly and everything she'd never wanted to be. "Of course, Cale," she said at last. "I won't bother you about it again." She smiled softly. "Or at least not for a while."

But instead of looking relieved, her eldest just looked even more exasperated. He picked up his cookies and mug and strode down to his bedroom.

"What was that all about?" Viola asked.

Sadie turned with a start. "I didn't see you there."

"I know." Viola continued to look at her intently.

Her knee-jerk reaction was to tell Viola not to worry about her brother and to stop eavesdropping. But that wouldn't solve anything. She had to stop hiding her head in the sand and face things head-on.

Thinking of the things Cale had said about his father, Sadie felt her mouth go dry. "How long have you been standing there?"

"Long enough to hear Cale say he's been working nonstop and deserves some privacy."

"I see."

Viola, her oh-so-confident daughter, folded her arms over her chest. "Well, I don't see why he didn't look happier. Mamm, why is he so upset?"

Sadie sighed. "I will talk to you about it eventually, but . . . I don't feel I can speak about it now, dear." Getting to her feet, she tried to smile. "Would you care for some cookies now? Maybe some hot chocolate?"

Viola's pretty gray-blue eyes scanned her face. "*Jah*, Mamm. That sounds *gut*."

"Wonderful. I'll fix that for you now."

"*Nee*, Mother. You sit."

"Viola?"

"Mamm, it's time I did more around here. It's definitely time I got myself a snack. Past time, I guess."

Her daughter's words were good to hear. Maybe in some ways a relief, too. There had been a time when she'd feared Viola would never stop being so self-centered.

But as she sat back down, she felt as if the bottom had just fallen out of her stomach. Perhaps Viola had heard her brother's speech and decided to make some changes on her own. If that was the case, it was probably a good thing. Surely it meant Viola was maturing. No, all of her children were growing up and changing right before her eyes.

But those changes hadn't been without consequences. It was obvious now that Cale hadn't been as oblivious as she'd thought to the type of man his father had been—or the type of marriage his parents had had.

Had Sadie really believed that?

As Viola walked around the kitchen, making her lunch for tomorrow, heating up water to mix with the homemade hot chocolate Sadie had made, and wiping down the counters, Sadie leaned back on the couch.

One day, in a very short time, all of her children were going to be gone, and she'd be on her own.

Alone.

six

Carson was running out of ideas and ways to accidentally converse with Jane. Deciding to invent a project for them to work on together, he leaned back in his mahogany desk chair and relaxed. She might say no to *him*, but his dutiful secretary would never say no to work.

—*Finding Love's Fortune*, page 99

Jason was still poking around with his homework when Cale entered their bedroom. "Hiya," he said, before staring at the plate in wonder. "How come Mamm let you bring your snack in here?"

That was his little brother. Snacks and which room he got to eat them in were still his priorities. "I didn't ask Mamm. I'm too old to ask her about snacks."

Jason blinked before putting down his pencil and turning to face him. "What's wrong?"

"Nothing." Cale sat down on the side of his mattress and took a sip of his hot chocolate. Of course, it was already lukewarm. Frowning, he put it on the small bedside table between their twin beds.

"It sure seems like something." Jason stuck the end of the pencil in his mouth then mumbled, "Did Mamm ask you to do more chores?"

"No. And for your information, I'm already doing a lot of chores."

"Sorry."

"Don't chew on the end of the pencil. That's gross."

Jason dropped the pencil on his desk. "Why are you being so grumpy? Are you mad at me, too?"

"I'm not mad at anyone."

Jason's expression told a different story.

Maybe his little brother was right. Maybe he was mad about a lot of things. "Don't worry about me none, Jason. Just do your homework."

"It's almost done."

They heard two raps at the door, then it opened quietly. Viola came in, her hands filled with hot chocolate and cookies. "I decided to come in here and talk to you."

"You get to carry around food, too? When did this start happening?" Jason scrambled to his feet. "I'm gonna go tell Mamm that I want my snack in here, too."

"*Nee*," Cale and Viola said together.

"How come?"

"You ain't old enough," Cale said.

"Plus, you didn't do your homework," Viola added.

"Did you do all of yours?"

"I did enough of it."

"Teacher's going to get mad."

Viola rolled her eyes as she took another sip from her mug. "The teacher's name is Bethany Anne. Don't call her 'Teacher.'"

Turning to Cale, she said, "Now, how come Mamm wanted to talk to you?"

"That ain't none of your business."

"I heard the last part of it. You sounded upset."

Glancing at Jason, Cale shook his head. "I *canna* talk about it now . . . even if I wanted to. Which I do not."

"Go get a snack, Jason," Viola said. "And when you get it, you stay in the kitchen and talk to Mamm for a bit. And don't get her upset, neither. Tell her something to make her smile."

"How come I've got to do that?"

Sometimes Cale couldn't believe how silly and self-centered his little brother was. He couldn't remember ever getting to only think about himself. "Because it's your turn to visit with Mamm. You know she gets lonely when none of us spend time with her," Cale said. "Now go."

When Jason looked at Viola for help, she stood up and shooed him out. After she closed the door at last, she sat down at the desk. "Now, what happened, Cale?"

Cale debated, then decided it didn't really matter if Viola knew about the room or not. Atle was going to be in the barn working soon. "Mamm wanted to talk to me about my Christmas gift."

Her eyebrows rose. "Really? What did you ask for?"

"I didn't ask for anything. Mamm hired Atle Petersheim to finish out the storage room in the barn and make it into my new bedroom."

Her eyes widened. "You get to move out there?"

Feeling even more self-conscious, he added, "Mamm asked him to build me a frame for a queen-size bed, too." Even though his toes practically hung over the edge of his current bed, he still couldn't believe it. "I know it's a lot, but I didn't know how to tell her no, Vi."

Instead of acting upset, Viola looked amazed. "I don't know why you'd ever want to tell Mamm no about that. Just think, you're going to have so much privacy. You can stay up as late as you want, and no one will ever know."

"I'll know when I don't want to get up in the morning," he joked.

"Oh, stop. You know what I mean. It's going to be like you have your own apartment or something."

He hadn't thought about it that way, but he reckoned she had a point. "I guess it would be."

"How come Mamm's doing that for you? And . . . why aren't you happy about it?"

"Mamm said she feels sixteen-year-olds need privacy and that I shouldn't have to always share a room with my little brother."

"That's true. I mean, it is true, right? Jason and I would fight all the time if we had to share a room."

"You two would. But I'm all right with it. I wish she wouldn't have done this, though."

"How come? It's a really *gut* gift," Viola said impatiently. "And what in the world is wrong with Mamm giving you a queen-size bed? Think of all the room you're gonna have to move around in. Why, I'd move out to the field if she wanted to give me a bed like that."

Yet again, his sister could exaggerate anything. "I don't know. It feels like it's a lot of money we don't have. And kind of a waste, too. I mean, it's not like I plan on living here a whole lot longer."

She smirked. "Cale, you're only sixteen. You can't go live on your own yet."

"I turn seventeen in two months. And since I can move out when I'm eighteen, I might only be here another year."

She started laughing, then stopped abruptly. "You're serious, aren't you?"

He nodded. "That's what we were talking about. Mamm started asking me about *rumspringa* and jumping the fence." He groaned. "Actually, she started acting like she wanted to talk about a lot of things."

"What did you say?"

"Didn't you hear me?"

"I only heard some. I heard you talk about doing chores." She swallowed. "And Daed."

Remembering the way their mother had looked so crestfallen, he shrugged. "I shouldn't have said so much. I wish I wouldn't have."

"I *canna* believe you brought up Daed."

"Why? He only died three years ago. It's not like we already forgot him."

Viola looked at him intently. "You know why. We don't talk about him because it makes Mamm upset, Jason sad, and you and me . . ." Her voice drifted off.

"What? Feel guilty because we're glad he's not here?"

She turned away but stayed silent.

This conversation was bringing up everything he'd kept carefully hidden and tried to never think about. But perhaps it was a good thing they were talking about their father. They might not like talking about him, but it wasn't like they were ever going to be able to wipe him from their memory.

Even though it hurt, he said slowly, "Hey, Viola, do you ever miss anything about him?"

"*Nee,*" she said quickly.

She wasn't looking at him. "Come on. Nothing?"

When she turned back to him, her blue eyes were clouded with pain. "He wasn't nice, Cale. He woke up every morning with something wrong, and we'd never know what it was. Mamm never smiled, and no wonder, because half the time she was wearing a bruise from his fists."

"Did you ever see Daed hit Mamm?"

"*Nee*, but I never saw him hit you, either. And he hit me more times than I care to count." Her voice barely above a whisper, she added, "Our father liked to hurt people in private."

"Mamm was afraid of him."

"She had good reason to be. We all did." A wayward tear slipped out from the corner of her eye, and she swiped it away angrily. "I *canna* even believe I'm crying over him. I promised myself I never would do that again."

He'd made the same promise to himself . . . but how hadn't he known that his sister had done the same thing? Feeling guilty that he hadn't been a better big brother, he said, "At least Jason doesn't remember him too well."

She rolled her eyes. "Oh, Cale. Where have you been living? Of course he remembers Daed. He was eight when he died, not a baby." She swiped her cheek again. "What's terrible is that you try so hard to forget all that."

"That's not fair. We all try to forget." He sighed. "How did we even start talking about this anyway?"

"Because you don't want a room in the barn because you have big plans to get away from here."

"Don't sound so bitter."

"Oh, Cale. I'm not. I want you to be happy. I'm just saying that it's not going to matter where you run off to. The memories are still going to be with you."

He was afraid that was the truth. "Don't hold your breath about me doing any of that right now. I need to stay around here and help Mamm."

"You're right. You do. But I think you need to accept the gift, Cale."

"How can I? It's no doubt a whole lot of money."

"Mamm watches her money and she's making a lot more with all her special foods."

"But still."

"Atle Petersheim is a nice man, and a fair one. Whatever price he gave Mamm must have been a mighty *gut* one. Otherwise, she wouldn't be so happy about it. And she wouldn't have talked to you if she hadn't talked to him about the cost, Cale. She doesn't do anything on impulse."

"You're right. And I hope you're right about me accepting it."

"If you don't believe me, then think about the alternative, Cale."

"Which would be what?"

"If you don't tell our mother her gift was a good idea and you're excited and grateful—" She paused for a second, then looked at him in the eye. "How do you think she's going to react to that, *Bruder*?"

He closed his eyes, hating to even think about her reaction. "She's going to be crushed, and then I'm going to feel terrible for hurting her feelings."

"She would be. Now, think real hard and decide if your pride and your made-up plans are worth it."

"And then?"

She smiled softly. "Then, you're going to need to do what we've always done. Move on."

"Have I told you I hate how smart you are?"

She stood up and gathered her empty mug and the napkin full of crumbs. "Not nearly often enough."

He could still hear her giggling after she closed the door behind her.

And later, after Jason had come in and Cale had taken a shower and crawled into his own very small bed, he realized he had already made his decision. Maybe he'd never even had a decision to make.

seven

Jane was nervous about being singled out for such an important assignment, but obviously there had been something about her secretarial skills that inspired Mr. Marks to ask for her help. Though traveling with him on a business trip to New York City did seem a little odd, she knew she was letting her imagination get the better of her. After all, what could possibly go wrong?

—*Finding Love's Fortune,* page 103

Sadie had stopped by his house early that morning, stood so stiff and proper on his doorstep, and handed him five hundred dollars in cash.

Atle had been so shocked to see the thick wad of bills—most of them were tens and twenties—that he'd taken it all from her before he thought to ask if she had enough money to see her through the week. He worried about her and attempted to take care of her in a multitude of awkward ways even though she never gave him any indication that she would welcome his courting.

It was obvious he had a long way to go in that department, too, since it was only when she was walking away that he came out of his trance and realized he should have invited her inside to get warm. He also should've put on a coat and walked her home. They might be neighbors, but her house was still a ways away. Instead, she'd trudged home by herself.

By the time he'd walked back inside, he was calling himself a great many names, all of which he deserved.

An hour later, he put on his coat and hat and walked the fifteen minutes to the top of his street. Right when he got to the crest, he breathed a sigh of relief. At least he had gotten the date and time right for the bookmobile's arrival.

Feeling almost the way he had when he'd finally gotten to the dentist to seek relief for an abscessed tooth, he stepped inside the vehicle.

He was getting help at last.

Sarah Anne was chatting with an English mother and her little girl. When she spied him, her smile grew to a grin. "Atle, I'm so glad to see you!"

"I'm glad to see ya, too. I was hoping you'd be here today."

"This stop is now on my permanent schedule. I wouldn't miss it unless I was sick."

"Good to know."

"This is Jessica and her daughter, Diana. Diana is five. Jessica and Diana, this is Atle."

He nodded at Jessica politely. "Ma'am. Miss Diana, pleased to meet you."

Diana waved shyly. "It's nice to meet you, too," Jessica said politely. "But now that we have our books—all eight of them!—we'd better get on our way."

When they left and he was alone with Sarah Anne, he shifted uncomfortably.

Luckily, she saved his pride.

"Atle, I've been thinking about your concerns and I did come up with an idea for you."

"I'm so glad. I wasn't sure if there was any hope for an old Amish bachelor like myself."

"First of all, you aren't old—you're a good twenty years younger than me! Secondly, this is just an idea, mind you. Take it or leave it."

"What do you mean?"

"Well, it's an idea a little out of the ordinary . . ." She appeared even more hesitant now.

"Perhaps you should just tell me, Sarah Anne."

"Okay, then." Taking a deep breath, she pulled out two books, each with a couple on the cover. "This is what I thought of," she said as she slid them across the counter toward him.

"I don't understand." He reached for one.

"They are, um, romance novels." When Atle dropped his hand

back to his side, she chuckled. "You can pick them up, Atle. They don't bite."

"I'm not going to read one of those books."

She frowned. "I was afraid you might say that."

"How could I not? Sarah Anne, most Amish men don't read fiction. I most certainly am not going to read anything like one of those books."

"Now, hold on please. I've read both of these books, and there's nothing offensive in either one. I promise you that. I would never give you something that would offend you."

But he was offended. "I asked you for help. I thought you might have some suggestions like a magazine or some such."

"As much as you might find it surprising, there aren't a lot of magazines offering advice for forty-year-old Amish bachelors." She picked up one of the books. "However, in both of these books, the gentlemen do court the ladies they are interested in. I thought everything they did was very sweet and heartfelt."

"Such as?"

"Oh, I don't know." Still holding one of the books, she glanced down at it, visibly trying to recall the story. "Oh! In this one, Dillon makes a garden for the woman he likes."

"I don't like to garden. What else does he do?"

"Atle, I am not going to give you tips from the books."

"Well, I am definitely not going to take either of these . . . these romance novels home!" What would his friends say if they spied one? What would Sadie think?

He shuddered to even contemplate it.

But when he gazed at Sarah Anne expectantly, sure she would start writing him notes and tips instead, he was taken aback.

Instead of looking helpful, the librarian had her arms folded over her chest and a mulish expression on her face. "I am sorry to hear that you are being so closed-minded. But I wish you luck with your lady friend, and do let me know if you ever need any help with anything else." Then she turned away.

"Wait. That's it?"

"That's all I *can* do. After all, I'm only a librarian, Atle."

He waved a hand. "You have access to thousands of books though."

Gesturing to a computer station, she lifted her chin. "So do you. I can help you access the circulation for the entire library system if you'd like to find something yourself."

He was familiar with computers—well, only a little bit familiar. But he sure didn't know how to use them to go about finding a solution to his problem.

Suddenly, it was as if the romance novels were beckoning to him, almost teasing him. He looked at the covers again and actually contemplated reading one of them. Checking out just one might be a good idea. And, if he hid it in a tote bag and only read it in the privacy of his sitting room, no one would ever know.

But then the door behind him opened, and Calvin Gingerich walked in. "Hi, Sarah Anne. Oh, hi, Atle. How are you?"

"I'm *gut*."

Calvin glanced at the table, noticed the two romances, and frowned. "Have you been helped yet?"

Well, there was his answer. There was no way on God's green earth he was ever going to admit to reading a romance novel. And since he wasn't a liar, the only way to handle this situation was to follow his instincts.

And his instincts said that no real man worth two cents would ever lower himself so much as to read one of those books.

So, without another word, he walked out the door and headed home. He almost felt good about his decision, too. Now he wouldn't have to worry about getting caught reading something so inappropriate.

It was only later, when he thought about Sadie and his absolute loss for what to say to her the next time they met, that he came to the conclusion that he might have his pride but he didn't have much else at the moment.

He still had no earthly idea how he was going to ever win her heart.

eight

Carson had been such a fool. Now he was not only going to have to act as if he was not infatuated with Jane while they were in meetings, but he was also going to have to sit next to her on the plane and pretend he didn't notice her gardenia perfume.

—*Finding Love's Fortune*, page 128

Sarah Anne's stomach sank as she put the books she'd been so excited about in the return bin. Though they were intended for a female audience, she'd gone to a lot of effort to find two novels she felt could appeal to a man. One of the books featured a firefighter and a lumberjack, and the other was *Finding Love's Fortune*—an old book from the 1970s featuring a debonair millionaire and his lovely, if somewhat oblivious, secretary.

She'd thought each of the heroes were a bit like Atle, too.

They were men's men. Tough and capable and brave. They were both rather awkward and shy around women, too. Kind of like Atle.

Now she'd scared him away because she'd been miffed he hadn't taken her suggestion to heart.

This wasn't about you, Sarah Anne, she told herself sternly. You're here to help other people, not to get compliments!

"Is everything okay, Sarah Anne?" Calvin asked.

Calvin was a new father to twins and a boy named Miles. She'd become friends with both him and his wife, Miriam, several months ago when they were going through some difficult times. And she was especially close to Miles, who had just turned eleven and occasionally came in to read to children.

"I'm all right, Calvin. What may I help you find?"

"Nothing in particular. I just happened to be in this area and saw your bookmobile. I couldn't pass up the chance to take a peek at your new books."

"I'm glad you came."

"How much longer are you due to be parked here?"

She glanced at the clock. "At least another fifteen minutes. But today's a short day, at least in terms of stops, then I'll be headed back to the main library campus this afternoon."

"I won't stay long."

She smiled at Calvin, enjoying the calming influence he always had on her. Though she was anxious to hear about his babes and Miriam, she kept quiet, giving him time to browse without her prattling on.

Ten minutes later, he approached with a stack of five books and his library card neatly placed on top. "I'm ready now."

"So you are." She smiled at him as she scanned his card and his books. "I hope everyone at your house is doing well?"

"We are. The babies are healthy and sleeping through the night. Miles has a new puppy that is driving our poor dog Paddy crazy. And Miriam is so busy she goes to sleep almost immediately the moment she rests her head on the pillow."

"Please tell her and Miles hello for me."

He gestured to her brand-new shiny gold wedding band. "How is married life treating you?"

"Wonderfully, thank you." She handed him his books. "Here you go, Calvin."

"*Danke*." He paused for a moment, then said, "Sarah Anne, did you think Atle was acting a little strange today?"

"I'm not sure," she said. Though she knew exactly why he'd been acting the way he had.

"Does he come in here often?"

"From time to time," she murmured, though she had a feeling he wasn't going to be back anytime soon.

Calvin seemed to think about that for a moment. "It's none of my business, but I always thought it was a shame he wasn't married. He's as steady as they come. He's always seemed kind, too."

"I've gotten that same impression, but I guess when the Lord decides the time is right, He'll provide."

Some of the worry faded from Calvin's expression. "You're exactly right, Sarah Anne. When I think how I had almost given up on having children and now I have three? It's obvious the Lord is in control and He helps us as much as He can . . . when the time is right."

"Amen to that. I guess we'll just have to hope and pray that the Lord will work some miracles for Atle soon, too."

Calvin grinned. "If that happens, our Atle had better hold on! He works in mysterious ways."

She chuckled, thinking that Calvin didn't know the half of it. "Indeed He does. Good to see you, Calvin."

After he walked out, Sarah Anne quickly started preparing the bookmobile for the road. As she put books away and secured the rocking chair she liked to have out, her words haunted her.

And she realized that they were very true. The Lord did work in mysterious ways, and miracles did happen when one least expected it.

Deciding that Atle might surprise her and come back in after all, she bent down and retrieved the romance novels from the return bin and fastened them with a rubber band and a strip of red construction paper. Then, she carefully set the books in the hold section. If

Atle did come back and he happened to change his mind about the books, she would know where they were.

It was a slim chance, but a good one, she decided.

Feeling better all around, she closed and locked the door, made her way to her driver's seat, and started the engine. Then, she set the vehicle in drive and pulled out of the parking lot.

All in all, it had been a very good day.

nine

Carson Marks was overbearing and a liar. She hoped she would never have to see him again. Well, at least not until Monday.

—*Finding Love's Fortune*, page 154

Saturdays were for catching up, making candy, and creating soup mixes for the Merry House, a little boutique that operated every year from November first to the end of December. Mary Troyer ran the place and she'd named it after herself, in a fun little play on words.

Over the years, Mary had become a friend, too. She and Sadie were close to the same age, and Mary also had three children. They had spent many an afternoon commiserating about the joys—and sometimes exhaustion—that accompanied motherhood.

Sadie had been so grateful to meet her shortly after Marcus passed away. Mary had been the one to encourage Sadie to make her treats and mixes to sell and had even suggested ways for Sadie to decorate the boxes and jars in order to make her goods look fancier. One day Mary had arrived at Sadie's door with spools of ribbon and an assortment of recipe cards and ink stamps. Together, they'd developed a wonderful look for Sadie's offerings to entice more customers.

And all of Mary's coaching had done the trick! Sadie now was selling more items than she'd ever imagined. Mary was pleased, too, announcing that Sadie's Sweets were some of her customers' most requested items. Mary had even recommended Sadie's treats to another shop owner in Holmes County, and now the Golden Bee was placing large orders for Sadie to fill as well.

The sales had certainly helped both her savings account and her shopping expeditions. Money wasn't everything, not by a long shot. However, there were things that smiles just couldn't buy, and Christmas gifts for the children were one of them.

All that said, Sadie worked long hours during the holiday season, and she expected her children to help as much as they were able.

That morning, to her surprise, both Jason and Viola got up early on their own, washed the breakfast dishes, and now were carefully measuring out ingredients for Sadie's three bean soup jars.

"Mamm, do you think your soup really is famous?" Jason asked as he tied the recipe card around the top of a mason jar.

"I don't think it's famous at all, though Mary says she gets a lot of requests for it." She smiled. "So, I suppose that means it's more famous than it used to be!"

"What about your kitchen-sink fudge?" Jason asked as he looked at the large sheet pans waiting on the other side of the kitchen. Sadie needed to carefully cut the fudge into squares and arrange them in tiny bakery boxes for the Golden Bee.

"If you're asking if people wonder if pieces of a kitchen sink are inside, the answer is no," she teased. "You know it's only called that because of everything mixed in with the chocolate."

"*Jah*, I guess so," Jason said. "But—"

"Jason, stop talking so much," Viola called out. "Mary and Stella are coming by later to pick all of this up, so we need to get moving."

Jason glared at his sister but kept much quieter.

Soon, the three of them got into a nice rhythm, and the evidence of their hard work showed in the completed boxes. Three hours later, Sadie knew her children had done enough.

"Let's stop for lunch," she said. "We deserve a break."

Pulling out the beginnings of the baked potato soup she'd prepared the night before, Sadie added milk and cheese and set it to simmer on the stove.

When Jason and Viola went out to the barn to check on Bonnie and Gwen, their horse and goat, Sadie thought again about how different her days were now as a widow. Marcus had been a hard worker but so very difficult. She'd never know what was going to set him off. Sometimes it was the weather or the price of oats for their animals. On some days, he'd yell at her if the house wasn't spotless. The very next day, he'd get mad if she spent more time cleaning than with the children. Then, there were times when he was as kind as he'd been when he'd courted her.

She'd been constantly walking on eggshells, hoping to escape her husband's ire and, of course, protecting the children as much as she could.

Unfortunately, there had been many days when she hadn't been able to shield Cale and Viola enough.

By the time the door blew open, the soup was finished, and she was in a reflective mood. Glad for her children's company, she greeted them with a big smile. "How are Gwen and Bonnie?"

"Bonnie seemed happy to get brushed with the currycomb and eat her oats, but Gwen wanted to trot around the barn," Jason said.

After she placed their bowls on the table, they bent their heads in silent prayer before resuming the conversation.

"Gwen is silly, ain't so?" Sadie asked.

"She is, but I don't mind," said Viola. "Watching that goofy goat makes me happy."

There was something in her daughter's tone that drew Sadie up short. "Is everything all right?"

Viola shrugged.

"She's upset because Gwen knocked into a box full of Daed's things," Jason said.

It was a struggle to keep her voice even. "Really? What did you find?"

"Just some of his old clothes and work boots," Viola said quickly. "It was a surprise, that's all. I thought all of his things were gone."

"Ah, yes. I had forgotten I'd packed up some of your father's clothes and put them in the barn. I think I thought that maybe your brother would want them one day."

Viola's eyes widened before she regained her composure. "He won't."

"I'll have to ask him later to make sure."

"Mamm, Cale isn't going to want anything of Daed's," Viola said. "You know that."

"All right. I won't ask, then."

Jason, who'd already finished his bowl of soup, frowned. "I might, though. What about me?"

"Jason, don't be stupid," Viola said.

"Wanting those things ain't stupid. I'm going to grow up one day and fit into his things. Right, Mamm?"

Determined to navigate the conversation as easily as possible, Sadie nodded. "*Jah*, you are right, Jason. One day you will be much bigger. It's no trouble to keep that box in the barn for safekeeping for you."

"When Cale gets his own room, I'm going to bring Daed's things into my room. That way I can have them nearby," Jason said.

"Mamm, *nee*," Viola said around a gasp.

Every bit of her wanted to shake her head and tell Jason no. But he had every right to want something of his father's. "All right, Jason.

Why don't we wait until spring? If you still want your father's things, you may bring them inside then."

His dark eyes turned stormy. "But—"

"Nobody else wants them, Jason," Viola said. "You're the only person here who misses Daed."

Jason pursed his lips and looked like he was about to argue, but then he blew out a breath of air. "Fine, but I don't think it's fair that I have to wait."

Sadie stood up. "Jason, we can talk more about this another time, but for now the three of us must get back to work."

"All right." He slid back his chair and went to the sink to wash out his bowl.

"Why does everything still hurt sometimes?" Viola asked as she stood up.

Sadie didn't have all the answers, but she did for this one. "Because we have feelings and memories and love in our hearts. And, every so often, life reminds us of that fact."

Her daughter nodded, washed her dish and hands, and then went back to work. When Sadie did the same, the silence felt like a balm to her frayed nerves. Then, little by little, hope filled the air again.

That was a gift, indeed.

ten

"You shouldn't have lied about the project," Dalton said.
"Women have a thing about liars. They hate them."

Carson mentally rolled his eyes. "Thanks for the tip,
buddy. Much appreciated."

—*Finding Love's Fortune*, page 162

Hope's parents had told her at breakfast that they were going with Anna to visit Aunt Hannah that morning but that she didn't have to join.

Instead, her *mamm* asked her to check on Cale from time to time, just in case he needed anything. Hope had barely been able to hold back her smile when she'd said she would be happy to do that.

That meant, for the first time ever, she and Cale were essentially alone. Well, her grandparents were there, too, but they were in their *dawdi haus* and wouldn't care if Hope was standing around talking to Cale anyway. They were the nicest people in the world.

After giving Cale a good hour to work, Hope decided it wouldn't hurt to go out to see him.

He stopped in surprise when she walked in in her new navy wool cloak and matching mittens. "Hey, Hope. I didn't know you were here."

"I didn't want to go over to my aunt's house. She always makes Anna and me look after her kids so she can chat with Mamm and Daed."

"Your sister won't get mad that you ain't there to help?"

"Nope. She likes babysitting Hannah's *kinner*. She's much better with little kids than I am."

Instead of looking pleased, Cale seemed mildly alarmed. "Who's here, then?"

"*Mei* grandparents. They're in the *dawdi haus*. Why?"

"Nothing. I mean, I was just wondering."

"This isn't the first time I've been left alone, you know."

"I know." He cleared his throat. "It's just that my *mamm* would probably think twice about you and me being alone together. It ain't exactly proper."

"I guess that would be true under other circumstances. But we're friends, right?"

"Of course," he said quickly. "I mean, *jah*. We are friends. *Gut* friends."

Even though she wished there was something more between them, she smiled like she was perfectly content with their current relationship status. "So, how are you?"

He shrugged. "All right, I guess." Before she could prod, he added, "My mother asked Atle Petersheim to build me my own room in the barn."

"Wow. For Christmas?"

He nodded. "It's my present. Well, that and a bed."

"You must have been really good this year," she teased.

"Hardly. I think it's more that she feels bad I have to share a room with Jason still."

"Well, that sounds exciting." Since Cale still didn't look too happy, Hope asked, "Are you upset about how much it'll cost?"

He nodded. Looking even more uncomfortable, he said, "*Danke*, for not making me say it."

"I know there's a reason you work here so much, Cale, and I know it ain't because you want to spend more time with Prudence."

As she'd expected, he grimaced. "That sheep. She drives me crazy. You know what? I think your father knew I was happy to be working in the just barn today."

Hope couldn't resist giggling. Her whole family knew Prudence and Cale didn't get along. None of them could figure out why, either. "He probably did. Prudence isn't shy about letting you know she doesn't like you much."

"One day I'll change her mind."

"I'm sure you will. One day." Noticing he looked much less uncomfortable now, she asked, "Do you mind if I sit in here with you for a spell?"

"I have to work on the livery."

"I know. But I could keep you company." Realizing how that sounded, she backtracked a bit. "Unless you'd rather I didn't."

"I don't mind." He picked up the rag he'd been using and started rubbing oil onto the saddle horn.

She watched him labor in silence for a few minutes, unable to focus on anything but the way his arm muscles moved, even under the thick shirt he was wearing. "Are you going to go to Caleb and Rachel's Christmas party?"

He stopped. "I don't know. Are you?"

"I was thinking about it." Caleb and Rachel were twins, and back when they were all still in school, they'd been some of the most popular. They'd embraced their *rumspringa*, and there were a lot of rumors circulating about some of the things they'd done. "I want to go, but I'm a little worried about what might happen. I mean, what if some of the kids get a little wild?"

"How about I promise to take you home if things get wild?"

"You'd do that?"

He rolled his eyes. "Of course I would, Hope. So, want to go the party together?"

Her heart just about stopped. Then she had to remind herself that he wasn't asking her out, like, on a date. He was just offering to go with her. It didn't mean anything. "Sure. I mean, if you want."

He smiled over at her. "I do."

She smiled back at him and tried to look calm and collected. But inside, she was practically jumping up and down. She had a date with Cale. At long last.

eleven

> Only an idiot wouldn't have realized his excuse to spend more time with her had been completely made up. Now Jane was giving him the cold shoulder. He didn't blame her—he would've treated himself far worse.
>
> —*Finding Love's Fortune*, page 170

Atle liked to believe he was the type of man who dealt with everything in a calm, matter-of-fact way. He made decisions in a steady manner, got along with most everybody, and was usually the person men gravitated toward at mud sales and horse auctions. Then, there was his work. Long before he'd gone into the construction business for himself, he'd worked for several big construction companies. He'd had no worries there, either. He'd talked to other men about projects, schedules, fishing, even his faith.

So, if he could do all of that with relative ease, how come it was so very difficult for him to have even the simplest of exchanges with Sadie Mast?

The moment she'd opened her door to his knock at seven that morning, still looking a little sleepy and warm, all coherent thoughts left his head.

In fact, it even took him a good two seconds of silence before he'd found his voice. "Hi."

Sadie slowly smiled. "*Gut matin*, Atle. I didn't expect to see you so early, but I'm glad you're here. Won't you come in?"

Should he? Was that proper? "Well, now . . ."

"Cale, Viola, and Jason are still here," she continued in that sweet tone of hers. "I'm sure they'd be delighted to get to know you better. Plus, I made cranberry-orange muffins. Would you like one?"

He wandered into the warm kitchen like a lost pet. "Thank you. I would," he said at last.

"Hang up your coat while I get you some coffee." She smiled over her shoulder. "You do like *kaffi*, *jah*?"

"*Jah*." Mentally giving himself a sure kick in the rear, he remembered his manners. "I mean, yes, I would like *kaffi*. *Danke*. And a muffin, too."

Instead of teasing him for his awkwardness—and surely there was so very much to tease him about—Sadie just looked pleased. "I'm so glad. Please, do sit down and get warm. It's bitter cold outside this morning."

"You don't have to wait on me, Sadie." There. That was a complete sentence, and he'd even used her name. Progress!

She looked surprised but then smiled again. "I don't think it's waiting on you if I'm hustling about the kitchen anyway. Just think of you sitting down as staying out of my way."

Fearing he was in the way, he did just that. Looking around the room, he noticed the walls were freshly painted a pale orange of all things! The woodwork was bright white, and there were all sorts of decorative touches. A wooden clock that had the words TIME TO EAT painted on the top. Pretty light blue ceramic canisters on the counter with the words FLOUR, SUGAR, and MORE SUGAR on them. In the corner was a large white ceramic jar in the shape of a cow.

"Is that a cookie jar?"

She had taken out a pretty cup and saucer with flowers decorating the edges and had just poured three cups. Looking over to where he pointed, she smiled. "It is."

"I've never heard of a cow cookie jar."

"I imagine not. I fear I like whimsical things."

"It seems so." He frowned at it, thinking about taking off the cow's head to get a treat. He wasn't sure if he would care for that.

Sadie looked vaguely embarrassed when she carried over his coffee and a large muffin on a flowered plate and placed it in front of him. Just as he was about to comment on the flowered plate—he really had no conversational skills around her—her youngest trotted in.

He came to a stop in front of Atle. "Who are you?"

"This is Atle Petersheim, Jason. He's our neighbor about a mile to our right, remember?"

"I remember, but I've hardly seen ya."

Atle reckoned that would be true. "I don't leave my farm much."

Jason took a moment to think about that. "If you don't leave much, how come you're here?"

Just as Atle was about to answer the boy, Sadie spoke again. "Son, don't be so rude. Now, sit down if you please. And where is Cale?"

Jason sat. "Still in the bathroom."

"And your sister?"

"I don't know. I haven't seen Viola yet today," he replied while Sadie placed a muffin, a carefully sliced apple, and a spoonful of peanut butter in front of him. Turning to Atle again, the boy asked, "Why are you eating breakfast here?"

When it looked like Sadie was going to speak for him yet again, Atle cleared his throat. "I can answer for myself, Sadie."

"Oh! Well, *jah*. Of course you can. I'm sorry."

Shrugging off the apology, Atle focused back on the little boy who was obviously trying to be so brave and protective of his *mamm*. "Jason, to answer your many questions, I'm here early because I'm going to build a room in the barn. I'm sitting here in your kitchen because your mother was kind enough to invite me. And I'm eating a muffin because I'm smart enough to never turn down anything your mother makes."

"Oh," Jason said.

"Now, give thanks and eat, child," Sadie said just as her two other children walked in.

The girl was a teenage version of Sadie. She had light brown hair and distinctive gray-blue eyes and was almost angelic looking. The boy had broad shoulders, dark hair, and light, almost silver-looking eyes. He looked like a younger version of Marcus. So much so, it was a bit disconcerting.

When both turned his way, he started to speak, but Sadie beat him to it.

"Viola and Cale, you remember Atle Petersheim, *jah*?" After both of the teenagers nodded, Sadie added, "He's going to be building Cale's room in the barn."

"Pleased to see you both again," he said politely.

"You, too." Viola smiled before tossing her books on the table.

"Morning, Atle," Cale said before walking to the percolator on the stove. After taking a large bite of one of the muffins, he started making himself eggs.

Viola tossed her head. "Mamm, Jason and I need to leave a little early. Is my lunch made?"

"It is, but if you've got to leave, then you'd best start eating quickly, *jah*?"

As Jason picked at his food, Cale put butter in a frying pan, and Viola examined the plate of muffins. Atle felt like he was almost forgotten as the children talked back and forth in what had to have been a long-rehearsed dance.

"I'll try," Viola said at last. She got herself a glass of milk and wrapped a muffin in a napkin. "Eat up, little *bruder*. We need to go soon."

"We *canna* go too soon. I still have an apple to eat."

Cale broke another egg into the pan. "Jason, we all know you play with your food. Stop messing around and eat."

Looking embarrassed, Jason shoved a wedge of apple in his mouth. Viola clucked her tongue. "The goat has better manners than you."

Atle bit his lip so he wouldn't chuckle.

"Viola, be kind now," Sadie murmured. "Why do you have to leave early? Is it because of Samuel?"

"*Nee.*"

"Well, then?"

"I want to see some of my friends before school. It's important."

"Ah," Sadie said.

Cale sat down beside Atle. After closing his eyes in a brief prayer, he looked at Atle. "Are you going to work on the room or the bed first?"

"The room. It will be best for me to work on the bed in my workshop in between my other projects."

"Where's your workshop?"

"In my barn." He watched in amazement as Cale quickly finished his third egg.

"Will you be here when I get back from work at two?"

After mentally calculating how long his plans for the day would take, Atle shook his head. "I don't believe so. I'll probably only stay here most days until lunchtime."

"Oh."

"But you are welcome to come to my barn any afternoon if you'd like to help me build your bed."

Cale's gray eyes lit up. "You'd allow that?"

"Of course. I'd enjoy the help."

"*Danke*. I would enjoy that, too," Cale said as he got up and placed his plate in the sink. When he moved to turn on the faucet, Sadie placed a hand on his arm. "I'll do that, Son. Get your lunch and be on your way to the Overholts'. You don't want to be late."

"*Danke*, Mamm. See you later."

"Have a good day, Cale."

To Atle's surprise, Cale kissed his mother's cheek before pulling on his coat and boots and hurrying out the door.

"Jason, we've gotta go," Viola said as she slipped on her coat and black bonnet.

"Fine." The boy carried his plate to the sink. "*Danke*, Mamm. See you later, alligator."

"After a while, crocodile." She bent down to kiss his brow.

"Jason, now!" Viola called out.

"Just getting my things. Hold on, Vi."

Viola shook her head but rushed to her mother's side. "I love you, Mamm. Bye."

"I love you, too. Goodbye." Turning her head, Sadie clicked her tongue. "Jason, you are going to make your sister late, which *isn't* going to make her happy at all. Hurry now."

"It ain't my fault Jimmy Brennamen has finally noticed Viola," he grumbled but soon threw on his coat and hat and rushed outside.

When the door slammed behind him, the answering silence was almost deafening. Sadie leaned back against the kitchen counter and exhaled. "At last, they are now on their way."

"Are things like this every morning?"

Sadie nodded. "Just about." Tossing him a sympathetic look, she said, "It might be best if you came a little later. My *kinner* are wonderful but not exactly quiet."

"They were just fine. Besides, I enjoyed watching you in motion."

"Oh?"

"You were like the ringmaster in a three-ring circus."

She chuckled. "I don't know about that . . . though I must say I don't exactly mind the comparison." She paused, then added, "I fear I encourage them to be themselves. Maybe a bit too much. When their father was around, things were different."

Atle wondered how Marcus had treated them, but he didn't feel comfortable asking for details. Instead, he stood up to take his plate and cup to the sink. "I enjoyed my breakfast, but you certainly don't have to give me coffee and muffins every morning. Tomorrow I'll probably just go directly to the barn."

"Oh." Looking flustered, she nodded. "*Jah*, I'm sure you would find that a better use of your time. Shall I walk you over there now?"

"I can find my way. Today I'm only doing prep work. Tomorrow wood is going to be delivered here, and then I'll be back on Wednesday to work all day."

"I understand." She bit her lip, then murmured, "Atle, may I walk into the barn and maybe see what you're doing from time to time?"

"It's your barn, Sadie. You can do whatever you want."

"All right, then." She lifted her chin slightly, as if she'd just made an important decision. "I think I'll walk out there in an hour or two."

"I'll look for you then." He smiled before putting on his coat and heading to the barn. The December sun was shining, and the air was crisp. It was quiet, too. Peaceful, even. His shoulders relaxed. This was what he was used to.

So, why did he feel himself yearning for more chatter, more busyness, more life?

twelve

It was official. She'd just received word that Mr. Marks had refused to let her transfer to another division of the company. She was going to be forced to see him every day unless she quit her job. He really was a tyrant.

—*Finding Love's Fortune*, page 178

Sadie had been watching the clock. Atle had been in her barn for three hours. During that time, she'd made her bed, carried the children's laundry to the washing machine in the basement, swept the kitchen floor, and combined all the ingredients for her hot chocolate mix in a large, five-gallon container.

All the while, she'd found herself peeking out the windows from time to time, checking to see what Atle might be doing. But she hadn't spied a sign of him. Finally she couldn't take another minute of worrying and self-doubt. Armed with a roast beef sandwich on a plate, she threw a wool shawl around her shoulders and went to the barn.

Bonnie and Gwen were the only two animals she had left. Bonnie was a lovely seven-year-old mare who acted more like a pet than a buggy horse. Gwen was her goat companion.

One of the first things Sadie had done after Marcus died was sell the cow, pigs, and chickens. She'd never liked when he butchered the animals and had dreaded all the work that came with it. Truthfully, she'd never even been all that fond of caring for the many animals. She'd found chickens to be messy and rather mean, pigs just plain difficult, and the cow expensive. She'd often felt the milk the cow produced never truly offset the price of feeding one.

It had been a surprise when she'd noticed Bonnie's happy and affectionate attitude take a downward turn several weeks after she'd sold all the other livestock. When she'd mentioned her worry to her friend Mary Troyer, Mary had said that Bonnie was probably lonely and Sadie might want to get the horse a friend. A goat friend. Goats were sociable creatures and enjoyed the company of all animals— not just other goats.

It had taken some convincing, but in the end, Sadie had taken Cale, Viola, and Jason to a nearby farm to purchase Gwen. The owners had claimed that Gwen was very sweet tempered and amiable. And, since she was rather young, would be just as helpful to the three children who'd lost their father as to the suddenly lonely buggy horse.

Sadie had been skeptical, but when she'd seen all three of the children's faces light up at the pretty little white and brown pygmy goat, she'd been willing to give it a try. Honestly, she would have done anything to help her children smile again.

Gwen had soon claimed all their hearts with her antics. One of her favorite activities was to hop up on the bench in the barn and sit next to whoever was sitting there. But the most wondrous thing had been that Bonnie loved her new friend.

They now shared a stall, and Sadie had found both animals sleeping next to each other more than once.

But she'd forgotten to mention to Atle just how chatty Gwen could be if she was ignored.

Walking inside the barn, Sadie was startled to see Atle sitting on the bench with Gwen contentedly perched beside him. Atle was talking to the little goat and running a hand down her side. When he caught sight of Sadie, he dropped his hand guiltily. "I was just taking a break."

Sadie felt a flutter in her chest and smiled at Atle carefully, disconcerted by her reaction to him—really, he was so handsome. "I see Gwen found you."

He chuckled, the deep sound making the whole barn feel a little warmer. "Gwen ain't a goat who likes to be ignored, is she?"

"I'm afraid not. She can be a handful at times. I hope she won't bother you too much."

"I don't see how she could. Besides, I'm the one invading her space, not the other way around."

He seemed to really mean that. Once again, she was struck by just how different Atle was from Marcus. Oh, not because Atle had never hit her or threatened the children. It was simply because he seemed so much more interested in everyone around him. It was quite a change from Marcus, who had often made a point to remind her and the children that they were living in his house and that they owed their food and shelter to him.

When she saw Gwen's dark, alert eyes glance her way, Sadie could almost read the little animal's mind. It was obvious Gwen was worried Sadie was about to separate her from her new best friend.

But there was no way she was going to irritate the goat without reason. Gwen was adorable, but she could also hold a mean grudge.

"Gwen is *gut* company, but don't be afraid to shoo her back into the stall with Bonnie. That's where she usually spends the majority of her days."

"I'll be fine." Gesturing to the plate she'd forgotten she was holding, he said, "Did you come out here for lunch?"

"Oh, *nee*." Realizing she'd been holding his roast beef sandwich like it was her new best friend, she held out the plate toward him. "This is for you. I thought you might be hungry."

His eyes darted toward the plate with a look of longing before meeting her gaze again. "You are paying me to work. It's not necessary to feed me, too."

"I guess I look at food as love." Realizing how that sounded, she felt her cheeks heat. "I mean, I have a habit of making food for people around me. But you don't have to eat the sandwich if you'd rather not."

He stood up and took the plate from her. "This looks *gut. Danke.*" After closing his eyes in a brief prayer, he took a big bite.

Pleased that he looked to be enjoying her offering, Sadie gave him a moment to eat another couple of bites before speaking. "So, how are things going in here?" She walked over to the corner of the barn where Cale's room would soon be located. On the floor were lines of blue painter's tape. "Oh, you've made progress."

"Some." The sandwich already consumed, Atle walked over to the space. Standing just two feet away from her, he lowered his voice. "This is where the door will be." He pointed to the section of dotted lines on the ground. "And in here will be a small closet."

"I didn't ask you to do that."

"I know, but the space calls for it, don't you think? Plus, all boys need some place to put their shoes and such. Ain't so?"

She nodded her head slowly and was suddenly struck by the thought that that closet might not be holding Cale's things for long if he decided to leave in a few years.

"What's wrong? Are you unhappy with the design?"

"Oh, *nee.* That's not it at all." Reminding herself that this was Atle, not Marcus, she cleared her throat. "I was just thinking that as much as I'd like for Cale to be here for a long time, he might only stay for a few years."

"He's only sixteen, though, yes?"

"Turning seventeen in February. Plus, he has big dreams." And, she thought, maybe a need for some space from his family.

Looking at her intently, Atle shrugged. "If he has big dreams, he's not alone. I think we all do."

"What are yours?"

When he looked taken aback, she held up a hand. "I'm sorry. Please forget I asked that. It's none of my business."

He stared at her a long moment before speaking. "My dreams aren't any secret, I guess. I have my own business, you see. I'd like to see it continue to prosper."

She was almost sure he was holding something back, but she quickly disregarded that notion. "I am looking forward to having a business of my own as well," she said.

"Your food business?"

"*Jah*. I make most of our spending money creating all of my little jars and tins."

"Ah."

Feeling a little let down that he didn't ask her more questions about her business, she added quietly, "Just to let you know, I've hired a driver tomorrow to help me make some of my deliveries, so I'll be gone three or four hours."

"Good to know." He handed her his plate. "Speaking of being gone, I reckon it's time I was on my way." He pulled back on his coat. "Don't forget that wood will be delivered tomorrow afternoon."

"I won't forget. I'll look for the wood." And, she realized, she'd be looking for him, too.

"If I don't see you tomorrow, I'll see you on Wednesday."

"Yes. Yes, of course." Walking him to the door, she said, "I know you are busy, Atle, but I'm mighty thankful for you building this room for Cale."

"I wouldn't have said yes to this job if I didn't want to take it."

"Of course not. Good day."

"Good day, Sadie."

Just as she was about to follow him out, Gwen bleated at her. Turning around and looking into the little goat's sweet, earnest expression, Sadie felt her heart melt. She rubbed the goat's head, in between her ears like she always did. "Oh, Gwen. Come on back in with Bonnie, if you will."

As if the goat understood every word she said, Gwen practically pranced to Bonnie's stall and waited patiently for Sadie to open the door.

Bonnie's ears wiggled when she saw her friend.

After making sure that Cale had watered them both last night, Sadie closed the door and picked up Atle's plate again. Then practically ran into him.

He was staring at her like she was something special. "You have a way with animals just as you do people, hmm?"

"*Nee*," she said before she thought the better of it. "I'm afraid where most things are concerned, I don't have much of a way at all."

Embarrassed now, she quickly turned and walked away.

She wished she still had some of the confidence she'd used to wear so proudly on her sleeves. Now, she realized that wishing for things like that did no good. After all, Sadie had learned the hard way that wishes and regrets were for fools.

❄   ❄   ❄   ❄

There was no reason to beat around the bush. Before he could talk himself out of it once again, Atle marched into the bookmobile, said a quiet prayer of thanks that Sarah Anne was completely alone, and then marched right up to her desk. "I'm gonna be needing a book after all."

Sarah Anne placed the pencil she'd been holding on the desk, stared at him for a beat, then turned in her swivel chair and reached for a wrapped pair of books. "Here are the two books I showed you the other day. Does either one interest you?"

Both had couples staring into each other's eyes on the covers. Neither appealed to him, but maybe that was part of his problem?

"Pick them up and read the back covers," she said as she nudged them across her desk. "I promise they don't bite."

After making sure no one had snuck into the vehicle without him knowing, Atle picked up both novels. One took place in the old west and the other seemed to be about some rich man and his secretary.

"Well?" Sarah Anne asked.

"I don't have a preference." Which one would help with a woman like Sadie? He had no idea.

"Ah, Atle, I don't want to pry, but maybe you could tell me about the lady you're hoping to woo? If I had more information, I could recommend one book over the other."

That did make sense. But did he really want anyone else to know so much about his love life? He could feel his face start to flush. That was the problem, wasn't it? He had no love life.

"The woman I'm hoping to court is a widow with three children. She lives near me." When Sarah Anne nodded encouragingly, he added, "She is real talented in the kitchen. She's real caring, too."

"She sounds kind. I think kindness is a wonderful quality."

"Sadie has that in spades. She got her horse a goat companion. Not too many people go to so much trouble for a horse."

"Atle, are you looking to romance Sadie Mast?"

Atle could feel himself blushing. *"Jah."*

"In that case, I think you should give *Finding Love's Fortune* a try. The heroine in the novel is a very kind person, too." She lowered her voice. "And don't worry. I won't ever say a word to anyone."

"Danke." Taking a deep breath, he picked up the book and looked at the cover, with the *Englischer* businessman in his suit. "Are you sure that reading this book will help me court Sadie properly?"

"I'm not a hundred percent sure, but I think it might, Atle." Smiling softly, she added, "At the very least, I can promise that it won't hurt your efforts."

It wouldn't hurt his efforts. Thinking about how hard it had even been to say Sadie's name, he knew he was being a fool to hesitate. If he didn't get some help, he was likely going to be an old man by the time he got up the nerve to actually pay a formal call on Sadie Mast.

Making the decision, he handed her the novel and his library card. "I'll check this one out."

Sarah Anne smiled, then competently scanned both items and handed them back. "Here you go."

"*Danke.*"

"You're welcome." Standing up, she said, "May I help you with anything else? Or, perhaps you'd like a cup of coffee before you head back outside?"

"*Nee.* I'm going to leave now."

"All right. I hope the book is helpful, Atle."

"I do, too," he said before turning on his heel and practically running right into Ruth Schmidt. As usual, she had a string of *kinner* by her side. All of them were staring at him. "Sorry, Ruth," he blurted. "I didn't see you there."

"No worries, Atle," she called out. "I hope you are doing well today?"

"*Jah,*" he mumbled as he strode toward the door. Horrified at the thought of the woman seeing *Finding Love's Fortune,* he stuffed the book under his coat and started walking away.

"Why's he so grumpy?" one of the *kinner* asked.

"I couldn't begin to guess," she replied. "Now, *kinner*, walk in quietly."

Laughter followed her command as they hurried into the bookmobile, making Atle almost feel sorry for Sarah Anne. Though, chances might be good that she would find their company easier than his nervous requests.

Repositioning the book under his jacket, Atle continued the two-mile walk back to his house. It was cold and there was a good amount of snow on the ground, but it didn't make him chilled. Instead, he realized that he was feeling warm from within, and it wasn't even from embarrassment. No, he was feeling excitement and maybe even anticipation, too. At last, he was taking steps to win Sadie's heart. He might never succeed, but that didn't exactly matter. What did matter was that he had hope again.

And hope in romance was such a wonderful thing.

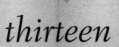

thirteen

"Jane, there's no need for you to come to work so early every day."

"I'm afraid there is, sir. Especially since I'd like to leave as early as possible."

—*Finding Love's Fortune,* page 186

"Why can't I go with you?" Viola asked Cale for something like the twelfth time since she'd discovered he was going to Rachel and Caleb's party on Saturday night.

"You know why. You're too young."

"I'm only two years younger than you." Putting her hands on her hips in that annoying way she did when she was sure she was right, Viola added, "And it's not even a full twenty-four months. Only twenty-two."

"Whatever. You're still in school." He lifted his chin. "I am not."

"I graduate in May. That's five months away."

"Yet it is only December." Though his mother would've chided him for sounding so smug, Cale reckoned he had every reason in the world to be that way. His sister loved to pretend she was far older and wiser than she was. She'd done that ever since he could remember. It was beyond annoying.

After checking to make sure their mother wasn't around, Viola flopped down on the couch. "Are you really taking Hope Overholt?"

"I really am." He didn't grin, but it took some effort.

"What did her parents say when you asked them?"

"It wasn't like that. She and I happened to be talking, and the party just came up."

Viola snapped her fingers. "Just like that, huh?" Pure doubt filled her tone.

"What is that supposed to mean?"

"I mean that everyone knows Hope has had a crush on you for years."

"Really?" he blurted before remembering who he was talking to. This was Viola, and she never forgot anything. Plus, she had a talent for bringing up things that were told in confidence—and at the worst possible times.

"Oh, *jah*," she replied, sounding like a wise, old *mommi*. "Everyone says Hope makes sure she's home whenever you are working there."

"Since I work there all the time, that isn't hard for her to do. I mean, it's not like she can be gone all the time."

"Do you like her, too?"

Yes, he did. "I'm not going to discuss Hope with you."

"Why not?"

"One, because you are my sister, and two, it's none of your business."

"What do you think is going to happen at the party?" Viola lowered her voice. "I've heard rumors that Rachel and Caleb's parents aren't even going to be around."

Cale had heard those rumors, too. It was one of the reasons he probably wouldn't have gone if Hope hadn't wanted to go. But there was no way he was going to say that to his sister. "I'm sure they will be," he said. "And it will most likely be like all the other parties when a bunch of Amish kids get together."

"Which is?"

"There's a lot of rumors . . . but nothing ever happens at all." He chuckled to himself. "One time, all the boys were on one side of the room, and the girls were on the other. We might as all have been sitting in church."

"Ha-ha."

"It's true." Feeling a little sorry for her, he gentled his tone. "So, Vi, you really have nothing to feel bad about. You won't be missing much."

"If it's going to be that boring, you could take me. Come on, Cale. Please?"

"No. I'm taking Hope." Liking how that sounded, he smiled.

"This really isn't fair."

"It is fair. You just don't like it." When Viola opened her mouth, obviously ready to argue some more, he blurted, "You'd best get up before Mamm walks in. She's going to be upset to see you lounging around when you're supposed to be helping with supper."

"I'll hear her before she walks in."

Cale looked at the spotless kitchen meaningfully. "What are you going to do about the fact that you haven't done anything? She's going to notice that."

Viola glanced around the clean kitchen and frowned. "Fine. I'll get up."

"What are we having for supper?"

"Tuna and noodles."

He groaned. "Can't you make something else?"

"Tuna melts?"

He groaned. He hated tuna fish. "Any reason supper has to contain tuna?"

"*Jah.* I forgot to thaw out anything to eat. So it has to be either tuna casserole or tuna melts because I don't know what else to make with a can of tuna fish."

"Tuna melts, I guess."

Sounding more enthused, she said, "Great! We'll have sandwiches and potato chips."

Viola was acting as if their mother was going to think that was a really good idea. Deciding not to give her any more warnings, he said,

"I'm going to go to the barn," and not worrying about a coat, walked out before Viola could ask him about the room or the progress Atle had made.

It was pretty dark inside the barn. Glad that his mother had bought a couple of battery-operated lanterns to use for the mornings and the evenings, he turned one on.

Bonnie and Gwen poked their heads out of the stall. Bonnie whickered softly. Gwen added a tiny bleat. Unable to resist, he walked into the stall with them. After checking to make sure they had water, he reached out to rub the mare's flank. "How're you doing today, Miss Bonnie? *Gut*?"

She pawed at the ground. "I know. You're probably ready to get out of here for a spell, ain't you? I'll take you out for a ride tomorrow."

Gwen bleated and butted him with her knobby head. He laughed. "Fine. I'll take you out for a spell, too, goat."

When the barn door opened again, he sighed in aggravation. "Viola, you better have done something in the kitchen before Mamm gets mad."

"Sorry, but it's only me," Atle said.

And . . . Cale was completely embarrassed. "*Nee*, I'm sorry. I should've looked at who I was yelling at. And, um, I promise I don't usually talk to my sister like that."

"I was an only child, but if I had been blessed enough to have a sibling, I reckon I would have talked to mine like that a time or two. It comes with the territory, *jah*?"

Cale nodded. "Viola and Jason are fine, but sometimes it's hard being the oldest."

"I reckon so."

Atle walked over and rested his elbows on the top rim of the stall. "When your mother showed me Bonnie and her goat, I thought it was the strangest pairing I'd ever seen. But they seem real close."

Still petting Gwen's soft white coat, Cale grinned. "I was pretty skeptical, but my *mamm* was right. They are best friends. Gwen has calmed Bonnie down a lot."

Atle clicked his tongue and held out a hand. To Cale's surprise, Bonnie walked right over and nuzzled him. "Hiya, girl. I brought you an apple." He fished in his pocket and pulled out a neatly quartered apple and fed her a fourth of it.

When Gwen sauntered over and bleated, Atle chuckled. "I didn't forget you, either, goat. Here you go." He gently fed Gwen another quarter of the apple.

"That's nice of you to bring them snacks."

"Sorry. I should've asked. You don't mind, do ya?"

"*Nee.* I was surprised, that's all."

"I figured since I'm going to be raising a racket all day with my hammering and sawing, I had better come bearing gifts." After feeding each of the animals the last of the apple, Atle said, "Sorry to catch you off guard, but your mother said I could come whenever I needed to. I'm only here to sort some of the lumber for tomorrow morning. I won't stay long."

"I only came to look at the room. Do you mind if I stay?"

Atle took off his hat and ran a hand through his fairly short salt-and-pepper hair. "Not if you help me move around lumber."

"I can do that." After getting out of the stall, he followed Atle to the pile of lumber. "I noticed all the lines you made yesterday."

"It'll be a good-size room for ya. Ain't so?"

Cale nodded. "It's going to be bigger than I imagined."

"It needs to be big enough to hold you and a queen-size bed frame."

Cale noticed that Atle's face held no expression. "Do you think this room is a bad idea?"

"Your mother hired me to build you a room, not share my thoughts about it."

"But, could you tell me what you think? When Mamm first told me about it, I tried to tell her it was a waste of money." Realizing how his words sounded, he blurted, "Sorry. I don't mean that your work ain't worth a lot of money. It's just that I don't think I need my own room."

Atle studied him closely and seemed to think about his words for a moment before speaking. "A lot of people smarter than me have told me it's wrong to correct a woman on a mission. And, well, your mother intends to pay me to build you a room and a bigger bed frame. She seemed real excited about it, too." He paused. "I could be wrong, but it doesn't seem like she's had a lot of practice making decisions like this."

Thinking of how his *daed* hadn't given their mother much say in family matters, Cale swallowed. "She hasn't. Not really."

"Then I think we should let her give this to you, Cale," Atle said in that calm way of his. "From everything she's told me, you've helped her out a great deal, and she feels the need to make you happy."

Atle's words struck a chord deep inside Cale. "You're right. I've been feeling guilty, but maybe my fussing is making things worse for her."

"Nah, I don't think you're making anything worse. But, well, Sadie's eyes shine when she talks about your Christmas gift. I'd hate to see that sparkle fade away."

Cale would, too. "I'll stop complaining. Sorry. Here you're coming over around suppertime and all you get is me sounding ungrateful."

Atle, who'd knelt down to inspect the wood, looked up at him. "You don't have to worry about me. Since I live alone, it ain't like suppertime is anything to be excited about. Plus, I know your words came from a good place. Now, are you ready to help me arrange some two-by-fours?"

"I am if you show me which ones those are."

Atle picked up a piece of wood. "See?" he said. "The thickness is two inches, and the width is four inches." When Cale nodded, he continued, "Most of these are two-by-fours. Pick one up and line it up this way." He arranged the wood on the ground. "Understand?"

"*Jah.*"

"All right, then. Let's get busy."

After Atle pulled out another piece of wood, Cale knelt down to do the same thing. Soon, they got into a good rhythm, neither of them speaking.

"Cale?" his mother called out after they'd been working together for almost an hour. "Are you in here?"

He straightened. "*Jah*, Mamm."

She appeared with a red wool shawl over her light gray dress. "Son, what are you doing in here? You're not wasting the batteries, are you?"

"I'm the one doing that, Sadie," Atle said.

"Oh! Atle, I'm sorry. I didn't realize you were here."

"I reckon not. I just wanted to frame out the room. Cale was in here, so I asked him to help."

"Oh."

"Don't worry now. We're almost done, and I'll be on my way."

"*Nee*, it's all right. Take your time. I just walked home with Jason. He was over at Samuel's *haus*. I'll need to go work on supper anyway."

"Viola's making supper, Mamm," Cale said.

"She is?" Happiness soon faded to doubt. "Ah, do you know what she has in mind?"

"Tuna melts."

"Oh."

"And potato chips."

"I see."

Cale reckoned it was a true sign of his maturity that he didn't mention how Viola had forgotten to thaw out anything better for supper.

"I've always been a fan of tuna melts myself," Atle said mildly. "Especially on a cold evening."

Cale grinned as he set another piece of wood down on the ground. He was beginning to think Atle was a really nice man. But when he glanced at his mother, he was stunned to see a look of wonder on her face. And then even more stunned when he heard what she had to say next.

"Would you like to stay for supper?"

Atle stood up so abruptly, he almost hit his head on the window frame. "Sadie, I didn't say that just so you'd ask me."

"I know. But we have plenty. I'll open up a can of soup, too."

For a moment, Cale was sure there was a look of longing in Atle's eyes when he looked at his *mamm*. But then, as if he was gathering himself together, Atle shook his head. "I appreciate the offer, but it's past time I was on my way. I'll be back in the morning. Thank you for your help, Cale."

"It weren't a problem," Cale called out right before Atle walked out the barn door.

When it was just the two of them, his mother looked down at the floor and then at him. "That was mighty strange, wasn't it?"

"*Jah*," Cale answered, but he thought maybe it wasn't such a big surprise. For a second there, he'd noticed the man had looked at his mother the same way Cale was sure he had stared at Hope before. If that was true, then he was pretty sure Atle had a crush on his mother.

Now *that* he hadn't seen coming.

fourteen

"Carson, we've played golf together a lot, but I have to tell you I've never seen you play so poorly," Dalton said.

"I know. I can't keep my mind focused on anything right now."

Dalton's teasing expression grew concerned. "Is the McCracken merger really keeping you up at night?"

"No. I've got bigger fish to worry about."

—*Finding Love's Fortune*, page 199

The moment Atle entered his house, he turned on a kerosene lamp, tossed his hat on the table, toed off his boots, and then wished he could turn right back around and apologize to both Sadie and her boy.

He'd made a cake of himself, there was no doubt about it. He couldn't believe he'd just bolted out of Sadie's barn all to stop himself from accepting her offer of a tuna sandwich. And he'd had a witness!

Her sixteen-year-old boy was probably laughing his head off, and Atle wouldn't blame him none, either. Grown men were supposed to be able to complete full sentences around women, not make up excuses like a scared child and run off. At this rate, he was never going to get around to asking Sadie out to supper.

Nee, at this rate, he was never even going to be able to speak to her in full sentences.

When his hands were warmer, he walked into the kitchen to rummage for his supper. Looking at the steak he'd thawed out that morning and seasoned with a special rub he had perfected years ago and the casserole of potatoes and cheese he'd made two hours ago, Atle realized he should have been the one offering to feed Sadie and her children. Tuna sandwiches and potato chips didn't keep *kinner* full for long. At least, he didn't think so.

He'd learned to cook out of necessity. His *mamm* had passed away when he was a small child, and his father had had no gifts in the kitchen. By the time he'd turned ten, Atle had started making their meals just so they could have something else to eat besides burned steak and chicken.

After turning on the gas oven and putting the potato dish inside, he poured himself a glass of water. And then he realized he couldn't put off the inevitable any longer. He had to become a better suitor so he could court Sadie. And there was only one way to do that. He needed to read his research book.

Opening up a tote bag, he pulled out the book he had checked out. And there it was: *Finding Love's Fortune*.

Right on cue, his face turned beet red. If only these romance books had more manly titles, like . . . like he didn't know what. But *"Finding Love's Fortune"*? It made him feel like a school-girl!

Opening up the book to the next chapter, Atle pulled out his notebook and got to reading. It seemed Carson Marks was back to circling Jane's secretarial desk like a hungry shark. At least he was acting like less of a jerk now. It was about time, too. Jane had been looking at the want ads for days.

Adjusting his eyes to the small print, he scanned the page to where he'd left off.

"Mr. Marks, you're back from golf already? That's a surprise."

Atle rolled his eyes. It definitely was *not* a surprise. The man had been lurking about her desk for days now.

"I had to cut the game short. I had some important calls to make."

Jane opened up his calendar. "With whom? I didn't see any calls scheduled, sir."

"These came up suddenly." Leaning against her desk, Carson gazed down at her. "Jane, it's time you called me Carson. Don't you agree?"

"Oh, brother," Atle said to the page.

"Well, I don't know. You are my boss. I mean, for now."

"For now? Please don't quit on me, Jane."

"I don't see how I have a choice."

"There's always a choice," he said in a deep tone.

Atle grunted. Just as he was about to skip to chapter four, because this stupid conversation was no help to his shyness around Sadie, old Carson made a sudden move.

"Jane, I think it's finally time I was honest with you. You've got to know I've only been stopping by your desk so much so I can talk to you. And instead of begging you to stay as my secretary, I would much rather take you out to dinner."

Atle gaped. That was really a pretty smooth move. Straight to the point. He was good at that.

Intrigued, he turned the page just to see if Jane was as impressed as he was.

Jane folded her hands over her chest. "Are you serious?" she whispered.

"He's serious, Jane," Atle told the book.

Carson straightened his burgundy silk tie. "Of course I'm serious, Jane. So, what do you say?"

Jane's violet-colored eyes widened before she turned her head away. "I'm not ready for a big step like that, Carson. I'm sorry."

"Can you tell me why not?"

"Well, first of all, you lied to me."

"I've already apologized several times."

"I realize that."

"What else do I need to do, then?" Impatiently, he added, "You know, forgiveness is a virtue."

Impressed with Carson deftly interjecting virtues into the conversation, Atle nodded. "Sorry, but he's got a point there, Jane. It's time to let his mistake go."

Carson leaned forward, so close she could smell the rich, woody scent of his cologne. "Won't you please at least try to forgive me?"

Her eyes widened. "I suppose I could."

Feeling triumphant, he said, "Then meet me tonight for a cocktail."

"I'm not going to meet you at a bar, Mr. Marks."

Afraid to lose his advantage, he switched venues. "How about we meet at the Ginger House for tea?"

"Just tea?"

"Just tea and conversation." Seeing her waver, he softened his tone. "All I want is to earn back your trust, Jane. Won't you give me that chance?"

"*Gut* job, Carson. She can't say no now."

Jane took her time responding, straightening the files on her already spotless desk. Finally, she spoke. "I suppose I could do that."

Carson stepped back and smiled. "I'll see you there at six o'clock sharp."

Carson left without asking if that time was okay with Jane, but he felt her gaze follow him out of the room. When he was out of her sight, he grinned. She might not like him yet, but she didn't hate him anymore. Progress had been made.

Even though the buzzer was going off on his oven, signaling that his potatoes were done, Atle closed the book and contemplated that scene. There were a great many things that irritated him about it, and it wasn't just the choice of meeting in a tearoom. But, he had to admit, he did rather admire Carson's confidence. Atle also appreciated the millionaire's patience as he gave Jane the time to regain her broken trust in him.

But the part that stuck with him the most was Carson's take-charge ways. That was what he needed to do, it seemed. He needed to give Sadie a little bit of time, make sure she knew his intentions, and then push a bit.

"What could go wrong with that plan?" he asked himself as he finally pulled the potatoes out of the oven.

He winced as he realized that a whole lot could.

fifteen

"I do forgive you," Jane said after they'd shared a whole pot of Earl Grey and Carson had explained the reason behind his lies. "But I don't think it will change a thing. There are just some people who aren't meant to be together. We might be two of those people."

—_Finding Love's Fortune_, page 208

Hope was wearing a new dress her mother and older sister, Anna, had helped her sew, and it had turned out rather well. It was an interesting color, a cross between dark cranberry and maroon. Her mother had called it festive without screaming out "Christmas dress."

Anna had simply whispered that Cale would be dazzled.

Dazzled was a pretty strong description. Hope didn't hold out any hope for that kind of reaction. But she was curious if Cale would think she looked pretty. Or if he would even tell her if he thought so. Cale was the type of guy who didn't say much. She'd always liked that about him, but it was sometimes frustrating.

When she came downstairs in her new black boots and dress, with her hair in a fancy twist under her white *kapp*, just minutes before Cale was supposed to arrive, she felt self-conscious but excited. Her parents and Anna were sitting in the living room watching her.

"Well, I guess I'm all ready," she said.

"You look mighty fine," Daed said.

"Indeed you do," Mamm said. "The color is flattering."

Anna winked at her and mouthed, *Dazzling*, before saying out loud, "Are you excited about going to Rachel and Caleb's party?"

"I am, but a little nervous, too."

"You aren't worried about going on Cale Mast's arm, are you?" her father asked.

Sometimes the way her father talked about dates was so old-fashioned. Not that this was a real date anyway. "Not at all. Cale is nice, and I'm comfortable around him."

"He's responsible, too. When he stopped by to talk to me about taking you, he was respectful," Daed said.

"I didn't know he talked to you about the party," Hope said. "When did that happen?"

"You don't need to know everything that happens in this *haus*, child," he teased.

"The fact is that you could do far worse than Cale Mast, even though his family doesn't have much money," her mother said. "He's smart and a hard worker."

"He's a lot of things, including gorgeous," Anna corrected with a smile. "But it's not like they're serious or anything, Mamm. I mean, Hope and Cale are only sixteen."

"Cale is almost seventeen, *jah*?"

"He has a birthday in February," Hope said.

"And yours is in April. Now, a lot could happen and you two could decide to choose different people, but then again, you might not. After all, your father and me fell in love when we were fifteen," their mother said with a fond look at their *daed*. "Right, Jeremiah?"

"I knew at fifteen that you were going to be mine, forever and ever," he said with a wink. "I'll never forget how pretty you looked on Christmas Day, Charity."

Anna groaned. "Here we go again."

Hope was so not up for hearing about their parents' Christmas courtship. "All we're doing is going to a party tonight," Hope reminded them all.

"I realize that," Mamm said. "All I'm saying is that it's good to be prepared and think ahead, dear."

Hope shared a look with her sister but said nothing more.

At least Mamm wasn't saying anything about her weight or how Anna was so much smaller than she was.

When the knock on the door came, it was hard to stay seated while her father answered.

"Cale, it's *gut* to see you when we're both not in the barn," he joked. "I hope you're doing well this evening."

"I am." He glanced in Hope's direction and smiled. "Hiya, Hope."

She smiled back at him. Cale looked freshly scrubbed and as handsome as ever. After she found her voice, she said, "Are you ready?"

"*Jah*. We should probably get there soon. I won't have her home too late, Mr. Overholt," he said.

"Oh, you two have a wonderful-*gut* time. We know Hope will be in good hands. Enjoy the party," Mamm said as she joined them. "How are things with your mother?"

"Good. And my siblings are doing well, too."

"I saw your mother's jams and hot fudge sauce at the Merry House. The manager said everything your mother brings in sells like hotcakes."

"She'll be pleased to hear that. She's home making granola now." He smiled. "Viola is helping her, which is nice for my *mamm*, but a disappointment for my sister."

"That's how it always is," Mamm said with a laugh. "Girls always want to be like their older siblings."

"I reckon so."

"Are you driving the buggy tonight?"

"I am. It's not snowing, so Bonnie won't mind it too much. She's a fair-weather horse, I fear." Looking over at Hope, he said, "I put a blanket in the buggy. I don't think you'll be too cold, though."

"I have my cloak and gloves, too. I'll be fine." She couldn't wait to get on their way.

Anna walked over with a tin of puppy chow. "Don't forget this."

"*Danke.*" After slipping on her thick black gloves, Hope said, "I'm ready, Cale."

"We'd best be on our way, then." He smiled down at her before looking at her *daed* again. "Have a good night."

When the door closed after them, Hope breathed a sigh of relief. "I'm sorry. My parents were in the mood to chat this evening."

"You know I like your parents, Hope. They've been mighty good to me."

She was surprised when she looked up to see the courting buggy. "Now I understand why you told me about the blankets."

"I like driving this one better. Plus, like I said, it ain't snowing, so the evening will be nice."

She tried to keep her happiness in check when he held out his hand to help her up and then hopped in after her. A courting buggy not only didn't have a top, but it was also much smaller. And the bench seat was shorter, making it impossible for the two of them to not be scooted next to each other.

After helping her arrange the blankets around them both, Cale released the brake and motioned Bonnie forward. "Have you talked to anyone who's going tonight?" he asked.

"*Nee.* I had assumed it would be the regular group of our friends."

"If it's not, we might have to leave." Cale sounded tense.

"You really are worried that Caleb and Rachel are planning something wild, aren't you?"

He shrugged. "Kind of." Staring straight ahead, he added, "*Rumspringa* is a strange time for people our age, you know? Some of our friends are going crazy; others are trying to be even more Amish than their parents."

Hope knew a couple of kids who were so strict about following the rules of the *Ordnung* that she sometimes felt they could be more pious than a bishop. "You're right," she said slowly. "It's a huge amount of pressure to make a decision about our future."

"But we're only sixteen. We've got time to figure everything out, right?"

She was tempted to share how her mother was practically ready to marry them off but didn't want to scare Cale. "What are you trying to figure out?"

"Oh, this and that. It's not like I have much choice about how I spend my days anyway."

"Because of your father's death?" she asked hesitantly. Cale didn't like to talk about his *daed* or how tight his family's finances were, but Hope knew both subjects were often on his mind.

"*Jah*," he said forlornly, his expression resigned. "I've always had to work to help my *mamm*. And, because I'm the oldest and a boy, I feel responsible for not just my siblings but my mother, too. I'd always planned to leave when I was eighteen, just to gain some independence, but now I don't know if I'll be able to."

Hope felt sorry for him. And maybe a little embarrassed about how she always visited him in the barn. Had she misunderstood all the conversations they'd shared over the last couple of years? Had she been imagining the warm looks he'd sometimes sent her way? Was he just being nice to her because he couldn't afford to lose his job? Maybe he didn't actually like her at all.

"Cale, I feel bad that you have to work for my family. I'm sorry if I haven't seemed more aware of your circumstances or acted like I was taking you for granted."

"You shouldn't. I like working for your parents."

"They like you a lot." She smiled at him in the moonlight. Maybe now he would say something about how he liked her, too.

"Good, because I need the job."

It felt like the bottom had fallen out of her stomach.

Old doubts about her looks settled in like old friends. Maybe Cale really didn't think anything about her other than she was his boss's daughter. Maybe he was only taking her to the party because he didn't feel like he could say no to her.

Hope was attempting to think of something to break the silence when she realized they were almost at the Beachys' home—and that there were a lot of buggies and a couple of older-looking cars in the field, too.

"I'm going to park the buggy over near the outside so we can leave early if we feel like it."

"That sounds good. Will you unhitch Bonnie?"

"*Jah.*" He pointed to a covered area where five or six horses were tethered to hitching posts. "Our old horse would've preferred to stay by herself next to the buggy, but Bonnie's real social. She'll enjoy the warmth and company of the other horses."

"Lightning always likes to be by himself."

"That makes sense. Lightning is a mighty opinionated horse."

She giggled. Cale wasn't exactly wrong. Lightning was obedient, but only if he thought the driver knew what he or she was doing. If someone was new to driving, he could be as obstinate and disagreeable as an old man in a crowded restaurant. "The first time I drove the buggy, I thought Lightning had turned into a bully."

"He probably was being one." Walking around, Cale held out his hands to help her down. When she leaned forward, he gripped her waist as she held on to his shoulders. It was only a moment, but it was much more personal than anything they'd done before.

When he dropped his hands like they were burning, Hope wondered if he'd felt their connection, too. Or, had it been something else? She hoped he hadn't been shocked by her weight.

Picking up the tin of puppy chow, she walked by his side toward the barn. The main doors were open, and they could hear light-hearted conversation and laughter from halfway across the parking lot. Off to the left was a firepit with about a dozen people standing around it—almost all boys.

"A lot of people are here," she said. "Wow."

"*Jah*, it sure seems like it."

As they approached, heads started turning their way, and a couple of people shouted out greetings.

"Hope! You did come. I'm so glad!" Clara called out as she hurried forward. When she saw that Cale was still standing protectively next to Hope, she smiled. "Did the two of you come together?"

"*Jah*."

"How are ya, Clara?" Cale asked.

"Great." She looped an arm around Hope's elbow. "I'll take care of her, Cale. Go on now, all the guys are probably already looking for ya. Most of them are around the firepit."

Cale didn't move. "Hope?"

"It's fine," she said. Though she'd been anxious to be by his side, she was also excited to join the other girls and finally be a part of the group. Summoning a bright smile, she added, "Go have a good time. I'll catch up with you in a little while."

He didn't look exactly happy about that, but he nodded. "I'll come find you in thirty minutes or so."

Embarrassed to say what she wanted in front of Clara—which was that she would look for him then—Hope smiled at him. After another moment's hesitation, he walked toward the firepit.

"Come on," Clara said. "Let's go into the barn. It's freezing out here."

The barn looked magical. Kerosene lanterns dangled from the

rafters, and someone had hung twinkling battery-operated lights along the sides. Tea lights were nestled in mason jars on every table, too. "Wow," she said again.

"I know. I *canna* believe how many people are dressed English."

Blinking, Hope stopped eyeing the beautiful decorations and noticed that Clara was exactly right. About half of their friends were wearing jeans and T-shirts. Others were wearing an odd assortment of half-English and half-Amish clothing. Several of the girls weren't wearing *kapps*, their hair either confined in a ponytail or hanging loosely down their backs.

A few of the girls glanced Hope's way and snickered.

She suddenly felt like the biggest wallflower there. Here she was, dressed up like she was going to a fancy dinner with her parents. At least Clara was dressed in her *kapp* and dress, too.

"Where are Rachel and Caleb's parents?" Hope whispered.

"Probably in their *haus.*"

"They don't chaperone? I thought they'd be walking around in the thick of things."

Clara giggled and shook her head. "*Nee.* They never do. That's why everyone wants to come over here for parties. It's the only time we can ever feel like normal teenagers, you know?"

Hope nodded, but she didn't exactly agree. She'd always felt like she was a normal teen.

"Hope! You came!" Rachel said. "I wasn't sure if you would."

"I was glad you asked."

"Did you and Clara come together?"

"Nope. Cale Mast brought her," Clara supplied.

"Really?" Rachel looked impressed. "Are you two courting?"

"*Nee*, we're just friends," Hope said.

"Hope might say that she and Cale are just pals, but they looked pretty close when I saw them walking in together."

Rachel smiled. "You've liked Cale for a while, haven't you?"

Hope felt her cheeks burn in embarrassment. She didn't want anyone to know the extent of her crush, but lying didn't feel right, either. She settled for a shy shrug and then realized she was still holding her tin. "I brought some snacks. Where are you putting all the food?"

"Oh, just put it over there," Rachel said. "Do either of you want some punch?"

"Sure," said Clara.

Next thing Hope knew, she was walking by herself to the snack table and feeling embarrassed all over again. There was her tin of snack mix in the middle of about ten bags of chips.

Realizing she was standing next to the trash can, she quickly moved to the side, not wanting to get her dress dirty. But as she moved, she realized that the trash was full of beer cans. Everyone was drinking.

She'd been so foolish. Cale hadn't seemed that excited to go but had volunteered to take her because she had wanted to be included so badly. Now, here she was, dressed wrong and feeling self-conscious while Cale was probably doing the same thing outside.

"Hey. It's Hope, right?"

It took her a minute to realize that the girl wearing jeans, leather tennis shoes, and a clingy top was Amanda, her sister's best friend from school. "*Jah*. It's me. How are you?"

"I'm good. I came in town for Christmas and decided to stop by Rachel's party to see what was going on. How's your sister?"

"She's good."

"Is she married yet?"

Hope tried to ignore the derision in Amanda's voice. "*Nee*. She and Hank do seem serious, though."

"I'm sure Hank doesn't want to let her go. Your parents have a lot of money, and she's really pretty."

"Anna is very pretty."

"I heard you showed up with Cale. Is he really dating *you*?"

Amanda's words were pleasant, but her tone was slightly derisive. Feeling even more uncomfortable, Hope clenched her hands together. "*Nee*, we're just friends."

"I figured as much. I mean, he works for your parents, right?"

Hope nodded, but resented Amanda for pointing it out.

"So, where is he? Hanging out with everyone else?"

Amanda's comment stung, though there hadn't been any rancor behind it. In a way, that was almost worse. It was like it hadn't even occurred to Amanda that a guy like Cale would want to seriously court a girl like her.

"He's out by the firepit," Hope said at last.

"Oh, he's out there drinking with all the guys," Amanda said knowingly.

"I don't think he's drinking. Cale doesn't drink."

"You sound so sure about that." For some reason that seemed to amuse Amanda. "Let's go see." She half pulled Hope outside to where they got a good look at all the boys. Her eyes went directly to Cale, then froze. He had a can of beer in his hand.

Amanda started laughing. "I guess you were wrong about him, huh? But I can see now why you two aren't a real match. No offense, but you are kind of a far cry from your sister. Ain't so?"

Hope spun around and sped back into the barn.

When Clara saw her and called her over, Hope hurried to her side, only to feel even more foolish when it became obvious she was the only person in that group who was completely sober.

"Here," Clara said, thrusting a red Solo cup into her hands. "At least look like you're having a good time."

Tentatively, Hope took a sip of the punch and tried not to wince. It tasted like Kool-Aid, but it burned her throat on the way down.

"Oh, good, Hope. You're finally relaxing. I'm glad." Rachel patted her on the back as she walked past.

Hope wasn't relaxing and she wasn't having a good time. But she was stuck there. And the only thing worse than being stuck was feeling like the person everyone was making fun of.

She took another sip and hoped Cale would come get her soon.

sixteen

They'd reached a détente of sorts. Despite her better judgment, Jane could not deny her attraction to Carson and had even agreed to accompany him to a few of his society functions, but only as his secretary. Unfortunately, standing by his side had felt awkward and uncomfortable. It didn't seem like anyone believed their relationship was strictly platonic, either.

That's why when Carson expertly parked his Bentley in front of her boardinghouse, Jane knew what she had to do.

"I don't think we should do this again, Carson. I think it only emphasized how you and I don't have anything in common."

Instead of accepting her words, Carson simply grinned. "I beg to disagree, Jane. The things we have in common are the only things that matter."

—*Finding Love's Fortune,* page 213

It had taken Cale about two seconds to realize that attending the party had been a really big mistake. From the moment Hope waved him off with a fake smile and walked into the barn, his sense of doom had strengthened. All he'd wanted to do was turn around and get out of there.

But next thing he knew, he'd gotten pulled into the crowd around the firepit and someone handed him a beer. He didn't drink, but he didn't want to make a big deal of it. He also hadn't known how to leave without either causing a scene in front of all the guys or embarrassing Hope if she was having a great time with Clara and the rest of her friends.

He ended up staying and biding his time. He told himself he would go check on Hope in thirty minutes, and if she looked un-comfortable at all, he'd get her out of there. Unfortunately, every time Cale tried to get away to see her, another person would ask him a question or tell him a joke, and he'd be stuck for another ten minutes.

It was frustrating in about a dozen different ways. Cale liked most of the people there. They had been his friends since he was a babe and had already confided that they were planning to get bap-tized when they were eighteen or nineteen. All they were doing now was just having a little fun. But the choices they were currently mak-ing weren't his. He felt like he was between a rock and a really hard place.

"What's up with you tonight?" Matt asked. "You look like a fox with his paw stuck in a trap."

That was a typical Matt comment. The guy was all about the outdoors. It didn't sit well with Cale, though. Not that it was a big surprise. His father had loved animals. Cale had always thought it ironic that his *daed*, who'd been such a bully around their house, had always been so gentle with wild animals.

Focusing back on the present, Cale shrugged. "I don't know. I guess I'm tired or something."

"I'd bet money on the 'something' part." Matt grinned at him. "Especially since you brought Hope here but haven't spent a second with her."

"I keep trying to get away, but I keep getting sidetracked."

Matt shrugged. "I wouldn't worry about it. She's probably with her own circle of friends, and you'd just be in the way. You know how girls are when they get together."

"Yeah, probably." He hoped that was the case.

"You want another beer?"

"Nah, I'm good." He'd only had a couple sips of the one Caleb had handed him when he'd first arrived.

Matt moved on to another group of friends, and Cale gazed into the fire. There was no real reason he shouldn't be enjoying himself. He liked a lot of the guys at the party, and it wasn't like he had a ton of opportunities to let loose and have a good time with his friends. The fact was that he hardly ever got moments like this. When he wasn't working, he was usually helping out at home.

That was probably the reason why he felt so disconnected. He didn't have a whole lot in common with most of his friends. His father had been abusive, which had forced him and Viola to grow up much faster than normal, and he had spent most of his time trying to shield his little brother and help his mother get through each day. Then, after his father's death, he had been burdened with the family finances.

Unlike guys like Matt, he hadn't grown up with a big extended family offering support and help with bills. It had only been him, his siblings, and his mother. While other kids were worrying about school assignments or acne or girls, he'd been wondering how to help get Viola a new pair of boots or pay for Bonnie's feed.

He knew his mother felt terrible about the burdens she'd shouldered him with, but he'd never blamed her. His mother was the sweetest person. It wasn't her fault her husband had not only been mean but also had left her with a mountain of debt when he died.

"Hey, Cale," Matt said, hurrying over to him. "You better go get Hope."

"What's wrong?"

"She's drunk."

"What?" He started walking toward the barn. "Are you sure?"

"Pretty sure," Matt said as he walked by his side. "A couple of the girls thought it would be funny to spike the punch, and I heard Amanda kept refilling her cup every time it got empty."

Though Cale wondered why Hope had been drinking in the first place, it wasn't the time to ask. "Where is she?"

"Rachel sat Hope in the back by the door and asked me to come get you and get her out of here."

"Great." He couldn't believe what had happened. Not only had he let Hope down, but her parents were going to be so mad at him. They'd probably fire him, too.

When he walked in the barn, he was greeted with a blast of humid air and the faint scent of sweet punch. Looking around, it was pretty obvious Hope wasn't the only person who'd had too much to drink. A lot of the girls were laughing and dancing to some song playing from a boom box.

Then he spied Hope. She was sitting alone in a corner and looked pitiful.

"See what I mean?" Matt asked.

"*Jah*. Thanks for getting me."

Matt lowered his voice. "I felt sorry for her, you know? A lot of the girls were making fun of how she'd never had a drink before and was wandering around all dressed up."

Cale had thought Hope was the prettiest girl at the whole party. No doubt a lot of people had thought so, too. Otherwise no one would have given her a minute's notice. He glanced at Matt. "I'm going to sneak her out the back. She needs to get out of here."

"That's probably a real good idea. I'm sorry all the girls were so mean to your date. You haven't had the best night, huh?"

Cale shrugged, though Matt was exactly right. The whole experience had been terrible, and he had a feeling it was only going to get worse.

Feeling more than a couple pairs of eyes watching, he sat down next to Hope. "Hey."

She turned to him in an exaggerated movement. "Hiya, Cale," she slurred. "You're back."

"We need to get out of here. Let me help ya with your cloak."

"All right." She attempted to pull it over her shoulders but seemed to be having trouble even doing that.

He leaned closer and pulled it around her, easily fastening the grommet.

When she swayed slightly, her eyes filled with tears. "I'm sorry. I'm so dizzy. I don't know what's wrong with me."

If there weren't so many people watching them, he would've told her. But at the moment, all he wanted to do was get her out of there. "I'm going to help you up and put my hand around your waist. We're going to go right out the back door. Okay?"

She nodded. "Okay."

"Come on." It was a blessing that Hope wasn't so far gone that she couldn't walk. She stayed by his side as they walked the short space to the back door and then headed around the side to where all the buggies were parked.

The cold air seemed to wake Hope up a bit. Slowly, her footsteps got steadier, and she didn't look as weepy. When they got to his courting buggy, he suddenly wished he'd brought his mother's real one. It would be warmer and give them some privacy, too. "Do you want to get in or stand here while I go get Bonnie?"

"Stand here?" She blinked at him owlishly.

"That's fine. I'll be right back." Glad that Bonnie was nearby, he quickly untied her from the post and guided her to the buggy. Bonnie, after nudging him with her nose a few times, walked by his side, though he could tell she wasn't happy he wasn't giving her the usual amount of attention.

"I know, girl," he murmured. "This is bad, right?"

He said a quick prayer of thanks that Hope was where he'd left her. "We'll be on our way soon."

"Do you want some help?" Hope called out.

"*Nee*. Just stay put." Luckily Bonnie allowed him to quickly hitch her up and didn't even paw at the ground as he maneuvered Hope into the bench seat and then finally hopped in beside her.

"It sure is cold," she said.

"*Jah*. Here." He tossed the blanket to her before motioning Bonnie forward. Right as they got to the road, he felt her hand grip his thigh. He jumped. "Hope, what are you doing?"

"I'm sorry. I was trying to get you covered, too."

"I'm fine. Remove your hand, okay?"

"Oh. All right." With the blanket hanging off the bench seat between them, she curved her arms around herself and bent her head.

She looked pitiful.

"Hope, hang in there. You're going to be okay."

He just prayed that was the truth—for both of their sakes.

seventeen

Carson decided to paint his basement. Yes, he had plenty of people on hand to do that sort of thing, but sometimes a man just needed time to think.

—*Finding Love's Fortune*, page 236

So far, the ride home had been a disaster. Hope was alternating between talking a mile a minute and looking like she was about to pass out. She was in a really bad way.

Cale started hoping they'd never get to her house, because as soon as that happened, things were going to get even worse.

After staying silent for five whole minutes, Hope blurted, "I don't feel *gut*, Cale."

"I know."

"I drank that punch, and it was so strong. But I didn't know what to do," she said as she started to cry. "Amanda was already making fun of me for saying I was there with you."

Even though Cale knew he should only think about trying to make her feel better, he was too curious to ignore what she was saying. "Why would she make fun of you about that? It was true. You did come with me."

"Oh . . . you know."

"*Nee*, I don't." When she somehow managed to look even more miserable, he said, "Talk to me, Hope."

"Because you weren't *with me*, with me. You were out at the firepit with all the boys."

"You said you were going to be in the barn with the girls. I thought you wanted to be separate."

"I didn't want you to feel you had to b-babysit me."

"Babysit you? You're not making any sense, Hope. I would've stayed by your side if you'd said anything."

"I couldn't."

"Why?" He was really starting to lose patience with her.

"Oh, Cale. You know why people couldn't imagine us together. It's because you're you, and I'm me."

She was right. He was the oldest son of a widowed mother who didn't have a lot of money. She was the prettiest girl in the county and had been coddled her whole life by her wealthy parents. "You're gonna have to explain that better."

"You're going to make me?" she asked in a high-pitched whine as if he'd said something really mean.

He had two choices. He could either let the whole conversation slide or he could push it. Since there was a real good possibility her parents were going to refuse to let him see her ever again after he got her home, he decided to push it. "Yep. I don't know what you mean."

"Fine. You're everyone's favorite. So handsome. All the girls want you to notice them. But I'm fat."

He couldn't help himself. He started laughing. "Yeah, right."

In the dim light of the almost full moon, he could see her eyes widen. "You are so mean!" she cried. And then she started bawling.

"Hope, don't cry."

"Why did you make me tell you that? Now you're going to hate me."

"I could never hate you."

When she glared at him, he could practically feel how upset she was. Even Bonnie seemed agitated. "And, for the record, I don't think you're fat at all."

Looking back down at her clasped hands, she mumbled, "Just forget it."

"I'm serious, Hope. I think you're the prettiest girl around. I . . . I like the way you look."

She sucked in a breath, then gasped. "Oh my word. I'm gonna be sick."

"Huh?" Belatedly realizing that "gonna be sick" was girl-speak for vomiting, he called out "Wait!" and pulled Bonnie over to the side. The moment he braked, she leaned over the side and threw up all over the ground.

Cale figured girls would throw up in a delicate way. Or at least quietly. That wasn't Hope, though.

He was so startled by all the noise, he gaped at her for a moment before realizing she needed help. Glad that Bonnie was such a *gut* horse and didn't seem in the mood to attempt to bolt, he loosely held the reins with one hand while he attempted to comfort Hope with the other. "Are you okay?" he asked as he carefully patted her back.

"*Nee,*" she said. "I'm not okay at all."

"Do you need anything?"

"Beyond another life right now? *Nee.*"

"We're almost at your *haus.*"

She didn't do much more than nod, though he was glad about that. He was already going over the different scenarios about to take place, starting and ending with Mr. Overholt firing him for not taking care of Hope.

Hope was sniffling, and he couldn't think of anything that was safe to say. So they rode the rest of the way in silence.

When he directed Bonnie up her drive, Cale knew he had to say something worthwhile before he never saw her again. "I'm really sorry about tonight. Everything that happened is my fault."

Hope only sniffled again in response.

When he parked Bonnie, the front door opened, and there were both of her parents standing in the doorway.

"Hi, you two," Mr. Overholt said in a merry tone. "We didn't expect you to be back for another hour or two."

Cale hung his head as he walked around and helped Hope down. Realizing there was nothing to be said but the truth, he murmured, "I'm sorry, but Hope is, um, not feeling too good."

The kerosene lantern by the front door illuminated Hope enough to see her tear-filled eyes and the faint stain on her dress.

Mrs. Overholt's face went slack. "What happened, Hope?"

It seemed to take Hope a second to get her bearings. "The party wasn't anything like I'd expected. There was drinking," she added with a faint slur. "I had too much punch, and I feel awful."

Her mother's eyes widened. "Hope Overholt, are you drunk?"

"I don't know." She glanced Cale's way. "I think I am. I mean, I just threw up on the road."

After shooting Cale a death stare, Mrs. Overholt ushered an unsteady Hope into the house. When the door closed, Cale was left to face Hope's *daed* all by himself. Not that Hope would have been much help.

With his hands on his hips, Mr. Overholt looked even more formidable than usual. "Cale, it's time you started talking. What, exactly, happened at that party, and how come my daughter got the worst of it?"

As hard as it was to do, Cale knew he had no choice but to be completely honest. "This was all my fault. When we got to the party, we split up."

"You left her side."

"*Jah*. I was by the firepit with the guys, and she went into the barn with a girlfriend." Feeling sick to his stomach, he continued, "A lot of the kids were pretty rowdy, and I guess the girls thought it would be funny to encourage Hope to drink a lot of punch. By the time I got to her, it was too late."

"I don't understand how you didn't know any of this was happening."

Since there was no way to excuse himself without making either Hope sound worse or ratting out their friends, Cale struggled to find the right words. "I know you don't, sir. I know you're disappointed in me, too. Even though I promised to take care of Hope, I didn't come close to doing that." He hung his head. "I don't know what to say."

"It doesn't seem like there is anything to say. Hope's mother and I expected better from you."

"I know you did. Worse, I know Hope expected more from me, too. I feel like I let a lot of people down this evening."

"You'd best get on home. I have a very sick daughter to take care of."

Cale nodded and turned around. He heard the Overholts' front door close as he freed Bonnie's reins from the hitching post. Bonnie whickered as he climbed into the buggy, released the brake, then clicked his tongue to direct her forward.

With no streetlights or vehicles on the road, his world seemed darker than ever. He supposed it was fitting, since it matched his mood. For the last year, he'd been biding his time until he could leave Berlin. He'd been ready to leave his job, leave the responsibilities of his house, maybe even leave Hope and the ties she represented.

But now, in a span of just a couple of hours, it felt like he'd just had everything pulled out from underneath him. All his big dreams seemed so elusive now. Why had he ever agreed to go to that party?

When he finally got home, the warmth of the barn was a relief. Thankful to be able to pull the courting buggy all the way inside, he turned on a flashlight, then unhitched Bonnie and carefully brushed her coat. Bonnie had been waiting for him for hours in the cold, and the journey home had taken a bit of time as well. She needed the attention.

When he was satisfied that her coat was cared for, he greeted Gwen, then allowed the two friends to reunite while he went to the house.

His mother was sitting in the hearth room with a cup of hot tea and a knitting project. She was wearing an old dark gray dress. It was a surprising sight. She'd worn that dress constantly after his father died. Once she'd gotten out of her mourning period, she'd worn far brighter shades. Cale had actually thought the dress had been long made into dustrags.

When she looked his way, Mamm smiled.

"Hiya, Mamm."

"Hello to you, too." Placing the yarn and knitting needles on the table beside her, she leaned forward. "Did you have a good time with Hope?"

Everything inside of Cale wanted to simply nod so he could go upstairs and be by himself. But he couldn't lie to her. Putting off the truth was only going to make things harder than they already were. "Not really. I should have never taken her, Mamm. I really messed up."

"Uh-oh. What happened?" She patted the cushion next to her.

"Way too much." As briefly as Cale could, he told her about the firepit and the beer and the Amish kids dressed English and Hope in her red dress. As was her usual way, Mamm listened without interrupting, though it was obvious from her deepening frown that his mother didn't like hearing much about his story.

"What do you think Hope is going to say about you taking on all the responsibility for the evening's events?" she asked when he finished.

He was confused by the question. "Probably the same thing I just did, Mamm. I really let her down tonight."

"Hmm." Looking like she was trying hard to rein in her temper, his mother stood up. "I think maybe we need some sustenance. Would you like some tea or hot chocolate?" She smiled slightly. "It might warm you up."

"*Jah*, sure. Peppermint tea sounds good."

"I'll be right back. Take off your boots and coat, Son."

As much as he didn't want to have a heart-to-heart with his mother, Cale did as she asked. At least this way he wouldn't have to go to sleep wondering what was going to happen in the morning.

She returned with two mugs within minutes. "Here you go."

Cale took it gratefully. The mug was hot in between his hands, warming him up even though he hadn't realized he was cold. After taking an experimental sip, he said, "Mamm, I don't know why your tea always tastes so good."

"I don't know, either. Perhaps tea always tastes better when someone else made it."

"Maybe so."

When his mother sat down again, the hem of her dark gray dress fluttered around her ankles. After a bit of a pause, she murmured, "Cale, I thought a lot about your story when I was in the kitchen."

"I bet."

"*Nee*, I don't know if you do." She set her mug on the table. "You see, I think you are being too hard on yourself."

"Really?"

She nodded. "While it is true that you are responsible and mature for your age, you're also only sixteen. In the grand scheme of things, that is not very old."

"Mamm, I'm almost seventeen."

"To be honest, seventeen isn't all that old, either. God gives you a childhood for a reason, and you're supposed to mess up from time to time right now. Otherwise, you'll never learn from your mistakes."

"Tonight's mistake was a pretty big one, Mamm." And what was he supposed to learn from it anyway?

"That may be true, but I don't know if anything too awful happened."

"Mamm, I brought Hope home drunk." When his mother's lips quirked up, he glared at her. "This isn't funny, you know."

"You are right. This isn't funny at all. I guess something about the way you said that caught me wrong." After visibly collecting herself, his *mamm* said, "Cale, Hope Overholt is a lovely girl, but she isn't a helpless one. She could've refused the punch or come to find you on her own."

"She hadn't been to a party like that before."

"Are you saying you are the expert? Do you go to a lot of parties, Cale?"

"*Nee*. You know I don't."

"All I'm trying to tell you is that I can understand why you feel badly, but I don't believe all the responsibility falls on your shoulders."

"Mamm, I told you there was drinking."

"I know you think I should be shocked, but I'm not. I'm disappointed, of course, but *kinner* have been experiencing their *rumspringa* for a mighty long time, Son. This party was not the first one with some Amish teens stretching their wings, and it's not going to be the last."

He wasn't sure about that, but even if his mom was right, it didn't change the fact that Hope's parents were mad at him. "I think I lost my job there, Mamm."

All traces of humor fled from her expression. "Surely not?"

"Mr. and Mrs. Overholt were really upset."

"What are you going to do on Monday? Did they tell you not to come to work?"

"I'm going to go, but I'm half expecting Mr. Overholt to tell me to go back home."

Looking more agitated now, his mother stood up. "Well, if that's the case, then that's what will happen. We *canna* prevent Jeremiah and Charity from making foolish decisions. It will be a shame if that's the outcome, though."

"I don't know what I'll do if they fire me."

"You will be disappointed, but you are strong and able-bodied. You can work around here for a few weeks and then go on a job hunt after Christmas."

"But what about my pay? I won't be making any money."

"I have money saved. Enough to still take care of your presents, too. Everything will be okay, Cale. I promise."

He didn't think so, but he was suddenly too tired to worry about it anymore. "I'm going to go to bed."

She hugged him tight. "Try not to worry, dear. I know you're upset, but everything happens for a reason."

He hugged her back and walked upstairs, ducking into the bathroom first to wash up so he wouldn't wake Jason. He wasn't sure what was going to happen next, but suddenly he didn't feel like everything was so horrible.

Perhaps he had needed that pep talk after all.

eighteen

Jane had been so distracted by her hot and cold feelings for Carson that she forced herself to go on two interviews at other companies. Unfortunately, neither was a good fit.

—*Finding Love's Fortune,* page 242

Sadie was a nervous wreck. Cale had left an hour ago to speak with Jeremiah and Charity Overholt and still hadn't returned. That could either mean that everything was fine and Hope's parents had simply wanted to chat with him a while or that Jeremiah had yelled at him, possibly fired him, and poor Cale was taking his time returning.

Cale carried so many burdens on his shoulders, Sadie knew her eldest would hate to bring home bad news.

She wished Cale was Jason's age again. Back then, she would've walked him to wherever he needed to go and wouldn't be in this awful spot where she had to let him grow up and handle his own problems while still feeling responsible.

Sighing, she gazed down the road but didn't see any sign of him. Maybe she should have gone with Cale anyway? Just to give him support? Would an almost-seventeen-year-old be okay with that?

She rather doubted it.

Atle came out of the barn. When he spied her, he walked over her way.

"It's a little cold out to be resting on the porch like you are," he called out. "Don't you want to go inside where it's warmer?"

"I'm not resting. I'm waiting."

His brow wrinkled. "Were you waiting for me? Did ya need something, Sadie?"

"*Nee*. I'm worried about Cale." She hesitated, then blurted what was on her mind. "I fear he's getting fired right now."

Atle's pure blue eyes darkened in concern. "If that's the case, then I reckon we'd better talk. Now, do ya want to go in the barn or in your kitchen? Both would be a sight warmer than this spot."

"I guess you're right." Though she hadn't been planning to share her worries with Atle, it was becoming obvious that she wasn't going to last much longer simply staring at the road. "How about we speak in the barn? At least then one of us will be able to get something done."

"Come on, then. At the very least, we'll be warmer there, *jah*?"

As her cheeks heated from his regard, she nodded shyly. It was becoming obvious that no matter how hard she tried to ignore her burgeoning attraction to Atle, it wasn't going to fade anytime soon.

"I'm looking forward to hearing your story," Atle said.

She followed him down the shoveled path and into the barn. To her surprise, Gwen was out of her stall and nibbling on a handful of pellets. "Gwen, what in the world?"

"Oh, sorry. I let her out. I hope you don't mind."

Reaching out to give Gwen's silky white fur a rub, she said, "Why did you take her out of her pen, Atle?"

"Well, you see, goats are sociable creatures, and Bonnie there was looking like she wasn't in the mood to entertain. So I decided to let Gwen keep me company for a spell." He looked embarrassed. "Don't worry. I was keeping an eye on her."

"She hasn't been trying to eat everything?"

"Given the choice, she likes food. Plus, she seems to like me chatting with her."

"I see." His comment was rather sweet. If she wasn't so worried about Cale, she would have been completely charmed.

"Gwen's all right. Now, how about you tell me about Cale instead?"

"Oh, well, it has to do with the party he went to on Saturday night. He took the Overholts' daughter Hope. Do you know Hope?"

"I do."

"Well, not to tell tales, but Hope got drunk at the party. And, since Cale was her date, her parents are upset with him."

He whistled low. "Oh, boy."

"I suppose you're shocked." Straightening her slim shoulders a bit, she said, "I promise, Atle, that I'm not in the habit of allowing Cale to attend parties like that."

"I am shocked, but not by the party as much as you worrying about Cale's job, Sadie."

"I feel the same way. Teenagers in the midst of *rumspringa* do all sorts of stupid things. We both know that."

"*Jah*, we do."

"It's just that . . . I know life isn't supposed to be fair, but Cale taking all the blame for Hope's drinking doesn't seem right. Of course, I *am* his mother."

"I happen to agree with ya."

Unable to help herself, she played with the edge of her apron. "Cale left the house this morning not knowing what was going to happen."

Still looking at her intently, Atle said, "What do you wish to happen?"

"What do I wish?" The question caught her off guard. It made her think a bit, too. "You know, I'm not really sure, Atle. I guess I should say that I am hoping and wishing Jeremiah Overholt won't decide that his daughter's problem with punch has anything to do with my son's work ethic. But I fear that's asking for too much."

His blue eyes softened. "Oh, Sadie. If you're that upset, I reckon you could go talk to Jeremiah and Charity. They're good people."

"I can't do that. Cale would get upset, and I would just make things worse."

"Because you care?"

She nodded. "And because I'm his mother. Mothers don't always make the best decisions when it comes to interfering." Walking over to Gwen, she ran her fingers along the goat's side. When Gwen nudged her hand with her head, obviously hoping for more pets, Sadie complied. She chuckled. "Atle, do you have a goat at home?"

"Not now. But we did have a couple when I was a small boy." Folding his arms across his chest, he continued, "Their mischievous ways always bothered my father something awful, but I found them entertaining. They were good company, too."

The image of a young Atle tending goats made her smile. Continuing to pet Gwen, Sadie watched Atle saw a piece of lumber, rest it on the ground, then pick up another and make a mark.

"What's the smile for?"

"Oh, nothing. I guess I was imagining you playing with goats when you were little."

He looked down at his feet. "I wasn't always old, Sadie."

The way he said her name, so low and soft, practically made all her nerves stand on end. "Neither was I," she whispered.

"You still look lovely as ever, though," he blurted. "I mean, the years have been kind to you."

Sometimes Sadie wished it was common practice to take photographs. She would like to have seen a photo from when she'd been married to Marcus. Would she look the same or different? She'd been so unhappy back then.

"I don't know what to say to that."

"Then say thank you."

"*Danke*," she said with a smile. Then her stomach dropped out when she heard footsteps approach.

Atle's hands stopped as well. They both stared at the doorway and seemed to cast a joint sigh when Cale appeared, upset and dejected.

It looked like her worst fears had just come true. She knew Jeremiah and Charity were likely disappointed, but she sure wished they would've thought about the consequences before taking out their anger on her boy. She was pretty sure that they'd forgotten Cale wasn't much older than their daughter.

Or . . . perhaps she was just imagining the worst? "What happened, Cale?"

"About what I thought." Cale looked worriedly at Atle.

"Don't worry about Atle, Cale. I just told him what happened, and he knows how worried I am about you."

Cale's dejected expression turned angry. "Mamm, you're telling everyone about what I did? About what *Hope* did?"

"*Nee*, she told me what was in her heart when I asked what was wrong, Cale," Atle interjected. "There's a difference. Plus, I've got no call to gossip about you. Whatever she said was in confidence."

Most of the bluster went out of Cale's body. "Sorry." He wiped a hand over his brow. "I don't know what I'm going to do."

"Do you want to go inside and talk?" Sadie offered. "Maybe between the two of us we'll be able to find a solution."

He looked at her for a long moment before shaking his head. "We might as well talk here." Looking at Atle, Cale added, "Maybe you can help me figure out what to do now. I *canna* believe it."

"I'll be glad to help if I can."

Watching him sit down on an overturned work bucket, Sadie once again was struck by the differences between Atle and Marcus. Where Marcus had been quick to erupt and cast blame on whoever was within reach, Atle acted as if he had a hard casing around him. Nothing seemed to crack that shell. Or if it did, he didn't let on.

Sitting on an old milking stool, Sadie gazed at her eldest in concern. "So . . . what happened, Cale?"

"I knew Mr. Overholt would want to talk about Saturday night, so I went over to the *haus* first thing and knocked on their kitchen door. Hope was there, but she got sent to her room before I got a second to say anything to her."

"And then?"

"And then Mrs. Overholt started saying things about how they thought I was different and better than I actually was and how I ruined Hope's reputation."

"Surely not."

Looking even more pained, Cale added, "Then Mr. Overholt

told me he didn't want me anywhere around Hope or their farm and I was fired."

"That seems awfully harsh," Atle said.

"That's not even the worst part," Cale said, looking so angry he was near tears. "Mr. Overholt said he would never give me a decent recommendation for another job. And when I asked him how I was going to get my paycheck for last week, he said never."

"'Never'?" Sadie was stunned.

"Never." Cale leaned back on the old wooden bench and kicked out a boot. "I worked forty hours last week, and Mr. Overholt is acting like it weren't anything at all." Her son got to his feet and started pacing. "Mamm, I know I'm not supposed to be, but I'm so mad."

"Of course you are," she murmured.

"*Jah*, and I'm really confused, too. I mean, all I did was take Hope to the party, leave her alone when she asked me to, and then get her safely home. It wasn't even my idea to go there. She's the one who wanted to go. But now I can't even talk to her, I lost my job, and her parents took a whole week's salary from me."

Sadie was so upset. She glanced at Atle for help.

He stepped right in. "I think you have every right to be frustrated," Atle said. "I'm real sorry about what happened, Cale."

"*Danke*." He shook his head. "I don't know what I should do now. I don't even know what I *can* do. How am I ever going to get another job if Mr. Overholt refuses to even tell people that I came to work on time and worked hard?"

There was so much despair in Cale's voice, Sadie wished he was still young enough to enfold in her arms and squeeze tight. But since he was too old for that, she made do with attempting to find the right words. If there actually was something right to say. "How they're treating you is shameful, Son. Taking away your paycheck is wrong, too. I'm going to tell them that, too, when I go over there."

"Mamm, you can't do that!"

"Of course I can." Just thinking about the way Jeremiah and Charity were treating Cale made her so angry. "Regardless of how they think you handled that silly party, they can't fire you, refuse to give you a decent recommendation, and keep your money. It's not right."

"If you go over to the Overholts' *haus*, you're only going to make things worse."

"I'm not sure how much worse it can get for you, Son." Looking over at Atle, who had been listening intently, she said, "What do you think?"

"Well, it seems to me that you need to ask yourself why they would be behaving like this. Cale, no offense to Hope, but do you think she lied to her parents about what really happened? Maybe she didn't want to get in trouble, so she blamed you."

Cale frowned. "I hope not."

"But?"

"But I don't know. She was pretty drunk. Maybe she doesn't remember everything too well?"

"If she had that much alcohol, her parents had to guess something was going on with her. I spoke with you when you got home. You weren't drunk at all."

Cale sat back down and slumped. "I just can't believe I lost everything because I didn't want to tell Hope no."

"You haven't lost everything, Son." He had her love. God's love, too.

"*Jah*, it only seems that way." Atle stood up. "Cale, no one is going to hire you before Christmas, so why don't you help me build your room and the bed over in my workshop? I could use the help, and you can use the time to think about what kind of job you want to do next."

Atle's words forced Sadie to think about the cost of the room— and Cale's lost paychecks. She didn't like to depend on her son's wages, but she did still accept half his earnings. Even with the extra money her food gifts were bringing in, she feared the room might be an extravagance they couldn't afford. "Atle and Cale, I hate to make a horrible day worse, but I'm afraid we might need to postpone this building project."

A flush filled Cale's cheeks as he stood up again. "You're right, Mamm. Building a nice room like this makes no sense right now. Makes no sense at all," he muttered before walking straight out of the barn.

Sitting down again, Sadie pressed her hands to her face. "Atle, I'm so sorry."

"About what?"

"About canceling the job. About Cale running out of here like that." About wasting his time.

"Sadie, stand up for a moment, wouldja?"

Confused, she did as he bid. Then bit back a gasp as he wrapped her in his arms for a hug. His body was warm and solid against hers. And his arms were holding her loosely, in a way that made her feel like she could pull away if she wanted to.

But right now, at that moment? She didn't want to leave.

Still holding her against him, he rubbed her shoulder blades. "I hope you don't mind, but it looked like you could use a hug. You know . . . to remind you that you aren't alone."

It was like he'd read her mind. She had been feeling like it was her against the world, and the world was winning yet again. But now? Now it felt like she had hope again.

At least for a little while longer.

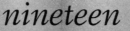

nineteen

Jane's mouth was dry, and her heart was racing. Surely what her mother was saying couldn't be true. But why would she make it up?

"I don't understand how Carson Marks's father could have been your boyfriend in college, Mom. My world couldn't be that small."

—*Finding Love's Fortune*, page 246

After sharing that brief hug, Atle told Sadie not to make any decisions about Cale's room in the barn. Then, afraid he was going to make a mess of promises he couldn't keep, he left for the day. It was cold out but not frigid, and he needed a walk to help his brain.

After stopping by his house to drop off his tools, he started walking. There was a small pond a bit more than two miles away. This time of year, it was covered with ice. Every once in a while, children would skate on it, but not like he'd used to. He wondered if it was

because parents nowadays worried outside ponds were too danger-
ous or because of children's lack of interest. Children—even Amish
children—seemed to gravitate toward more daring activities now.

Thinking about children stretching their wings brought him
to thinking about the party Cale and Hope had attended. It was a
shame what had happened, to be sure. However, he'd known a great
many teenagers during his own running-around years who had done
much worse. That didn't excuse bad behavior or drinking, but he
personally didn't believe that Cale needed to be fired from his job
because of it. He reckoned both Cale and Hope had learned some
things and would make better decisions in the future. Atle's *daed* had
often said that a nail in the foot was more memorable than a half
dozen warnings.

But then again, he was a bachelor with a rather solitary life.
Perhaps he simply didn't understand what it was like to be a parent.

Atle wished he had known what to say to the boy. The teenager
had looked like he'd just lost everything he'd ever cared about.

Continuing to walk, he kept an eye out for cardinals, robins,
and hawks. At one time the land was slated to be the site of a new
firehouse, but folks in charge had elected to build it a few miles to
the east. Since then, it's stood empty, only getting a bit of mowing
a couple of times a year. Some people griped about the waste of
valuable farmland, but Atle had always felt that the open space was
valuable in its own way. There were far too few places in the area
where a person could simply walk, enjoy God's blessings, and think.

Catching sight of the pond in the distance, Atle spied some Canadian geese on the banks. Perhaps it wasn't frozen solid after all?

And then he saw a lone girl sitting on the bank. When she looked up, he once again was reminded that the Lord God was wondrous, indeed.

Because sitting right in front of him was the young lady who seemed to be on many people's minds that day. None other than Hope Overholt.

When she spied him and then looked like she was going to hurry away, he took a chance. "Hiya, Hope. How's the pond today? Frozen through?"

Hope looked like she wasn't sure she wanted to answer, but she did at last. "It's frozen pretty good, but not in the center yet. The geese and a pair of mallards are taking advantage of that."

"I'm surprised to see the ducks here. It's late for them to be in the area."

"*Jah.*" She shrugged. "Maybe they decided to stay for a spell instead of going home."

That sure seemed like the opening he'd been waiting for. "I can see that. I come here quite a bit whenever I need a break from home."

"Me, too." She paused, looking sheepish. "I mean, I only just discovered it, but I aim to come back real soon."

He sat down on a rather uncomfortable rock. Close enough to

not have to yell but far enough away not to invade her space. "I just came from the Masts'."

Her head popped up. "You're making Cale a room or something, right?"

"That's true. Or rather, I *was* building him a bedroom. That's stopped, though."

"You're not going to build it for him anymore? How come?"

Hating to tell her the news but not wanting to fib, he said, "His *mamm* thought maybe I should stop the project since Cale is now out of a job and all."

Hope's already glum expression turned crestfallen. "I didn't realize that would happen. I mean, my parents told me they'd fired Cale, but I didn't think about the consequences for his family. I bet he's so upset." She slumped. "I bet he hates me now, too."

"I don't think he hates you at all, Hope."

A look of longing flashed in her eyes before she blinked. "I hope he doesn't, but I wouldn't blame him if he did. This . . . this whole situation is such a mess."

Keeping his attention on the ducks, Atle nodded. "I reckon so."

Hope picked up a pebble and tossed it onto the ice. It skittered a couple of feet until it slowed to a stop. "I was so mad at my parents that I ran over here to get a break from them. Now I'm probably going to get in trouble for doing that, too. They're driving me crazy."

"Should you head back? They're likely worried about you."

Hope seemed to think about it for a moment, then shook her head. "*Nee*. I still need some space. They're being really unreasonable and don't want to listen to a thing I say." She shrugged. "Besides, I doubt they even know I'm gone."

"Forgive me if I'm prying, but why are they blaming Cale so much?"

"I don't know."

"Are you sure?"

She shifted and wrapped her arms around her knees. "I didn't blame him for anything, if that's what you're asking. I promise you, I didn't."

"I'm only asking—and you don't have to reply."

"*Nee*, I should probably tell someone what happened on Sunday morning. It's been hard keeping it all inside."

"What happened?"

She took a deep breath. "My mother woke me up earlier than usual and told me to come downstairs. I did what she asked, but I felt terrible. My head was pounding." Her blue eyes darted to his. "I've never gotten drunk before. It isn't fun."

"I imagine not," he murmured.

"Anyway, as soon as I got downstairs, both of my parents were there. Next thing I knew, they were yelling at me and blaming Cale for being such a bad influence. At first, I tried to tell them he didn't have anything to do with my actions. I mean, he wasn't even there when I accepted that cup of punch. But they didn't want to listen." She looked down at the ground. "It was like they needed him to be the bad person instead of me."

"What did you do then?"

"Well, after it was clear they wouldn't listen to me, I didn't say anything. I just sat there until they said I could leave."

"That's it?"

Looking miserable, Hope nodded. "I know it sounds childish, but I didn't mean to act like a baby. I just . . . Well, I know how my parents are. They like to be right, and sometimes they find it pretty easy to make me feel like I don't do anything right."

"I'm sorry about that."

"Me, too. But it's no big deal, I mean, not for me. I sure didn't think they were going to fire Cale, though."

Atle had no experience dealing with teenagers, but he had once been a teenage boy.

"Hope, ignore me if you want, but I gotta tell you that I think you're being mighty selfish."

Looking shocked, she shook her head. "That's not true, Mr. Petersheim."

"Are you so sure? Instead of admitting that Cale did nothing besides abide by your wishes and then take you home, you let your parents twist everything and blame him. Now, he not only feels terrible about what happened, but he doesn't have a job. The boy needs a job, Hope."

"I know, but—"

"They even refused to pay him last week's salary. That's a full week's worth of work."

Looking angry, Hope got to her feet. "That's not my fault. I didn't know they took Cale's salary. I feel terrible about everything! I really do."

Atle got up, too. "Forgive me, but does that even matter?"

"Of course it does."

"If it really does matter to ya, then you'd best figure out what you're going to do now. Maybe you're going to have to tell your parents some things you don't want to say and they don't want to hear . . . if you want to help Cale Mast." After giving her a pointed look, he got up and started walking back home.

Atle knew he probably should've walked her back or apologized for speaking to her so bluntly. But he couldn't help but feel that telling her about her parents' decision was the right thing to do. If she knew how they treated Cale and she didn't do anything, then that would say a lot about her character.

But if she did somehow manage to make things right, then that would help Cale and his mother.

And as for his part in it? Well, he would say an extra prayer before going to sleep. Maybe Jesus wouldn't have wanted him to interfere, but perhaps He would understand his motives.

He might not be a hero in a romance novel like Carson Marks, but he was determined to do his best to help out a certain mother and son in distress.

twenty

This new development in their relationship shouldn't have blindsided Carson. But he supposed he shouldn't have been so caught off guard. So far, everything that had happened with Jane had taken him by surprise.

—_Finding Love's Fortune_, page 250

The right thing to do would've been to go home, but Hope wasn't ready to do that. Atle's words had shaken her, and she needed some time to think about them before she faced her parents again. The ten-minute walk back home wasn't nearly long enough.

However, she was feeling too restless to simply sit still. When she was sure Atle was long gone, she started walking toward town. The wind was blustery and cold, but the sun was out, a rarity in central Ohio in the middle of December. Figuring a walk in the sun was as good an excuse as she needed for continuing to be so disobedient, she kept going.

Fifteen or twenty minutes later, she saw the bookmobile in the distance. Curious to see if Sarah Anne was there, Hope quickened her pace. At the very least, she could step inside and get warm for a few minutes.

Just as if Hope had conjured her up, Sarah Anne was in the vehicle. She was sitting all alone, too.

The librarian seemed startled to see Hope, but her shocked expression quickly turned to a broad smile. "Hi, Hope. Now, isn't this a nice surprise to see ya."

"I was out walking when I spied the bookmobile. I had to come in and see if it was you."

"It's a rare day when I'm not driving it," Sarah Anne said with a chuckle. "Though, I have to share that you caught me off guard. This isn't a usual stop, you know. I just had an extra half hour before my next stop, so I decided to have some coffee and a snack."

Embarrassed that she barged in without a second's pause, Hope backed up two steps. "Oh! Well, I'll let you go, then."

"No, I don't want you to do that at all! What's the point of a bookmobile if I don't see patrons while I travel? Now, what can I help you with?"

"Nothing, I don't think," Hope said honestly. "When I spied you, I wanted to say hello but also get warm." She held out her empty hands. "I don't even have my library card with me."

"Of course you don't, if you weren't planning to see me. But if you do want to check out a book, I can find your library card online."

When Hope hesitated, Sarah Anne added, "Or you can simply stay inside a few and get warm while I finish my coffee."

"*Danke.*"

"Oh, where are my manners? Would you like a cup of coffee, too? Or, I can make tea or hot chocolate." Looking pleased with herself, the librarian said, "I've recently upgraded my beverage selection. It's getting rather fancy, if I do say so myself."

The offer was too good to pass up, especially since it was cold out and she was a pretty good distance from home. Seeing the coffee bar Sarah Anne now had, Hope smiled. "I'd like a cup of coffee, if you wouldn't mind."

Looking pleased, Sarah Anne motioned her over. "I'm going to show you how to work it." She popped a button. "First, put the pod in here, then the paper cup here . . . and snap the lid."

Hope snapped it. "And now do I push the flashing button?"

"Yes! You're doing swell, dear."

Swell? Hope giggled at the librarian's delight. When the coffee started dripping seconds later, her mouth watered. "This smells really good."

"It's hazelnut. My favorite." Sarah Anne motioned to the container of creamer sugar. "Help yourself to sugar and cream as well, then take your time and look around. Who knows? Maybe you'll find a book after all."

After Hope fixed her coffee with a whole packet of sugar, she carefully sipped the hot brew and wandered among the shelves.

Sarah Anne was sitting down again, eating a scone and glancing at her phone's screen.

Taking another sip, Hope slowly felt herself relax as she scanned the fiction shelves. She was a hot and cold reader. Sometimes she would read three or four books in a month. Soon after, she might not think about reading again until several weeks passed.

She was just about to turn and look at the small selection of magazines Sarah Anne had stacked in the back when she realized she was likely going to have a whole lot more time to read now that Cale wasn't going to be around.

She probably did need to have some books on hand. She began to scan the titles in earnest.

"Have you found anything of interest?" Sarah Anne asked. "Don't forget, I've got some new titles in the front."

"*Danke*, but I don't need anything new. Just something to hold my attention for a while."

Sarah Anne stood beside her and scanned the titles. After a moment, she pulled out two books. "I would recommend both of these. One is a historical novel about Lewis and Clark, and this one is a mystery about a woman searching for her sister."

Neither sounded appealing. "I think I need something more romantic. Do you have any books like that?"

Sarah Anne's eyes lit up. "Do I ever." She motioned Hope to follow her to some books wrapped and set near her desk. "I have a patron who has been interested in reading romances featuring admirable heroes, so I've been pulling some of my favorites." Picking up a stack of three, she scanned the titles, then plucked one out. "I think this might appeal to you, dear."

Hope took the book but didn't even glance at the title. "I'm sorry, but isn't it reserved?"

"The patron I was referring to reads rather slow. One book will be enough for him for now."

"'Him'? It's a man who is reading romances?"

"On the sly."

That sounded rather weird to Hope. "Why?"

"He's hoping the books will help him with his courting, you see."

Thinking of how badly she'd messed up with Cale, Hope sighed. "I could use some help in that regard, too."

"Really? Well, then this book is definitely for you, dear. It's about love conquering all."

Love conquering all did sound perfect for her—but also unattainable. After all, she was only sixteen. But when she finally read the title, it seemed to speak to her. "*Ruth's Last Chance*?"

Sarah Anne nodded. "Poor Ruth has to overcome a lot of obstacles to finally get her man."

Ruth's life sounded like hers! "I'd like to check this out, please."

"Of course, dear. Tell me your birthdate, would you please? That's how I arrange all my patrons."

Hope finished her coffee while Sarah Anne checked out her book. Soon after, she was on her way home.

❅ ❅ ❅ ❅

When she walked through her front door almost an hour later, both of her parents were standing in the entryway.

"There you are!" Mamm exclaimed. "We've been worried sick. Where were you?"

"I went to the bookmobile."

"You went to the library without asking for permission?"

That question was the last straw. "Mamm, Daed, we have to talk. You're treating me like a child." She took a deep breath. "I also am pretty upset with the way you treated Cale."

Her father crossed his arms over his chest. "Cale Mast is none of your concern."

"Oh, yes he is. Especially since I heard you not only fired him but also stole his money."

"I didn't steal anything." But it was obvious that Daed looked uncomfortable.

"It's true, though, isn't it? You actually refused to pay Cale for last week's work because I made a stupid choice at a party. That isn't fair at all."

"What did you do, Jeremiah?" her mother asked.

Now Hope was really shocked. "Daed didn't even tell you about how terribly he treated Cale, Mamm?"

"I know Daed told Cale he should've looked after you better."

That news made Hope even angrier. "You didn't even have the

nerve to share with Mamm that you both fired Cale and took his pay?" When her father continued to look embarrassed, Hope waved a hand in the air. "Daed, I think you owe Cale an apology."

"You need to watch your tone, Daughter. I don't like how you're speaking to me."

Hope placed a hand on her hip. "Well, I don't like finding out from a practical stranger that you cheated a sixteen-year-old who is working here to support his *mamm*. I didn't like discovering that because you fired Cale, he now can't have the new bedroom Atle Petersheim was building for him because they can't afford it." She drew a deep breath. "Now Atle won't get paid for his work."

"Oh, dear," Mamm murmured. "Jeremiah, I think we need to have a discussion."

"Hmph," Daed said. He folded his arms over his chest but there was a new, wary expression in his eyes.

Hope knew she should stop, but she was on a roll. "I especially don't like that you both refused to listen to me when I said that Cale didn't have anything to do with my drinking all that punch." She pulled her shoulders back and stood up straight. "I know I made a lot of bad decisions and I know you two are disappointed in me. But at least I was with Cale. He is the one who got me out of there. He is the one who took me home. He is the one who even told you everything. If I hadn't been with him, I don't know what would have happened."

"Hope, did you just go out to secretly meet Cale?"

"*Nee*. Cale is likely never going to want to speak to me ever again. And who can blame him?" Breathing hard, she said, "Mamm, Daed, you might be disappointed in me or wish I was a better person . . . but right now I'm pretty disappointed in the both of you, too. Now, I'll help make supper, but first I'm going to put this library book in my room."

While they gaped at her, she walked upstairs to her room. After she closed the door, she smiled at the woman on the cover of her book.

"I don't know what you had to do, Ruth, but I have a feeling you're going to be in good company. I've just stood up to my parents for the very first time, and it felt pretty good."

twenty-one

Jane was so overwhelmed that she decided to stop
interviewing for other jobs. She might not be exactly
sure about her feelings for Carson, but at least he was
a devil she knew.

—*Finding Love's Fortune*, page 279

Sitting through church in the Weavers' barn had been excruci-
ating. Even though Cale had been in the back row with all of his
friends like he usually was, nothing felt right. Not the whispered
gossip about what had happened at Caleb and Rachel's party after
they'd left, not the fact that Mr. Overholt was sitting three rows in
front of him, and definitely not that Hope was sitting almost directly
across from him.

Every time he looked straight forward, he was staring directly at
her face. And, to make matters worse, she seemed to be trying her

best to look anywhere but at him. Boy, was she going to refuse to even acknowledge his presence now?

There were so many emotions running through his head, he felt kind of sick. He was mad at both Hope and her parents, upset that he still didn't know where else he could work, and envious of his friends who didn't have near as many problems as he did.

Though he felt guilty for even thinking it, he wondered why he had to be the one in the crowd God had given so many problems to. How come he'd had to have an abusive father? How come that father had to then die and leave his *mamm* with no money? How come he'd had to start working on the weekends before he'd even finished eighth grade but Viola only had to help out their *mamm* around the house?

And how come Hope, who he'd basically had a crush on for years, had turned out to be so stupid?

"Cale," Reuben whispered. "Preacher Andrew is staring at you. Look more interested, or he'll pull you aside later."

Cale sat up straighter. Though he'd actually only heard of Preacher Andrew cornering a teenager once after services, they all lived in fear of being his next victim.

After mentally apologizing to the Lord for blaming Him for all his troubles, Cale listened harder.

And then it felt like Preacher Andrew was talking to just him.

"God is not unjust," Preacher Andrew said. "It says in chapter six, verse ten of Hebrews that 'He will not forget how hard you have worked for him and how you have shown your love to him by caring for other believers, as you still do.'" The preacher paused. "What does that mean to you? How have you shown your love by caring for other believers?"

Cale drew a blank. He'd tried to care for his family and Hope and her family. He tried to care for his friends and the people in his community. But maybe, sometimes, he spent a bit too much time caring for just himself.

During the last week, he'd only been concentrating on his loss and his hurt. Not on the bigger picture, which was that he'd been blessed to have that job for so many years already.

Taking a deep breath, Cale lifted his head and looked at Hope. She looked miserable and so alone. He wondered then if some of the people who'd been at the party had teased her about getting drunk. Even he had noticed that some of the kids had smirked at her pretty red dress. It was like they had put her down because she hadn't tried to be something she wasn't.

Still watching her, Cale noticed her sigh and look at the other girls, then look his way again, freezing when she caught him staring.

Driven by instinct—or maybe it was because his heart speaking instead of his pride—he smiled at her. Hope blinked and then, as if she was gaining her courage, smiled back.

And just like that, everything started to feel better in his life.

"Cale, why are you staring at Hope Overholt?" Reuben asked.

"That is none of your business."

"You should ignore her, Cale. Everyone has been talking about how drunk she got last Saturday night."

He might still be mad about a lot of things when it came to Hope, but there was no way he was going to let anyone he knew say one word against her. "I hope you put a stop to it, Reuben. Those girls got her drunk on purpose."

"Why would they do that?"

"Why wouldn't they? You know how some girls are. Everything is a joke to them." Lowering his voice even further, Cale added, "Besides, you know how innocent Hope is. Some girls like to make fun of that."

"I reckon you're right, but still . . ."

"But nothing," he fired back. "I took her to the party, and she wasn't planning on drinking. What happened is their fault."

Reuben put up his hands. "Okay, okay, I hear you." Looking at him curiously, he added, "What's gotten into you?"

"I don't know. I guess Preacher Andrew got me thinking about things."

"Really? I guess I should start listening more when I'm here."

Cale fought back a smile. He'd been thinking the very same thing.

An hour later, after the service had ended and everyone was standing in line to get sandwiches and soup, Cale found Hope. She was standing next to her sister, Anna, and looked like she wanted to be anywhere else. "Hey," he said.

"Hi." Darting a look around, she said, "Do you need something?"

"*Jah*, I wanted to talk to you for a couple of minutes. Is that okay?"

She leaned closer to her sister. "Anna, where are Mamm and Daed?"

"They're over at the back table with the Hershbergers. They're not going to be getting up for a while."

Cale folded his hands behind his back. "Anna, do you mind if I speak with Hope for a little bit? We won't go far."

"Cale, I'm not upset with you at all. I don't know what you have to say to Hope, but I don't have a problem with you two being friends."

Feeling relieved, Cale said gently, "Hope, what do you say?"

"I guess that would be okay." She looked around, noticing, like he did, an empty table in a back corner. "We could sit over there if you want. It's pretty private."

"Sure." He led the way and sat down on the bench beside her instead of across from her. Just as he was about to start talking, he noticed her eyes were filled with tears. "What's wrong?"

"What isn't? I ruined your life, Cale."

"You haven't." To his amazement, he realized that was true, too. No, things weren't easy for him right now, but he'd been through worse. A lot worse.

"I heard you won't be able to get your room or a better bed now because my father fired you. This is all my fault."

When he'd woken up that morning, he probably would've said the same thing. Now he realized that he'd been really unfair. And focusing on all the wrong stuff. "It doesn't matter."

"It does." Her bottom lip trembled. "I'm really sorry, Cale. I can't say that enough. I'm going to miss you, too."

And that was what really mattered, he realized. They'd been friends for years, and there was something special between them. "I didn't want to leave my job, but maybe it's for the best. I didn't want to work for your parents the rest of my life." Feeling more certain, he added, "Actually, I'm starting to think that one day I'll look back and be glad your parents fired me. It's going to force me to think about my future."

"I understand."

But she didn't. Not really. "Hope, even if I'm not working at your farm, I'd still like to be friends."

Happiness flared in her eyes before she looked away. "I'd like that, too, though I don't know how we'll be able to ever see each other."

"We can work something out." Thinking quickly, he remembered a hollowed-out tree by the pond near her house. "I've got an idea. I'm going to write you a note and put it in the old tree by the pond. Do you know the one I'm thinking of?"

"I think so."

"You can write me back, and maybe sometimes we can figure out places to meet, too."

For the first time since they'd been talking, amusement lit her eyes. "You want to write secret notes to each other?"

"I know. It sounds stupid, but it's the best I can do for now. Do you have anything better in mind?"

"Nope."

"Okay, then. Look in that tree on Tuesday."

"Hope, come on," Anna called.

"Okay," Hope said to Cale.

His lips curved up. "You sure?"

Looking a whole lot more confident, she nodded. "I'm very sure."

"Great."

"Ah, hey, Cale?"

"*Jah?*"

"Thank you for talking to me today."

If he could have, he would have pulled her close and given her a hug. "Don't thank me for that. I wanted to see you."

Standing up, Cale noticed Viola, Jason, and his mother all waiting for him. They'd been patient, but he knew they wouldn't want to wait much longer. "I've got to go, too. See ya, Hope."

"*Jah.* See ya soon."

When she smiled at him, he felt like everything was going to be okay after all.

twenty-two

Carson Marks seemed just as confused about their future. He'd only stopped by her desk thirteen times that week. Not that she was counting.

—*Finding Love's Fortune*, page 290

Sadie had a lot on her plate. Late on Saturday, two different shops had left her messages asking for more of her snacks and mixes to sell. Whitney, the manager of the Merry House, had gone so far as to say that she would gladly come to Sadie's house to pick up the goods, and would pay her up front instead of waiting for them to sell first. She was that certain she could sell Sadie's products.

The other manager didn't offer to pick up anything or to pay up front, but she said she was going to start charging a dollar more per item and pass on the additional profit to Sadie. Now all Sadie had to do was figure out how she was going to make everything.

Then, of course, there was Cale. He'd been so blue over the

last week that she'd begun to really worry about him. At first, Sadie had wanted to give him space, but now she was wondering if she needed to encourage him to think about apprenticing for one of the businesses in town. He was going to need to be skilled in some-thing, and it was almost past time to get started on that.

But, she realized, what was really keeping her up at night was Atle. His hug had made her believe there was something between them that she'd been missing. She wasn't sure what their future held, but she now knew she wanted to explore it.

The only problem was that she didn't know how to go about doing so. Now that he wasn't going to be coming over to work on Cale's room, it was unlikely she would see him very often.

She needed to figure out what to do . . . or if she was just being silly and should put her friendship with him out of her mind.

"Finally," Viola said. "I was starting to think Cale was never going to get done talking to Hope."

"I don't think they were chatting for more than ten minutes, dear."

"It felt a lot longer." She frowned. "Mamm, aren't you surprised he's even talking to her in the first place? It's all her fault he lost his job."

"That isn't our business. And I, for one, don't happen to feel that all of Cale's troubles are Hope's fault."

"Sure they are."

"I'm afraid you're going to learn one day that everyone makes mistakes."

"I know that, but some mistakes are hard to forgive, don't you think?"

"Not if you are Amish, dear," Sadie gently reminded her daughter. "We believe in forgiveness, remember?"

"I remember." Viola looked rather disgruntled about that, though.

"I hope one day you'll remember it is better to turn the other cheek and move on instead of dwelling on the past."

"I will. But that's still hard to do, don't you think?"

Remembering the many years she'd prayed for help with Marcus, Sadie nodded. "I think it's a very hard thing to do. But, then, no one ever said forgiveness was easy, did they?"

Viola shook her head with obvious reluctance.

Still, Sadie reckoned that was a win for both of them. It wasn't always easy to persuade a fourteen-year-old to agree with a parent. "Ah, here's Cale." Raising her voice, she said, "Are you ready now?"

"*Jah*. Sorry to keep you waiting."

"It was no bother, especially since the day is nice."

Jason trotted over to Cale's side. "Are you going to drive the buggy today?"

"I reckon so. Why?"

"No reason . . . unless you'd like me to take a turn."

To Cale's credit, he didn't even crack a smile. "*Danke*, but I'm good today."

Sadie chuckled as they walked to the field where all the buggies had been parked. Due to the nice weather, they'd let Bonnie stay out in the sun next to the hitching post. She was chewing grass when they approached. "Bonnie, you are enjoying your day, too, aren't you?"

Bonnie's ears perked up, but she continued to eat like they'd forgotten to feed her breakfast. Sadie was chuckling at their horse's antics when she noticed Hope's parents approaching.

"Now what do they want?" Viola muttered.

Cale glanced in the direction his sister was staring and seemed to pull himself up a little straighter.

As far as Sadie was concerned, Cale might be close to being a man, but he was still her son. Before he could speak, she smiled at the Overholts.

"Good day, Jeremiah and Charity. I hope you are doing well."

Her sunny greeting seemed to take them aback, but Charity recovered quickly. "Hello, Sadie." A little less uneasily, she added, "Hello, Cale, Viola, Jason."

"Hi," Viola said as Jeremiah Overholt joined them.

"Hello, Mr. and Mrs. Overholt," Cale said, slowly nodding.

"We were just about to go home," Jason added. "Church was real long today."

Jeremiah smiled. "Don't tell nobody, but I kinda agree. Preacher Andrew can be long-winded from time to time. We won't keep you too much longer." Turning to Sadie, his expression faltered. "I'm afraid we owe you an apology, Sadie."

"Whatever for?"

He looked even more uncomfortable as Hope walked over to join them. "I said some things to Cale that weren't exactly fair."

"Weren't exactly fair" didn't describe their actions well at all. Though she didn't want to start a fight, she needed to be honest, too. "Jeremiah, Charity, you two have been good to my son. His job has been a godsend for our family in many ways. And Cale has liked working for you. That said, deciding to take his paycheck because you didn't like the way he behaved at a party with Hope? Well, in my opinion, it wasn't just not 'exactly fair.' It was plain wrong."

Charity's eyes widened, but she merely stared at her husband. Jeremiah cleared his throat. "You are right, Sadie. I shouldn't have taken Cale's pay. I would like to make that up to him." Turning to her son, he said, "Cale, I would like to hire you back. On Monday, when you return, I'll pay you what you're owed."

Cale exchanged a glance with Sadie before turning to Jeremiah. "Mr. Overholt, *danke* for the apology, and I am grateful to get my paycheck. But as far as the job goes, I think it would be best if I didn't come back to work on your farm."

Charity looked stunned. "Oh, Cale. Did we really upset you that much?"

"You did. I care about Hope, and I wouldn't have knowingly done anything to make her sick or upset. I was hurt that you thought I wouldn't take my promise to you seriously."

Looking crestfallen, Hope stepped forward. "I told Cale I tried to tell you the evening was my fault. I should've tried harder."

"Hope, you don't need to get involved in this discussion," Jeremiah said.

"Oh, Daed. Of course I do! All of this happened because of my mistakes and my bad decisions. However, I'm making amends. I've already apologized to you and to Cale." She bit her lip. "The only person I should have apologized to as well is you, Mrs. Mast. I'm sorry for the trouble I caused."

"Your apology is accepted, dear."

"*Danke*."

"Now, about work—" Jeremiah began.

"Mr. Overholt, I would appreciate you paying me for the money owed, especially since *mei mamm* counts on that to help with the household. But I think it's time I looked for a different job anyway. I need a job that gives me more responsibilities as I grow older."

"I see."

"I would like your permission to still court Hope, though."

Sadie had to stifle back both a gasp and a chuckle. Honestly all three members of the Overholt family looked shocked, and who could blame them? Her dutiful, serious son had just turned rather cheeky.

"I don't know if Hope is ready to be courted, Cale. I mean, my goodness. You two are still young," Charity said.

"Hope has told me a lot of stories about when the two of you were courting. I believe you began calling on Mrs. Overholt when you were just fifteen, Mr. Overholt. Ain't that right?"

Looking almost amused, Jeremiah nodded. "I suppose it is. I couldn't stay away."

Charity's eyes widened at her husband's sweet statement. Sporting a sudden blush to her cheeks, she murmured, "It seems Cale does have a point, Jeremiah. We were awfully young when you started knocking on my door, but maybe not too young."

"But things are different now, aren't they?"

"*Nee*," said Hope.

After sharing a look with Hope, Cale said, "I promise I won't take Hope anywhere until you give me permission. I'll just visit at your *haus*."

Looking even more conflicted, Jeremiah added, "I'm not sure if our daughter is ready for a caller."

Remembering how things had been all those years ago when Marcus had sought her out, Sadie clicked her tongue. "Perhaps what really matters is if Hope wants Cale to come calling."

Charity turned to her daughter. "Hope, Mrs. Mast does have a point. What do you want?"

Hope's eyes widened, but then she seemed to get even braver. "I do want you to come calling, Cale." She turned to her mother. "Please, Mamm?"

"We'll talk about it at home, Hope."

"All right."

"We should be on our way," Sadie said. "I wish you all a *gut* afternoon. *Danke* for speaking to us."

"Cale, come over tomorrow to get your pay," Jeremiah said. "I'll have it in an envelope waiting for you."

Her son grinned. *"Danke.* I'll be over 'round mid-morning."

Just as they turned around, Sadie caught sight of Cale whispering something to Hope, which made her blush. If she was a betting woman, she would put money on Cale and Hope having a Christmas courtship this December.

twenty-three

It wasn't that Carson's actions didn't make sense. It was that they were breaking her heart, and Jane had no idea what to do about it. It shouldn't have been a surprise, though. After all, she'd never been in love before.

—*Finding Love's Fortune*, page 298

Atle didn't much enjoy his new activity. Actually, he'd taken to comparing his morning routine of reading *Finding Love's Fortune* to taking bitter-tasting medicine. It didn't feel too good going down, but the benefits were very nice.

With a sigh, he opened up the novel and tried to get interested in the way Carson was attempting to win Jane back after being so aloof. As for himself, Atle was firmly on Jane's side. If he were Jane, he wouldn't give that Carson Marks the time of day. After all, Carson knew how to make money, but not much else. He sure didn't know beans about wooing.

Old Carson was inventive, though, he'd give him that. Unfortunately, he was also a bit of a goof. Who else would attempt to make brownies for the woman one was courting?

"Jane doesn't want your half-burnt brownies, you idiot," Atle said to the page. "She wants you to stop caring what your parents did and stop keeping all of your feelings inside."

As he heard his words, Atle practically heard Carson laughing at him. He deserved it, too. So far, he hadn't done too well in sharing his true feelings with Sadie.

However, because he was indebted to Sarah Anne, Atle flipped the page and hoped for the best. But it didn't go well, especially since Carson had shown up at Jane's boardinghouse uninvited, and his brownies were essentially hard as rocks.

> "Carson, you shouldn't have gone to so much trouble," Jane said, attempting to extricate a small piece. After doing her best to swallow the bite, she set it on her desk.
>
> "It was no trouble. I want you to know how much I care."
>
> "I didn't know you baked."
>
> Looking smug, Carson gazed into her eyes. "I wanted to do something special for you."

"This ain't it," Atle said. "Plus, if you really want to show her how much you care, you should've helped her fix her car. She needs new brake pads, you know."

Jane's expression warmed as she gazed at the burnt brownies. "You really do care about me, don't you?"

Atle groaned. "He's been running around in circles trying to please you, Jane. Of course he does. He's just an idiot who can't bake."

Reaching for her hand, Carson pressed her slim, perfectly manicured fingers in between his own. "I do," he said. "More than you'll ever know."

A small line formed between her brows. "But you never said."

"That's because I didn't think words mattered as much as actions," Carson said in a deep voice.

"They do. At least, to me."

Just as he was about to make fun of Carson and Jane again, Atle realized that Jane had made a really good point. "I reckon you're right, Jane. Sometimes a woman needs to hear the words, don't she?" Especially, if, say, her first husband had been an abusive jerk.

He flipped the page, anxious to see what Carson had to say about that.

Jane's hand felt so perfect in his. They were completely alone in her small, rather run-down room. Her violet eyes were wide with expectation . . . and, could it be, longing?

Carson couldn't wait another moment. "How about if a man does both?" he whispered.

She stared at him in wonder. "What are you going to do?"

"This," he said. Then, without waiting another second, Carson leaned close, pulled Jane to him, and kissed her passionately. She melted in his arms.

When Carson stepped back at last, he whispered, "I care for you, Jane Cousins. No, I more than care for you. I love you."

Looking supremely happy, Jane smiled into his dark eyes. "I love you, too, Carson."

When the verbose author wrote another three paragraphs about how wonderful it was to be in love and described how they couldn't stop gazing at each other with stars in their eyes, Atle tossed the book down.

That couple really was too much.

But, just as Atle put *Finding Love's Fortune* away for the day, he realized he had learned two things. One was that women needed words. And the second was that it seemed a kiss didn't always mean a man was looking forward to getting his cheek slapped.

That one kiss had moved things forward in a way that burnt

brownies had not. Maybe Jane had just needed a little bit of passion to realize her true feelings.

Atle wrote down some notes, determined to keep this in mind for future reference. Though, if he was going to be completely honest with himself, he didn't need any prodding to think about kissing Sadie.

That was something he'd been thinking about for some time.

❄   ❄   ❄   ❄

There were some things more important than money, and his promise to Sadie was one of them. With that in mind, or simply because Sadie seemed to always be on his mind these days, Atle arrived at the Masts' house at eight the next morning.

Not wanting to risk scaring Sadie by simply walking to the barn, he knocked on her front door. When there was no answer after a full minute, he knocked again.

At last, the door opened. "Atle? Oh, hello. Come on in." Sadie looked harried but as pretty as ever in a dark forest-green dress and a white apron. Her sleeves were rolled up, and her cheeks looked flushed.

"What's going on?" he asked.

"Hmm? Oh, nothing." She chuckled. "*Nee*, that's not true. Everything seems to be going on right now."

"Mamm, it's boiling!" Viola called out.

"Keep stirring, Vi!" Turning back to Atle, Sadie motioned him forward. "Come on into the kitchen. I'm gonna have to talk to you while I work."

Curious as to what had her in such a dither, he toed off his boots and followed her down the hall. The closer he got to the kitchen, the more his mouth watered. The hallway smelled like caramel, and there was a hint of butterscotch and chocolate in the air.

"Hi, Atle," Viola said as she stirred a saucepan on the range.

"Hi there, Viola. Um, shouldn't you be in school today?"

"*Jah*, but I decided to skip."

"Really?"

"It's no problem. We weren't doing too much anyway," Viola said as she moved the pan off a burner.

"This is my fault," Sadie said as she read a candy thermometer carefully before setting it back on the counter. "I have a big Christmas order and I needed an extra set of hands."

"More like fifteen sets of hands," Viola said. "Mamm has a lot of cooking to do."

"A whole lot." Sadie gestured to the countertops surrounding her.

He realized then that he'd been so intent on what the women were doing at the stove that he hadn't taken a moment to look at the other counters. What he saw practically made him gasp. At least a hundred jars were neatly lined up, their lids still in a pot, obviously just sterilized.

"What in the world are you making?"

"Butterscotch and caramel sauces and turtles. And my specialty bars," Sadie added with a smile.

"What are those?"

"Mamm mixes up rice cereal, caramel, peanut butter, marshmallows, and chocolate," Viola explained. "They're really good."

"I reckon they must be sweet, too."

"They are, but who cares?" Viola quipped. "Everyone loves them."

Sadie chuckled as she pulled the saucepan from the stove and immediately stuck a thermometer into another pot. "I shouldn't have said yes to two different stores, but I was so excited about the opportunities."

"Mamm is going to make a lot of money this December," Viola said proudly. "Maybe even the most she's ever made."

"I know I shouldn't have said such a thing," Sadie murmured. "It's prideful."

"It is prideful, but I can't help but think that many a man would say the same thing. Having a successful business is the product of many hours of hard work and ingenuity. There's nothing wrong with that. Ain't so?"

"See, Mamm? I told you it wasn't bragging."

Sadie looked even more flustered, which was rather cute. "I'm not going to be too proud if I don't get all of this done. The manager of one of the stores is coming by soon to pick everything up."

"I'm happy to help. I mean it. What can I do?"

"Oh, Atle, that's so nice." Still looking flustered, she said, "I really should say no."

"Don't say no."

"Well, if you're sure . . ."

"He's sure, Mamm," Viola said from her spot at the stove.

Grinning, Atle said, "What Viola said is true. Now, stop protesting and give me a job."

She chuckled. "Fine. Would you mind spooning the hot caramel sauce into the jars?"

"Of course not." He looked around for a spoon, and Sadie dug into a drawer for him.

"Here's a *gut* one to use."

Just as he was reaching for it, Viola snatched it away. "You have to wash your hands first, Atle," Viola said. "And put on gloves. That's important, too."

"Indeed it is." He turned on the faucet and started scrubbing his hands with enough fervor he reckoned he could go into an operating room.

"Here you go," Viola said, handing him two paper towel sheets. "And now you are ready to begin."

He nodded his head. "*Danke*, Viola." Her answering giggle made him smile. He'd never had much reason to be around teenage girls, but he was enjoying Viola's spunk and sweetness. It was obvious she was proud of her mother, and pleased to be helping her as well.

Taking the large pot from the stove, he rested it on the hot pad

Viola had set out and slowly began filling the first jar. "This much, Sadie?" he asked when there was about a half inch left at the top.

She eyed it carefully. "About a spoonful more, please." After he did as she asked, she smiled. "*Jah*. That's perfect."

Pleased to have the sample, he got to work.

After perhaps ten minutes passed, Sadie said, "Atle, I never asked. Why did you stop by this morning?"

"I decided to still work on Cale's room," he replied after filling the jar he was working on. "I want to do the work even if you can't pay me."

"That is most generous of you, but—"

"But nothing. We're neighbors and friends." He was tempted to admit he had already been giving her such a discount that he wouldn't have missed the money she would have paid him anyway. But because that sounded like it was opening a whole new can of worms, he added, "Please don't argue."

"I won't, because our circumstances have actually changed," she said. "Cale is over at the Overholts' now, collecting his pay."

"And probably flirting with Hope," Viola said.

Sadie clicked her tongue. "There is nothing wrong with Cale visiting with Hope. Be nice, Daughter."

"I am being nice, Mamm. I like Hope a lot, and it makes sense my brother would like her, too." Then, looking all-business, Viola turned back to Atle. "All I'm doing is stating the facts, Atle."

"I see," he murmured.

"You see, Cale likes Hope so much, he asked permission to court her in front of everyone."

"Who was 'everyone'?"

"Our whole family and Mr. and Mrs. Overholt. He did it yesterday after church. After they apologized for being so mean to him."

"It sounds eventful."

"It was," Viola said. "Atle, you should've seen Mamm. She almost looked like she wasn't gonna forgive Mr. and Mrs. Overholt."

"But I did forgive them, Vi." Looking apologetic, Sadie said, "I'm sorry. I am sure this is more than you wanted to know."

"I am interested." *Especially after speaking with Hope*, he thought, but he kept that to himself. "I'm glad Jeremiah and Charity apologized. What they did wasn't right."

"I hadn't thought so, either." Smiling again, Sadie added, "Anyway, since he's getting his paycheck and I'm going to be selling so many of my syrups and such, we can hire you again."

"It all is working out, then."

"It is."

"Only if we can get all of your jars filled, sealed, and decorated, Mamm," Viola said.

"We'd best stop talking so much and get to work, then," Sadie said. Suddenly looking horrified, she turned to Atle. "I'm sorry. I don't mean to order you around."

"You aren't ordering me to do anything." He winked. "Now hush."

When Viola started giggling again, Atle felt his heart fill with happiness. He had hated seeing the look of fear on Sadie's face when she was so worried about her finances and hoped that in time, he could turn all the hardships she'd endured at Marcus's hand into faded memories.

That would be his honor, he knew, but witnessing her eyes glow with only happiness would be a sight to see.

twenty-four

"Carson, what's up with you, man?" Dalton asked. "You barely said a word during the whole meeting. And, what's up with the bandage on your hand?"

"I've had a lot on my mind lately," Carson muttered. Holding up his hand, he added, "And this is nothing. Just a burn."

"A burn?"

"It's harder than one would think to pull a hot cake pan out of the oven."

"You've taken up baking?" Dalton looked incredulous.

"It turns out some women don't want diamonds and mink coats. They want baked goods instead."

—*Finding Love's Fortune*, page 303

Hope had on a pale purple dress that made her blue eyes look bluer and her dark brown hair look even shinier. But Cale supposed she could have been wearing an old burlap sack and he still would have thought she looked really pretty, mainly because she was smiling at him.

After Mr. Overholt had given Cale his pay, he'd chatted with him for a few minutes before suggesting Cale visit with Hope for a bit. He'd taken that as a sign that eventually he was going to be able to start courting Hope in earnest.

Now he and Hope were sitting in her living room, supposedly alone, but he knew both her mother and Anna were within hearing distance. He didn't know if they were staying so close because they didn't trust them or if they were just being nosy. Maybe a little of both.

"These cookies are really good," he said. "Did you make them?"

"I did. Last night." Hope looked like she was about to say something else but glanced toward the kitchen and grew silent.

"What's wrong?"

"Oh, nothing."

"Hope, you can tell me. What?"

She lowered her voice. "It's nothing. Just that, um, well, my mother doesn't like me to bake so often."

"How come? You're really good at it."

She looked even more uncomfortable. "Oh, you know."

"Hope, we've talked about everything, so I know a lot about you. But I *canna* read your mind." He wanted to say he'd even confided in her about his feelings when his father died. If he could talk about his confusion and grief, couldn't she at least talk to him about something like baking cookies?

She pursed her lips. "I just meant because of my weight." Lowering her voice, she added, "I need to be careful that I don't get any bigger."

Peeking over her shoulder, he saw Anna standing in the doorway looking upset. He wished he could tell Anna to give them some privacy, but he knew that was pushing his luck. Why, just a few days ago, he'd thought he wouldn't ever be allowed to talk to Hope again.

Realizing Hope looked really embarrassed, Cale pushed aside all thoughts of her eavesdropping family and reached for her hand. When her eyes widened and she tried to pull it away, he stopped her. "Stop. I don't care if your parents see me holding your hand. This is important."

"What is?"

"What I think about you." Before she could get upset with him, he started talking faster. "Hope, I've liked you forever. I love how sweet you are and how you always made a point to come out to say hi to me whenever I was here." He took a breath. "But, I don't just like you because of how nice you are. I think you're really pretty."

Instead of looking pleased, Hope looked even more uncomfortable. "You don't have to say that."

"*Jah*, I do. I like your hair and your blue eyes. I like how you blush so easily . . . and how the rest of you looks, too." Though he was probably saying all the wrong things, he added, "For the record, I wouldn't change a thing about you, Hope."

Her cheeks were bright red now, but she was also smiling. "*Danke*."

"I'm not the only person who thinks that, either. All the boys used to talk about how pretty you are, but they left you alone because they knew I liked you."

She rolled her eyes and giggled. "All right, Cale. I hear you."

"I hope one day you'll believe me, too."

"I will. I promise."

"*Gut*." Cale squeezed her hand before releasing it at last.

When she smiled at him, he could practically feel sparks in the air. He knew he'd have to wait a long time to kiss her, but Cale sure wished he could at that moment.

Instead, he decided he needed to get on home before he said or did something that was going to get him barred from her house. "Listen, *mei mamm* has two big Christmas orders to get ready by tonight. She's going crazy. I should go help her."

"Does she need more help?"

"She does. Mamm's orders are really big. But can you get away?"

"I'm not sure, but I could ask."

He stood up. "Let's go ask."

Hope gathered their mugs of hot cider and napkins, and picking up the plate of cookies, Cale headed toward the kitchen.

Anna was smiling at him, but Mrs. Overholt was looking at him in a perplexed way. Since he no longer had to rely on Hope's parents for employment, he looked right back at her without a shred of embarrassment.

Hope rushed in with her mugs. "Mamm, Mrs. Mast needs some help cooking this afternoon. May I go over with Cale and help her?"

"*Jah*. I think that would be a fine idea. We all need to help Sadie as much as possible. It's *gut* of you to do that."

Beaming, Hope turned to Cale. "I guess I can go, Cale."

"I'll walk her back in a couple of hours," he promised.

"No need to do that," Anna said. "I'll come get her." She glanced at her mother. "What do you think, Mamm? Four-thirty?"

"That would be good. It will only be starting to get dark then."

"I'll go put on my boots and be right back, Cale," Hope said before she hurried down the hall and up the stairs.

Mrs. Overholt looked at the cookies. "Would you like a plate of cookies to take home?"

All he wanted to do was get out of there, but his mother had taught him there was only one answer to give. "*Danke*."

She tore off a piece of foil, laid it out flat, and started neatly stacking the cookies in the center. "That was quite a speech you gave to my daughter, Cale."

"I reckon it was." He tensed, half waiting for her to tell him to cool his heels.

Instead, she smiled at him softly. "It sounded like you were speaking from the heart."

"I guess I was. I mean, I've always thought Hope was both the sweetest and the prettiest girl I've ever met." He felt his cheeks heat. It seemed now that he had to face her mother, he wasn't quite as brave as he was sitting with Hope.

"I'm glad about that."

"I'm ready, Cale," Hope said as she hurried in. She'd taken the time to change her boots and her dress, too. Now she was wearing one of her older dresses that he knew she liked to wear whenever she was doing a lot of work.

"Let's go, then." He picked up the folded foil. "Your *mamm* wrapped me up some cookies to take home."

She darted a look at her mother, but simply smiled. "*Danke*, Mamm."

"I'll see you in a few hours, Hope. Have fun."

Cale kept his mouth closed, but in his mind, he felt like cheering. Maybe at long last, all of them were coming to a new understanding.

When they were about halfway to his house, he reached for Hope's hand and linked their fingers together.

"We're going to be holding hands twice today, Cale?"

"We are." He grinned.

"Did my *mamm* say anything about you holding my hand on the couch?"

"*Nee.*" He hoped she wouldn't ask him if her mother mentioned anything else because he didn't want to lie.

"God sure acts in strange ways, doesn't He?" she asked instead.

"*Jah.* You aren't wrong about that."

"I would've never thought you'd be courting me, Cale."

"I guess that means I can surprise you."

"It does." She chuckled. "Two days ago, I was sure everything between us couldn't have been worse."

"I felt the same way, but I'm thankful things are better."

When she smiled up at him, he squeezed her hand. They were alone now, and she probably wouldn't even get upset if he kissed her. But it wasn't the right time for that.

Holding hands was good enough. More than enough.

twenty-five

It was Carson's third attempt at brownies that melted her heart and led her to finally agree to going on a real date with him. However, things were still far from perfect. Jane was finding it harder and harder to have both a romantic and a professional relationship with Carson.

Especially when two coworkers caught sight of them kissing in his office.

It was time to start interviewing again.

—*Finding Love's Fortune*, page 322

Her mother had been acting strangely all evening. Normally talkative and opinionated, she had been quiet and seemed deep in thought. Mamm had even forgotten about the gravy on the stove until it had boiled over. To Hope's shock, her mother had hardly seemed to care about the mess at all.

Hope wasn't sure if her mother was still fretting about everything that had happened during the last week or if there was something else going on.

Even when they'd all sat down to supper, which was thirty minutes late, her *mamm* kept looking out the window and picking at her meal.

Hope was pretty sure Daed suspected something was really bothering Mamm because their normally quiet father started talking about the price of wool. That somehow led him to recall a story from his childhood, when he'd helped to deliver a lamb. At another time, Hope probably would've found the glimpse into her father's childhood sweet and interesting. However, all the story had done was make her more confused, and she kept glancing at Anna to see if her older sister felt the same.

Anna, though, had been on her best behavior. She'd sat demurely while her father spoke about their grandfather and then dutifully shared how Julie, her *Englischer* girlfriend, was doing during her senior year at the high school.

When at last supper was over, Hope practically ran into the kitchen to do dishes. She needed time to think about her mother's strange attitude—and her afternoon in the Masts' kitchen. That, at least, had been wonderful. Even though there had to have been some hard feelings toward her and her family because of all they'd recently put Cale through, she'd been greeted like a friend and had been put to work pasting labels on jars and tying bright red and gold ribbon around the lid of each one.

Cale had helped his mother make her special dessert bars and then packaged the caramel chocolate turtles into gift boxes, which left Hope even more in awe of him. Never once had he acted as if baking or working in the kitchen wasn't a job for a man like him.

Just as Hope had begun to scrub the crusty remains of a squash casserole from the baking dish, Anna appeared in the doorway.

"Looks like I get to finish cleaning up, Hope. Mamm and Daed want to speak to you."

"Why? Do you know?"

Anna, usually so open, shook her head. "Not really."

"That's all you're going to tell me?" Panic set in. "Am I in trouble?"

"Just go on into the living room, Hope. They're waiting."

"Sorry I haven't finished all the dishes yet." Years ago they'd agreed to take turns washing the supper dishes. Neither of them liked giving up their nights off.

"You're almost done. Besides, it's not like you can help it."

"I'll make it up to you tomorrow night."

"There's no need. Now stop procrastinating and go talk to Mamm and Daed before one of them comes in here to get you."

Spurred on by her sister's warning, Hope hurried out of the kitchen, through the dining room, and into the living room where her father was sitting in his recliner and her mother was sitting on the couch.

A cheery fire was crackling in the fireplace, and a bolt of red ribbon had just been tacked onto the wall above the mantel. As the month progressed, her mother would put each Christmas card they received on the ribbon. Last year they'd gotten so many cards, they had to hang up ribbons along the banisters, too.

Both of her parents turned to look at her when she entered.

"Ah. There you are, Hope," Daed said.

She nodded. "Anna said you wanted to speak with me?"

"*Jah*. Sit down."

Normally she would've sat next to her mother, but she felt the need to be able to see both her parents at the same time. So she took her grandmother's old wooden rocking chair facing the fireplace. Sitting in the chair, with its embroidered cushion, provided her a sense of comfort she needed.

After exchanging looks with her father, her mother spoke. "Hope, I'm sorry to say that I eavesdropped on you and Cale today. It wasn't right, and I'm embarrassed about it. We all know I would've gotten upset if I had discovered you listening to a private conversation between your father and myself."

"I knew you were there, Mamm. Cale did, too."

"I see." Her throat worked, and she looked like she'd just swallowed a bitter pill. "Well, then I suppose you have an idea what I wanted to talk to you about."

Oh, Hope knew. She was about to get a lecture for holding Cale's hand. Though she thought her parents were being ridiculous, she decided to agree with everything and act sorry so this little chat could be over as soon as possible. She was going to do whatever it took to keep seeing Cale. "I have a pretty good idea."

"Hope, I have to admit that at first I was shocked. But after giving it some thought, I realize I shouldn't have been shocked at all."

"I feel the same way," Daed said.

Oh, for Pete's sake. Even though she'd just cautioned herself to keep quiet, she said, "I think everyone has known I've liked Cale for years. Holding his hand couldn't have been that big of a surprise."

Her father cleared his throat. "Hope—"

She just kept talking. "And, I'm sorry, but it's not like Cale was kissing me or anything."

Her father's eyebrows rose. "You and Cale were holding hands?"

"*Jah*, but . . . Wait. That's not what you want to speak to me about?"

For a moment, her mother almost looked amused. "*Nee*, dear. And just so you know, I don't happen to believe hand holding is very shocking, either."

Now Hope was really confused. "What did I do wrong, then?"

"You didn't do anything wrong. Um, I'm referring to your conversation about baking cookies."

"Oh." Now it was clear. She had heard Hope complaining about her mother's fixation on her weight. And, she supposed, Mamm had also heard Cale's sweet speech about how he liked her appearance.

"Hope, you don't have anything to say?" Daed prodded.

"*Nee.*" She was beginning to lose patience with the conversation. Her mother had never been the type to beat around the bush, and Hope had no practice trying to read her mind. "Mamm, I wish you'd just go ahead and tell me what I did wrong."

"You didn't do anything wrong, Hope. I'm the one who owes you an apology."

Hadn't they just gone over this? "Mamm, like I said, I knew you were listening."

"Hope, what I'm trying to say is that hearing your perspective on . . . on all my comments about your weight made me realize just how judgmental I've sounded." She clenched her hands together. "I felt terrible, and then when I heard Cale's words, I realized he was exactly right. You are a pretty girl, and there is nothing the matter with you."

Maybe the best thing to do would be to smile, to tell her mother not to worry about it, and to assure her she wasn't upset. But Hope couldn't help but wonder if the only reason her mother was apologizing was because she'd heard a handsome boy defending her looks.

"Mamm, all my life you've compared me to Anna, and I've felt like I've come up wanting. I'm not as thin as her, so therefore I'm not as attractive. I didn't do as well in school as she did and I don't have many talents. I can't be a wonderful-*gut* seamstress like her. The only thing I ever felt like I was good at was liking Cale, and—"

"That's not true."

"Mamm, when you helped me make that red dress and braid my

hair for the party, it was one of the first times I can ever remember feeling you were proud of me." She shook her head. "And it wasn't because of anything I'd done, either. It was simply that Cale liked me enough to take me to a party where a lot of the popular kids were going."

"I was happy for you because you were happy."

"How can you expect me to believe that? When I came home, feeling terrible, guilty, and drunk, you never even let me explain what happened. You didn't care enough to let me tell you how the other girls decided to play a trick on me or how everyone else was in English clothes and reveling in the freedom of *rumspringa*!"

"I didn't realize that was what happened," Daed said.

"Of course you didn't. Because you never asked."

"Hope, all I'm trying to do is apologize."

Hope got to her feet, exasperated. "Then I accept your apology. Now, may I leave?"

"I fear there's still a lot you're upset about."

"There is, Mamm. I'm through with feeling bad about myself. I've accepted me for who I am, and I just wish you would, too." She paused, then added, "You know what? When I went to the Masts', Mrs. Mast, Viola, and their neighbor Atle were in the kitchen, and for over two hours, the five of us worked hard and joked around. When the folks from the Merry House came to pick everything up, I stood off to the side with Cale and Viola and Atle while they complimented Mrs. Mast on how wonderful everything looked. And, for a few minutes, I even felt full of pride because I knew I helped Mrs. Mast achieve her goal."

"I imagine it was a good feeling," Daed said.

"It was, because I wasn't trying to please anyone or be someone other than myself. All I was doing was trying to help, and my help was valued." Looking at her parents, she felt all the frustration that had been brewing for sixteen years bubble up to the surface. "I love you both, and I hope one day you'll value me for being me. For being Hope."

"We already do value you, Hope," Mamm said.

"If that's true, then I'm glad," she murmured before walking up to her room.

Amazingly, her parents didn't follow her, ask her to come back, or say another word.

When she sat on her bed, she kicked off her shoes, laid down on her side, and wondered what the Lord had in store for them next. It had already been the strangest December she could remember.

twenty-six

"You'll never guess who I interviewed today to be my personal assistant," Dalton said over the phone. "Jane Cousins."

"You interviewed my Jane?"

"Sorry, buddy, but I don't think she's yours anymore. She just accepted my offer."

—*Finding Love's Fortune*, page 348

It was the last week of school before Christmas break. Once again, Sadie was scurrying around the kitchen. Cale had already been out to the barn to do chores and was showering, Jason was lollygagging over his bowl of oatmeal, and Viola wasn't downstairs yet.

All things considered, it was a typical Monday morning.

Noticing that Jason was playing with a grain of rice left on the table from last night's supper, Sadie cleared her throat. "Jason, eat now, if you please."

"Fine." He picked up his spoon. "But I'm getting real tired of oatmeal," Jason said. "Can you make waffles tomorrow?"

Oh, that son of hers. Some days he spoke to her as if she were his short-order cook! She often wondered why the Lord had decided her third child needed to be such a flighty dreamer. Torn between chuckling and firmly reminding him to mind his manners, she took a deep breath. "*Nee*, Jason. I'm afraid I cannot be making you waffles tomorrow. One needs a waffle iron for that."

"Oh." He spooned in another bite of oatmeal that now looked a bit like glue since he'd eaten so slowly. After he swallowed, he said, "Can you get a waffle iron?"

A waffle iron would necessitate electricity or a desire to heat the waffle form on the stove. Neither was going to happen. "*Nee*, I cannot."

"Great." Jason ate another bite and sighed.

Just as she was going to chide him yet again, Sadie realized he seemed particularly out of sorts.

Taking her cup of coffee to the table, she sat next to him. "What's wrong, child? For some reason I don't think you're too worried about waffles."

"Nothing." He ate another bite.

She took a sip of coffee. "I know something is wrong, Jason. Now, would you care to try answering me again?"

"Fine. I feel like everyone is looking forward to something besides me."

Usually, all Jason did was count down days until Christmas. "I'm afraid you're going to have to give me some examples of what you're talking about."

"You know. Viola is going to graduate school in May, and she's looking forward to seeing all her friends when we're on break."

"I'm sure you'll have time with your friends, too, Jason."

"Then, there's Cale. He's moving out of our room." Looking even more miserable, he added, "He *canna* wait to do that."

Now she understood. "You're going to miss your brother, aren't you?"

He shrugged before nodding. "I liked things the way they were."

"I know, but your brother is much older. He needs more space."

"*Nee*, Mamm. Him moving was your idea. Cale would've been fine staying with me, but you're making him leave. He's going far away, too. Being out in the barn is a lot different than being in the *haus*."

"Jason, if Cale really didn't want to leave, he would've said so. In any case, you need to prepare yourself for when he moves out on his own in a couple of years."

"He might not."

"That is true, but there's a good chance he will. He is practically a man now, you know."

"Cale is not!" Jason said just as both Cale and Viola appeared. Both of her older children gaped at him.

"I am not what?" Cale asked after a few seconds passed.

"You are not practically a man." Looking up at Cale, Jason folded his arms over his chest. "You ain't, Cale. I don't care what you think."

Cale stared at him for a moment, then rolled his eyes. "May I have some oatmeal, Mamm?"

"Of course. Viola, do you want any oatmeal this morning? I saved you some."

"*Nee*. Just coffee and an apple."

"How come she gets to have that breakfast, and I have to eat this?" Jason held up his spoon and let a chunk of cold oatmeal plop into his bowl. "Nothing is fair around here."

All three of them stared at Jason in shock.

Sadie had just reached the end of her patience. "Jason, I suggest you speak to me in a different tone. I would appreciate an apology as well. The sooner the better, if you please."

But instead of apologizing, Jason just scooted out his chair. "Everyone else gets to do fun things except for me."

Just as Sadie was about to speak, Viola cut in.

"You don't know anything, Jason," she said. "You've got things so easy and you don't even appreciate it."

"I do not. You got to take a day off school last week, but I had to go."

"I was here working all day! You know that."

"I still had to walk Samuel back and forth all by myself. It wasn't fair."

"Jason, get up, rinse out your bowl, and get ready for school. Now," Sadie said.

Her little boy's eyes widened, then seemed to come to a decision. "*Nee*. I'm not ready yet."

Cale reached down and pulled Jason to his feet. "I don't know what's wrong with you, but you'd better apologize to our mother right now. If Daed were here and heard you speak that way to Mamm, he would've spanked you something awful. You're sounding mighty spoiled and ungrateful, too. I'm ashamed of you."

And just like that, Jason burst into tears and ran out of the kitchen.

"Oh, dear," Sadie said. "I guess I'd better go fetch him."

"Leave him alone, Mamm," Cale said. "He'll get over it."

Viola groaned. "Now he's going to be miserable the whole way to school. Cale is right. He's so spoiled, Mamm."

"He's having a bit of a difficult time, I fear."

Viola rolled her eyes. "With what? Jason hardly has to do anything. And now, of course, I'm going to be late because my little brother can't even eat a bowl of oatmeal without complaining."

Making a decision, Sadie said, "I'll take Jason today. You get your apple and get on your way to pick up Samuel."

Viola smiled before glancing back at her hesitantly. "Are you sure, Mamm? I can wait. You know I don't really care too much if I'm late."

"I appreciate that, but I'll manage." She kissed her daughter's brow. "I'll see you when you get home. Don't forget your lunch."

Five minutes later, Viola had on her cloak, her lunch and apple were packed in her book bag, and she was out the door. After it closed, Sadie shut her eyes and prayed for patience.

"Are you all right, Mamm?" Cale asked.

"Of course. I was just thinking that Jason is going to need a little bit more patience than I have at the moment."

"I don't see why you have to give him so much patience anyway. He was being a brat."

"He might have been, but he's just a child." When Cale raised his eyebrows, she chuckled. "*Jah*, I know. You could've never gotten away with half the things he does."

"It's true, but that doesn't mean he gets to speak to you like that, Mamm. It's not right," he added as a knock sounded at the door and Atle poked his head in.

"*Gut matin.*"

Sadie waved him inside. "Come on in, Atle. Would you like some coffee?"

"*Danke.*" Looking at Cale, he grinned. "Ready to continue framing your room today?"

"*Jah.*"

"We can go out and get started as soon as I finish this," he said as Sadie pressed a cup into his palm.

"Okay."

"How are you, Sadie?" Atle asked.

He was truly the kindest man. Sometimes when he looked at her, she felt like he wasn't aware of anyone else in the world. "I've been better," she replied. "My son is having some growing pains today."

He looked at Cale. "Really?"

"Not me, " Cale said. "Mamm is talking about Jason. He's decided to be difficult this morning."

"Oh? What happened?" Atle asked.

"I'm afraid he had a bit of a fit about oatmeal," Sadie answered, though that explanation didn't do justice to the tantrum.

When Atle blinked in confusion, Cale chuckled. "Exactly."

"I decided to give Viola a break and walk him to school this morning, which means I better go get him back downstairs."

"Do you need help? I could walk him to school for you."

"I can do it, but *danke*." She squeezed Cale's shoulder. "I used to walk this one to school many a day. The walk and the time with Jason will do me good. I'll see you when I get back," she said over her shoulder as she went to fetch her youngest. She just hoped she'd have a chance to see Atle before the day was over.

There was just something about him that she was drawn to.

❋　❋　❋　❋

Twenty minutes later, she and Jason were about halfway to school. They hadn't said much, but she could tell he still had a lot on his mind. At first she'd been thinking that it would be best to keep her words to herself so she wouldn't upset him before school. But now that she realized whatever was bothering him wasn't fading away, Sadie decided to push a bit.

"Are you feeling any better, Jason?"

He shrugged. "I don't know."

"Perhaps it would help if you talked about what is really bothering you. I am fairly sure it isn't oatmeal or your unfair life."

"I told you. I don't want Cale to leave."

"Why is that?"

He looked down at his feet, then kicked a rock. "It feels like everyone's leaving."

"Who else?"

"You know. Daed."

"Ah." She tried to act sympathetic, but it was hard.

Jason raised his eyebrows. "See, that's the problem. I don't think you even miss him. Viola and Cale don't miss Daed, either. But I do."

Oh, boy. Realizing it was time to put her feelings to one side, Sadie chose her words with care. "I mourned for your father. And . . . well, I miss the man he could have been." The man she'd thought he was when he'd been courting her so long ago.

"What does that even mean?"

Though she ached to protect him from her true feelings, Sadie realized that shielding him wouldn't help him understand her feelings or how his siblings felt. "It means that your father became an unhappy person. He found fault with a lot of things, Jason. And when that happened, he took out his anger on me and sometimes even your siblings."

"Viola and Cale said he hit them, but he never hit me."

"I'm grateful for that."

A line formed between his brows. "I don't know how I'm supposed to feel. Sometimes I just wish I still had a father."

"That's a good thing." Though sometimes thinking back to her life with Marcus felt like jumping into a muddy hole, Sadie forced herself to go there. "Jason, I never wished your father to die. I never hoped for you, Cale, and Viola to be without a father. But I cannot deny that I prayed more than once that he would have been nicer to me and treat you, Cale, and Viola better."

Looking troubled, Jason nodded.

"There is something you need to keep in mind, Son. And that is that the Lord decided your father had lived enough time on this earth. And there's nothing we can do to change that fact."

"I'm the only boy I know who doesn't have a father. Soon I won't even have Cale."

"There's nothing anyone can do about you not having a father. And Cale has his own journey to take. One day he might even move away. But the Lord wouldn't have taken your father and given Cale the choice to leave if He didn't think you could handle it."

"Really?"

"Oh, for sure. He never gives us too many burdens that we cannot hold." Pressing a hand on his back, she said, "That means you might have some growing to do, but you are strong enough to handle whatever happens next."

Jason's eyes widened. But then he nodded.

She felt like she'd just won a battle she hadn't ever intended to fight.

As they turned the corner and approached his school, she asked, "Do you want me to walk you inside?"

"*Nee*. I'll talk to Miss Wendy on my own."

"Have good day, then, Son."

"Okay."

Just as Sadie was about to turn around, he called out, "Mamm?"

"Hmm?"

"I'm sorry about the oatmeal." He swallowed. "And for being so mean. Cale and Viola were right. I wasn't being nice."

"Thank you for apologizing, Jason. Have a good day now."

He smiled at her before trotting to the building.

Sadie stood on the sidewalk until he disappeared from view. And then she exhaled . . . and realized that Jason wasn't the only person who had needed that talk.

At last, all the ghosts were firmly behind her, and she had brighter days ahead.

Smiling, she headed back home.

twenty-seven

"Jane, open the door. We need to talk."

Jane turned the knob. But she was only allowing him in so he wouldn't disturb her neighbors. Phyllis from accounting had told her all about how Mr. Marks had taken her to a very expensive and private lunch.

—*Finding Love's Fortune*, page 377

Now that it was Wednesday and they'd put in several long days together, Atle was wondering how he'd ever gotten along without Cale. Not only was the boy a huge help, but he was also good company, which made the hours fly by.

Just as importantly, the teenager did a good job. "Cale, I think you might have a gift for carpentry," Atle said when they finally broke for lunch.

Cale rolled his eyes. "Yeah, right."

"I'm serious. You are a hard worker and have an eye for details, too. Come look." He pointed to some of the cuts Cale had made with the saw and the line of nails he had neatly hammered in a row. "I've seen work by men with far more experience that doesn't look as good."

"I've been liking the work. I'm learning a lot, and it's much better than working with sheep."

Atle chuckled. "Sheep can be trying, and that's a fact."

"Even though I'm missing the pay, I'm glad I told Mr. Overholt I needed to do something different. I wasn't very happy with farm work."

"I was the same way," Atle said. "My father was a gifted farmer, but no matter how hard I tried, my skills never came close to his. Carpentry was more for me."

"Maybe it's a better job for me, too."

Encouraged by the look of optimism in the boy's face, Atle said, "Perhaps on Friday, you'd like to come to my workshop and help me sand the pieces of your bed frame."

"I would. I'd like that a lot."

"I'll count on it, then."

"Hey, Atle?"

The boy sounded almost tentative. "*Jah*, Cale?"

"*Danke* for all your help."

"Oh, I haven't done much. I'm glad things are going better for ya, though."

"Me, too."

"I'm guessing things are better now with you and Hope?"

He nodded. "I got to pay a call on her the other night. It was my second one."

"And it went well?"

"*Jah.*" He smiled. "I don't care if some of my friends think I'm too young to be courting Hope so seriously. I like spending time with her."

Atle never thought he'd get to this point, but he asked, "What did you talk about?"

Cale looked at him like Atle was asking him to reveal confidential secrets. "Nothing bad. Why?"

"I *wasna* asking to be nosy. I was asking for myself. I'm afraid I haven't done much courting before." Atle knew his face was as red as a tomato, but there was no denying the truth.

"You're interested in going courting?"

"Well, *jah.*" When Cale still gaped at him, Atle added, "I'm not *that* old, you know."

"I know. Sorry. I guess I never thought of someone your age doing that."

His age? He was forty-two! "Well, I am interested in courting, and I don't want to mess it up."

Cale smiled, then quickly attempted to look serious again. "I wasn't making fun of you or anything." Setting the piece of lumber that Atle had just handed him in place, he picked up a nail. "I don't have much advice. The only girl I've ever really liked was Hope, and she's different than everyone else."

"Really? How?"

"Well . . . She's shyer, I guess. She doesn't joke around like some of the other girls we're friends with. Or, say, Viola." Looking a bit aggrieved, he added, "My sister is the type to tell you exactly what she thinks, you know? Hope ain't like that."

"So you're saying that different women need different types of courting." For a moment, he thought about Carson and Jane in *Finding Love's Fortune*. Their relationship was filled with games and lots of give-and-take. That type of relationship wasn't for him.

"I guess," Cale said. "But like I said, I'm no expert."

"Thank you anyway." Picking up another piece of lumber, he measured, made a mark, and then neatly cut through the wood. Just as he picked up another piece, Cale spoke.

"Who do you want to court?"

Atle froze. Though it was tempting to brush off Cale's question with a brusque reply, he couldn't do that. The boy had been through enough of his own drama, plus, if things ever did happen with Sadie, Cale would feel betrayed.

He mentally rehearsed several ways to share the news, but there didn't seem to be any way to say it besides plain speaking. "Your mother," he said at last.

Cale's hand slipped, and the nail fell to the ground.

Atle turned to him in concern. "Did you just hit a finger?"

"*Nee.*" The boy's voice sounded choked.

Feeling more embarrassed, Atle tried to rectify the situation. If it was salvageable. "Sorry for not, ah, leading up to that better. I guess I shouldn't have said that so bluntly."

Cale coughed. "Was there another way to tell me that you like my mother?"

"I doubt it. Ah, that's why I decided to tell it to you straight."

"Is that why you're here?" He gestured to the room they were framing. "Is that why you're doing this with me? So I'll help you court my mother?"

Shocked, Atle shook his head. "*Nee.*" Walking to his side, he added, "Your mother approached me for this job."

"But you took it."

"Indeed, I did. And, if you want the whole truth, I'd probably do whatever your mother asked of me. Even something as big as building her son a room of his own and a bigger bed."

"So you didn't do it for the money."

Deciding to come clean—after all, he didn't have anything to lose now—he said, "Cale, I'm only charging her for the materials. I would usually charge a customer double or triple the amount she's paying me."

"Why? So she'd like you more?"

Atle didn't like how Cale was making him out to be. "I'm not that kind of man," he said quietly. "I'm not conniving, and I don't do things just to get someone to like me. Not your mother and not you."

"Then—"

"Boy, even if I didn't want to court your mother, I would have helped her out. She's a widow raising three children. She also is working hard and has the sweetest disposition of anyone I've ever met."

Cale still looked torn. "I feel like I should tell Mamm. She should know."

"Go ahead, if that's what you want. She is your mother, and you must do what you think you need to do. But be advised that all you're going to do is hurt her feelings."

"You just said yourself that it's best to be honest."

"I also feel that it's best to be kind and not hurt someone intentionally." Looking at Cale intently, Atle added, "And, forgive me, but that's what you would be doing."

Looking confused, Cale picked up the nail that had fallen and hammered it in place. Atle picked up several of the pieces of wood he had just cut and methodically hammered them in place as well. There was tension between them, but to his relief, the boy's anger had dissipated and now he only seemed to be thinking hard.

Knowing the power of silence, Atle let the boy think in peace while he berated himself for not foreseeing that this discussion would have come up in a matter of time.

Perhaps he really was a hopeless case. He couldn't seem to emulate a romance hero's actions any better than he could calmly discuss his admiration of Sadie with her own son.

"Does my mother know how you feel?"

"I doubt it."

"Well, when are you going to say something to her?"

"I don't know." Trying to keep up with the boy's train of thought—hadn't he just made his displeasure known?—he added, "I'm waiting for the right time."

"You should probably do it soon, you know."

"*Nee*, I don't. You just acted like you wanted me to stay away from her."

Looking embarrassed, Cale shifted on his feet. "I was probably wrong about that. I mean, it's hard to think about my *mamm* dating you."

"Thank you," Atle said dryly.

Cale chuckled. "I don't just mean you. I mean anyone. She's . . . She's my mother."

"I would feel the same way, Cale."

"But, that said, I guess she is really nice. And, uh, pretty? I mean, pretty for a woman her age."

Atle hid a smile. The boy was acting as if Sadie was in a nursing home, not the beautiful, active woman she was. "Your mother is both of those things."

"I never thought about her being alone, but I don't think she would like that. So, I suppose if she has to be courted by anyone, it might as well be you."

That was faint praise, indeed, but better than Atle had first thought things were going to go. "Are you saying you won't dissuade me if I come calling?"

"I guess not. I don't think Viola or Jason will mind, either. But if Mamm doesn't want you to be her . . . um, suitor, I expect you to honor that," he warned.

"Of course I will. I want Sadie to be happy."

Now looking amused, Cale said, "When are you going to make your move, then?"

Atle sighed. "As soon as I get up my nerve."

Cale grinned. "Well, you're pretty old, you know. If you wait much longer, it'll probably be too late."

Atle raised his eyebrows. "Are you really teasing me about my age?"

"Maybe."

"I suggest you tease less and hammer more, boy. We've got a lot to do if you plan on sleeping in here by Christmas."

"You really think it can get done by then?"

"For sure I do. After all, I promised your mother that it would."

"When you finally come over to see my *mamm*, bring her some flowers. She likes flowers."

"I'll do that. *Danke*." He took a deep breath. "Now, let's stop for lunch, and then I'll show you how to put up drywall."

"Sounds good."

Atle breathed a sigh of relief. That had been awkward and a little bit painful, but at least everything was out in the open.

All he had to do now was get some flowers and go calling. Well, that . . . and hope that Sadie wouldn't laugh in his face.

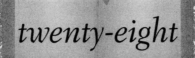

twenty-eight

There were so many things Carson wanted to tell Jane when she finally let him inside, but when he looked into her violet eyes, he blurted, "I'm not going to let you work for Dalton."

—*Finding Love's Fortune*, page 380

Three days after Sadie had walked Jason to school, things seemed to settle down around their house.

Cale had started working with Atle both in the barn and at his workshop, and when he wasn't working hard, he was eating everything in sight, sleeping, or paying calls on Hope.

Jason had returned to his usual self. He was agreeable, seemed to be looking forward to Christmas, and even occasionally spent an hour or two after school in the barn helping Cale and Atle. And Viola was busy making plans with her friends for the Christmas break.

As for herself, Sadie was still cooking, but now for gifts

instead of merchandise for the stores around town. She'd even hired a driver and gone into town one day to buy Christmas gifts for her children. Each child would receive new pajamas and slippers, a book, and a couple of small items that might make them smile.

Everything was going so well that she wasn't sure why she'd begun to feel a little bit lonelier lately.

She had just sat down after supper when a knock came at the door. She stared at the door in confusion before getting to her feet.

And there was Atle, holding a bouquet of flowers. He looked as awkward as she was surprised. For a long moment, they stood there staring at each other. Well, they did until she remembered it was near freezing outside.

"Atle, come in."

After closing the door behind him, he thrust the flowers at her. "These are for you."

Feeling completely puzzled, she took the bouquet of pink roses and carnations from him. "*Danke.*" Unable to help herself, she held them to her nose. "They smell lovely. They're really pretty, too." When he still looked worried, she added, "Pink roses are my favorite flower."

He smiled at last. "I'm glad you like them."

"I do."

Seconds passed. Atle continued to look at her intently. So intently, she was beginning to think she'd forgotten something important. Feeling desperate, she said, "Um, is there a reason you're here?"

"There is." He stuffed his hands in his pockets.

"Mamm, Atle's come courting," Cale said from the stairway.

She turned around in alarm. "Cale, you shouldn't be eavesdropping."

"Of course I should. If it was up to you and Atle, you two would still be staring at each other in the entryway ten minutes from now. Invite him in, wouldja? It's freezing out there."

Sadie turned back to Atle. "Is Cale serious? You've come courting?"

"I reckon so." He sighed. "I can't think of another reason I would have come over here with a bouquet of flowers."

"I see." Sadie tried to bite back a smile. "Please come into the living room. I've got a fire going. Would you like some coffee and maybe a piece of cake?"

"*Jah.*"

Grateful for the chore, she smiled. "I'll be right back, as soon as I put these in water."

Hurrying to the kitchen, Sadie prepared a pot of decaf and set it to brew. Then she carefully placed the flowers in a vase she found under the sink, stood back to admire them, and sliced two thick pieces of cake. She was going to need as much sustenance as she could get to calm her nerves.

Five minutes later, she was holding a tray with two cups of coffee, a dish of cream, a jar of sugar, and cake.

When she appeared, Atle walked to her side. "I'll take this for you. It's heavy."

"Thank you. Um, just set it on the coffee table."

He did and sat back down again while she served the cake and poured coffee. "It's decaffeinated," she said. "I like decaffeinated coffee after one or two in the afternoon."

"I don't remember the last time coffee kept me up, but that's a good idea."

"I don't seem to be too affected by regular coffee, either."

"I, um, guess that's because I've drunk so much over the years."

"Me, too." She smiled, pleased to find they had something in common . . . until she remembered that the majority of their friends probably would say the same thing.

And, now they'd exhausted the coffee conversation.

After eating half his slice of cake, Atle set it down again. "This is a *gut* cake, Sadie."

"*Danke.*"

"You're mighty talented in the kitchen."

She smiled at him. "I'm happy in the kitchen, so I guess it shows." Just as she picked up her plate, she recalled that Cale had been the one to spur them forward. Since Atle's appearance had been a surprise, she knew she hadn't been the one to tell Cale about the visit.

That left only one other person to blame. "How did Cale know you were here courting?"

Atle covered his mouth to stifle the cough that rang forth. "Well," he sputtered as soon as he caught his breath. "There's a bit of a story there."

"I'd be interested to hear it."

"I'm guessing you would." He cleared his throat. "Well, you see . . . he and I were working on the room together, and he mentioned how he has been courting Hope Overholt."

"Yes?"

"Well, one thing led to another, and before I quite knew what was going on, I told him I was interested in courting you."

"I see," she said, but she wasn't sure if she was embarrassed or rather charmed. She would've never expected Cale to open up about anything, let alone his relationship with Hope or Atle calling on his mother.

"I suppose you probably ain't too happy about that. I didn't mean to tell Cale all my business, but, um, I thought it might be a good idea."

"I'm not sure what I am . . . except surprised." After peeking toward the stairs to make sure none of her three children was listening, she said, "Atle, I had no idea you, ah, liked me." And now she sounded as awkward as a teenage girl. Definitely more insecure.

He rested his elbows on his knees and looked at her intently. "Sadie, we have been neighbors for some time. Even though we never talked all that much, I was aware of you always. And with the way Marcus treated you from time to time."

"Oh."

"I'm sharing this because I want you to know I came over here with my eyes open. I realize you might not want to ever be married again, just as I realize that even if you were interested in one day marrying, it might not ever be with me. But, during all this time, I've admired you." Looking pained, he said, "I would have never said a word to you if you were still married. That said, I can't deny that I hoped and dreamed I would one day be sitting here with you."

"I don't know what to say." Everything Atle was sharing was beautiful. But how did she respond to that?

"You can say whatever you want. I want to get to know you better, Sadie. Perhaps, you would like to get to know me better, too. But if that isn't something you want or are comfortable with, all you have to do is let me know."

"And then you'll leave? Just like that?"

His expression softened. "Then I won't ever pop over here without an invitation again. I'll work on Cale's room and bed, but I won't expect anything more."

She knew he was speaking the truth, too. Atle Petersheim didn't play games. She smiled at him. "Did Cale suggest the flowers, or did you think that up?"

"That was Cale. I went down to Cindy's and asked her to prepare a bouquet."

"I haven't received flowers in a long time. I do like them."

"I'm glad about that." Atle drained his coffee cup. Then, looking uneasy again, he sighed. "I think it would be best if I left now."

Letting him go would be the easy way out. She could keep to herself, cling to the memories of Marcus's many flaws, and use those memories as a way to hold any other relationship at bay. Atle was enough of a gentleman that he would probably never mention this visit again. But she didn't want to be that person. More importantly, she didn't want Atle to leave at all. He made her feel girlish again. No, he made her feel hope for her future.

He made her feel again, which was something she thought was needed.

All that was why she smiled at him. "Atle, if you leave now, we'll never get to know each other better."

"You want to do that?"

"I do. Besides, it would be a shame to let those flowers go to waste," she teased. "I mean, Cindy probably put a lot of effort into them."

"That's true." His eyes lit up. "She said that bouquet took her almost fifteen minutes to arrange."

Leaning against the couch, Sadie folded her hands in her lap. "Atle, you know a lot about me, but I don't know much about you. How about you tell me a story?"

"*Jah.* Sure. I can do that."

Then he proceeded to talk . . . and Sadie realized she didn't regret her decision to ask him to stay for a moment.

twenty-nine

Jane gazed at him with a hurt expression. "When you say things like that, I remember exactly why I need to move on. I can't do this anymore."

He shook his head. "You can't mean that. Not after everything we've gone through."

"I'm sorry, Carson, but the problem is that we haven't gone through enough. Relationships are more than gifts and expensive nights out."

—*Finding Love's Fortune*, page 386

"Atle! It's good to see you!" Sarah Anne called out.

Sarah Anne had a knack for greeting people like they were long-lost friends. Atle had wished more than once that he had even a small inkling of her warmth and good humor. Or, perhaps it was her ease with conversation he was jealous of.

"It's good to see you, too," he replied. "I'm sorry it's been so long since I've stopped by." Looking down at the book he held in his hands, he added, "I fear I owe you money for my overdue book."

Sarah Anne took the novel from him and scanned it on her machine. "I'm afraid you are right. That will be a dollar twenty-five, please."

Happy it wasn't more, he pulled out the exact amount and placed it on her desk. "Here you go."

She clicked another button on the computer and then placed the book carefully in the deposit bin. "Have you been sparse because of the book or for other reasons?"

"I've had a job that's taken up a lot of my time." That was the truth, too. But it also wasn't the whole story. It was actually Sadie and her three *kinner* who'd consumed him of late.

Sarah Anne folded her arms across her chest. "Well, now, that sounds interesting. What kind of job is it? Are you working on another kitchen remodel?"

"Not this time. I'm building a bedroom in part of a barn . . . and crafting a bed frame as well."

"You are certainly gifted, Atle. I've never heard of a craftsman who could craft both furniture and rooms."

He shrugged. "I enjoy it. Plus, I've had help," he added with a smile. Cale wasn't exactly much help at the moment, but he certainly made Atle's days go by faster.

"I didn't know you had a partner. I thought you liked working alone."

He was starting to become very aware that not only had the librarian remembered a lot about him, but he had also been something of a chatterbox around her. "This is a special circumstance. Cale Mast has been giving me a hand."

Her eyes lit up. "You've been getting help from Sadie's son."

"*Jah*. See, it's his room and bed I've been building."

"Ah."

Atle could practically see her mind clicking as she put everything together. He forced himself to stand there and not turn away in embarrassment. After all, if he could discuss courting with a sixteen-year-old and then show up at Sadie's doorstep with flowers, he could handle Sarah Anne's questions, too.

She didn't disappoint. Clasping her hands together, she grinned. "Does that mean things with Sadie Mast have been progressing?"

"It does." Unable to help himself, he shared his news. "I've begun courting her."

"You have?" Sarah Anne hurried around her desk. "Atle, I'm so excited for you!"

"There's nothing to be too excited about yet. We're taking things slow."

"Oh, of course."

"Her *kinner* are still getting used to me, too, you know." Though, that wasn't exactly the truth. He and Cale were becoming good friends, and Jason was a rambunctious boy who could likely get along with a tick if he was of a mind. As for Viola? Well, things between them might be moving at a slower pace, but he was at peace with that. He had much to learn about teenage girls.

"I suppose Sadie is going to need some time, too, since she's a widow and all."

"She does seem a bit careful. But she seems amiable to me calling on her again, so I reckon I haven't messed things up too much yet."

"I'm sure you haven't. You are a good man, Atle. One of the best, I think."

Her praise was embarrassing him, mainly because he knew he hadn't done anything special. More importantly, he felt as if the Lord had had more to do with the progression of things than anything he had done. God in His wisdom had decided that Atle and Sadie could be happy together.

He cleared his throat. "Well, now. I just wanted to return the book to you and apologize for being late."

"Did you read it?"

"Yes. Yes, I did."

Her eyes brightened. "And . . . did it give you any ideas about courting?"

Sarah Anne looked so hopeful, he wanted to give her good news. But to be honest, he wasn't sure if it had or not . . . until he started thinking about how interested he'd been in the characters' romance and imagining what he would do in their stead. "I think it did."

"You're not sure?"

"It might have inspired me more than anything." Thinking of Carson and Jane's on-again, off-again antics, he added, "I started figuring that if those two could make a go of it, I might have a chance with Sadie."

"They do have some issues, that's a fact," Sarah Anne said with a laugh. "I liked their story because I thought it might give you some hope. They never gave up on a future together." She sighed. "Plus, Carson Marks was just so dashing."

Atle believed Carson was a bit too full of himself, but he couldn't deny that Jane liked him.

Now that he thought about it, their trials and tribulations had been encouraging for him on many levels. They were proof that there was someone for everyone.

"I don't intend to give up on Sadie anytime soon."

"I like hearing that. Well, it's good to see you, Atle. Good luck to you both."

"*Danke* for your help and time," he said as he walked out the door.

"Hi, Mr. Petersheim!" Hope Overholt called from the sidewalk as he closed the bookmobile door behind him.

He walked to meet her halfway. Today she had on a bright red dress, a black cloak, and mittens and a scarf with different colored snowflakes on them. "Hiya, Hope. How are you doing today? And call me Atle. We're friends, after all."

"All right, Atle. I'm well, *danke*." She smiled. "I wanted to thank you for your help with my parents."

"I didn't do anything."

"We both know you did. Thank you for helping me reason with them about Cale."

"A little bird told me he's been given permission to visit you?"

"*Jah*, which is so silly now." Looking even happier, she giggled. "When Cale was working on our farm, I went out to see him all the time. Sometimes I would sit on an upturned watering trough and chat with him while he tended the sheep and horses. Now we have to sit in the living room, and my mother hovers in the kitchen."

Atle smiled. "That sounds rather trying."

"It is, especially since it seems my *mamm* has no qualms about eavesdropping—and then speaking to me about what she's heard."

"What does Cale have to say about that?"

"He doesn't seem to think it's as irritating as I do. He keeps saying my *mamm* is hovering because she cares."

"Perhaps you should believe that?"

"I suppose." She shrugged. "Her eavesdropping did encourage the two of us to have some good conversations, so I'm grateful for that."

"There you go. It's better to look on the bright side of things."

She nodded. "Were you just in the library?"

"I was. I had an overdue book to turn in. If you're headed there, you'd best get on in before Sarah Anne moves to her next stop."

"I will. See you soon, Atle." Her smile turning brighter, she said, "That same little bird told me Cale's not the only person going courting these days."

Atle chuckled. "Christmas season is a time of miracles, for sure."

He heard her giggle until he was halfway down the path. Few things had ever sounded so sweet.

thirty

Carson was so distracted by their most recent argument
and by the way Jane's eyes had looked so luminous
through her tears that he didn't see the car veering into
his lane. His last thought before losing consciousness
was that he hoped Jane would be okay.

—*Finding Love's Fortune*, page 405

One of Hope's favorite things about visiting the bookmobile
was having the chance to chat with Sarah Anne. Hope considered
Sarah Anne to be a combination of fairy godmother, wise grandmother, and the girlfriend everyone always wished they had but
rarely did.

When she entered the vehicle, the librarian didn't disappoint.
"Hope Overholt, now isn't this a nice surprise."

"Hiya, Sarah Anne. I've been trying to get over here for days. I'm
glad I made it before you left."

Sarah Anne looked at her watch. "You caught me but not for too much longer. I have one more stop to make after this one."

"I'll hurry."

"Are you looking for anything special? If so, I can point you in the right direction."

"I was hoping for a good love story. Do you have anything in mind?"

Sarah Anne seemed to consider things for a moment, then nodded. "Actually, I do," she said as she reached under her desk. She disappeared for a second, then popped her head back up. "Here we go. Hope, someone just returned this book. It's one of my favorites."

Hope stared at the silhouette of an English couple standing in a doorway on the cover, then read the title out loud. "*Finding Love's Fortune?*"

Sarah Anne chuckled. "I know, the title does seem a bit over the top. But the story is appealing, and the hero and heroine never give up. I've always felt like they needed to be together, no matter what."

"Really?" That was how Hope felt about herself and Cale. They'd already had a lot to overcome, and she had a feeling that the obstacles in their future weren't over yet. If she could find some inspiration and hope in a book, she wanted to do just that. "I'd like to give it a try."

Sarah Anne smiled like she'd just called out the winning number in a Bingo game. "I'm so glad," she said as she placed it on the counter. "Do you want to look around now? I can probably stay here ten minutes more."

"*Danke*, but this book is enough for now," she said as she handed the librarian her card. "Thanks for your help."

"Of course! That's why I'm here." She smiled sweetly. "Don't forget that I only got married a few months ago. If an old bird like me can find love at the bookmobile, anything can happen."

Hope giggled. "I reckon so."

As she walked back home with her new book in hand, Hope kept hearing Sarah Anne's parting words in her head. Though she knew Sarah Anne had been teasing, she found a lot of comfort in what she'd said as well. Anything could happen, if one believed it could. She just had to keep hoping and praying that the Lord would guide her through, one step at a time.

She found Anna sitting on the porch with a bag of yarn and a crochet hook in her lap. "What are you up to?"

"I decided to make Hank a scarf for Christmas."

Hope frowned. "I thought you were making him some caramel corn."

"I am, but it didn't seem personal enough," she said as she continued to organize the yarn. "What are you giving Cale for Christmas?"

"I don't know," Hope answered before panic set in. "I haven't thought of anything."

"Really? Well, you better start. I mean, I'm sure Cale is going to give you something, Hope."

"He might, but I'm not sure Cale is the type who thinks of gifts."

"Come now. He asked Mamm and Daed if he could come calling. He told you he thought you were pretty. Of course he's going to give you a Christmas gift."

Anna had a point. "I'm not sure what I should get him." Sitting down on the front porch, she started thinking about her options. Not a lot was coming to mind. Time was running out, too.

Their mother opened the door. "Back so soon, Hope?"

"*Jah.* Sarah Anne had another stop to make after ours. I'll come in to help in the kitchen."

"We've got time. We're going to make some Christmas cookies for the widows' baskets."

Hope loved that project. Every year all of the women put together large boxes of canned vegetables, soups, homemade bread, cookies, and small items like toothbrushes and shampoo for the elderly women in the area. Every family in their church district worked on something to contribute. Her mother was the one who spearheaded the effort, too, which reminded Hope that while they might sometimes have their differences, her mother really did have a wonderful, giving heart.

"Mamm, Anna and I were just talking about Christmas gifts. She's making Hank a scarf, but I don't know what to give Cale."

"Uh-oh. That is a problem." Her mother sat down next to

her on the steps. "You don't have much time for anything big, I'm afraid."

"I know. I should've thought about this earlier." Why hadn't she? Had she really been so selfish . . . or was it that she'd been afraid to believe the two of them could actually have a chance together? Maybe a bit of both, she decided.

"You are a good baker," Anna said. "Cale said that when he was over, remember?"

"I remember."

"So, how about you bake him something?"

Hope considered making Cale a cake but then promptly rejected that idea. She wanted to make something for him that wouldn't be gone in a couple of days. "Baking something doesn't seem special enough. Besides, his *mamm* is one of the best bakers in the county. He's probably surrounded by baked goods."

Anna frowned. "True."

Her mother snapped her fingers. "I've got the perfect idea. You can finish the quilt you've been working on forever and give it to Cale."

"Oh, Mamm. You know what that quilt looks like."

Anna giggled. "The bane of your existence."

"It isn't . . . but it's definitely been a source of hardship."

"Oh, we know," Anna said.

Hope felt her cheeks heat, but she couldn't deny her sister's and mother's knowing looks. Because, in truth, she had a love-hate relationship with the quilt. It was a simple enough design, an around-the-world pattern in blocks. When she'd started it three years ago, she'd decided to use all types of red, white, and blue fabrics—mainly because those fabrics had been on sale after the Fourth of July. Unfortunately, she'd soon learned that she wasn't always as precise as a quilter needed to be. She'd mismeasured, sewn crooked lines, and sometimes even pinned them a little off-kilter. Every time she'd shown her mother what she'd done, Mamm had clicked her tongue, pointed out the flaws, and encouraged her to fix them. Hope's thirteen-year-old self hadn't liked that one bit. More than once she'd argued that pulling out stitches was a waste of time, but even Anna had agreed with their mother.

"I want Cale to like me. I don't think giving him such a sorry-looking quilt is going to do that. Plus, I still have a lot to go on it."

"Cale already likes you," Anna said. "He likes you a lot. A whole lot. Don't you remember him standing up to both Mamm and Daed in the parking lot after church?"

"*Jah*. Of course."

Her mother smiled softly. "Dear, while your father might never tell you this, he and I have both known that Cale has liked you for quite a while now."

"You knew? How?"

"It wasn't hard to figure out. The boy watches you whenever you are in the room."

Anna nodded. "He's done it for years, too."

"I didn't realize that." Hope wasn't sure whether she was embarrassed that her whole family had been watching her and Cale or that they'd known what he'd been feeling before she had.

"Hope, dear, I think a quilt is a good gift for a beau, especially since it's in red, white, and blue and not pink, purple, and yellow."

"That is true. He could put it in his new room, too."

"Indeed he can. Go fetch it, and we'll devise a plan on how to finish it," Mamm said.

"Okay, but I'm afraid it's going to look even worse than I remember it."

"It might look better. One never knows what will happen if one doesn't try," Mamm said softly. "Have faith, child. Remember, it is the season for miracles."

Her mother's words rang in her head as she headed upstairs, her purse and her library book in her hands, and she felt a sense of peace and happiness wash over her when she stepped into her bedroom. Her walls were a creamy vanilla color, just two shades off white. There was a window seat with a comfortable cushion covered in pink roses, and laid on her bed was her grandmother's pride and joy, a white quilt dotted with appliquéd roses, daffodils, and pansies. She'd spent many an hour running a hand over the worn, soft fabric and thinking about her grandmother working on the quilt in the mornings when the light was best.

In the bottom drawer of her dresser was her own quilt and a large plastic sack of all the scraps, patterns, thread, and a seam ripper. Though it was tempting to open it up in private, Hope made herself hurry back downstairs. If she let her doubts get the best of her again, she'd never be brave enough to attempt to finish it by Christmas.

As she hurried, she said a little prayer. She was going to need a lot of help over the next few days!

"Do you have it?" Anna called out from the dining room.

"I do," she said as she stood next to Anna and her mother.

"How does it look?" Mamm asked.

"I don't know. I haven't had the nerve to look at it closely yet."

Chuckling, her mother picked up the project. "Come now. You need to think positively." Shaking it out, she spread it out on the table.

There were supposed to be twelve squares, and she'd finished eight. She had only four to go. That was the good news. The bad news was that the squares she had completed were full of flaws. The three of them silently stared at it for a good two minutes.

"You've got a lot of sewing to do, Hope," Anna said.

"But if Anna and I help you some, it won't be too terrible of a job."

The project felt daunting. "It's not going to be easy, though. We'll still need to put a backing on it and then quilt it together."

Her mother pursed her lips. "We'll need more help for that. I'm going to have to call in reinforcements."

"But I wanted the quilt to come from me."

"Dear, as much as I admire your resolve, the fact is that there's not enough time for that."

"Everyone is busy, though."

"That is true, but all the women I know will get behind a quilt for a beau. It will be a nice break and a good reason to get together."

"I'll start asking around," Anna said. "The first person on the list is going to be Viola."

Viola did beautiful work, and she was only fourteen. "Do you think she'll come?"

Anna grinned. "Of course she will! She's a fourteen-year-old girl itching to finally be included with the rest of us."

"Thank you both so much."

"No need for that, dear. We might have our differences from time to time, but we all love each other. And that's what matters, right?"

Hope nodded as she finally directed her attention to the project at hand. Of the eight squares that were completed, six looked well enough, one was a little odd and crooked, and the last had so many things wrong with it. Holding it up, she turned it to the right then the left, attempting to find a way to make it better. She honestly didn't know if that was possible. "What am I going to do about this square?"

"Let's keep it as it is. If you have time after piecing together the other squares, you can get out the seam ripper and rework it," Anna said.

"I can do that."

"*Gut.* Now, let's get out the fabric and start cutting. We have no time to waste."

Hope did the only thing she could. She followed her mother's directions right away. The only thing worse than finishing a poorly made quilt in a hurry was not finishing it at all.

thirty-one

Jane's hand was shaking as she placed the phone back in the receiver. Carson was in intensive care. Running to her closet, she quickly changed her clothes. She wanted to look her best when he woke up again.

—*Finding Love's Fortune*, page 415

Soon after Sadie had joined her children at the table and they'd finished bowing their heads in prayer, Viola made an announcement.

"So, Anna Overholt came over to see me today."

Cale, who'd just been spooning mashed potatoes onto his plate, looked at her in concern. "What did she want?"

"Some ladies are planning a quilting bee, and she asked me to be a part of it."

Sadie smiled at her headstrong daughter. "That is wonderful-*gut* news, dear. The ladies must have been talking about how talented you are."

"Why did Anna ask *you* about joining?" Cale asked.

Looking like the cat who had gotten all the cream, Viola grinned. "Because she's helping Hope with a special quilting project."

Now Cale looked really confused. "She's helping Hope?"

"She is."

When her eldest frowned again, Sadie began to get puzzled, too. "Why do you look so confused, Cale?"

"Because Hope doesn't sew. She likes to read books and sometimes writes stories and such. And bake, of course."

"Maybe you don't know her as well as you think you do," Viola said in a singsong voice. "Because this quilting bee is definitely to help Hope finish a very special Christmas gift."

When Cale frowned at his sister again, Sadie decided to help clear the air a bit. "Viola, you are teasing us all. What has gotten you looking so mischievous?"

"Because I know who the quilt is for, and it's for someone at this table."

Cale put down his fork. "Hope is making a quilt for me?"

"Maybe."

"'Maybe'?" Cale echoed. He frowned. "Viola, stop being annoying. Just tell me who Hope is making the quilt for and be done with it."

"I would, except I'm not supposed to tell you about the quilt."

Jason started giggling. "Now you know, Cale."

"But don't forget that I didn't actually tell you," Viola said. "You guessed."

Sadie felt like rolling her eyes in exasperation. "Daughter, you are terrible at keeping secrets."

"I know, but in this case I have a really good excuse for letting my secret slip."

"And what might that be?" Sadie asked.

"Because Cale needs to know Hope is planning to give him this quilt as a Christmas present."

Her eldest frowned. "I could have probably handled opening the gift without your warning, Vi."

"Okay . . . But what are you going to say when she looks at you expectantly for your gift? Or, have you already gotten Hope something and we don't know about it yet?"

"I haven't gotten her anything." Looking panicked, he pressed a hand to his face. "Was I supposed to get her something?"

Just as Sadie began to nod, Jason spoke up.

"You're courting her, aren't you?" Jason asked.

"You know I am."

"Then you've got to give her candy or something," Jason said, like he was the resident expert on such things. "It's expected, and if you don't give her anything, she's going to be real upset."

"How do you know this, Jason?" Sadie asked.

"Because *mei* friend Roland's big sister Emma has a suitor, and all Emma talks about is that he is going to give her something really fancy for Christmas."

"Jason's right," Viola said.

"He's really right." Turning to Sadie, Cale said, "Mamm, what am I going to do? I need to figure out what to give Hope."

"See, that's why I told you about Hope and her quilt," Viola said, triumph in her eyes.

Sadie was just about to chastise Viola for being cheeky when she realized that Cale wasn't the only one who was courting . . . or who hadn't given a moment's thought to what to give a person who meant so much.

"I think I might have to give Atle something, too," she said half to herself.

All three of her children turned to stare at her. Their expressions were so incredulous, Sadie feared she'd upset them. "It was just an idea," she murmured.

"Mamm, you really haven't gotten Atle anything yet?" Viola asked.

"*Nee.* I . . . I don't know why."

"But he's courting you," Jason said. "He brought you that big bunch of flowers."

"It's called a bouquet," Viola corrected. "And, um, actually . . . I think Atle is courting all of us. He always makes time to talk to each one of us when he comes over."

"He did help me feed Gwen the other day," Jason said. "And he and I shared a bunch of knock-knock jokes."

Sadie gaped at him. "Atle knows knock-knock jokes?"

"Oh, *jah*. He knows lots of them," Jason answered. "He's really funny, Mamm."

"He's practically saved my life," Cale blurted. "He talked to Hope, and he gave me a job. I've got to give him a gift, too."

"But you're the most important to him, Mamm," Jason said. "You've got to give Atle something special because he likes you the best."

"I don't know if that's true."

"It is," Cale said. "He really likes you, Mamm."

"You know, we have never really talked about Atle and me. Does, um, me seeing him bother any of you?"

"By 'seeing' do you mean liking him?" Viola asked.

"She means kissing," Jason corrected.

"I do not mean that, Jason. I haven't kissed Atle. We're only talking right now."

"But you're planning on it, right, Mamm?" Jason asked. As Sadie's cheeks turned a bright scarlet, he added, "And don't act like you're never going to kiss him, because that's what people who are married do."

Viola gaped at Jason. "How come you know so much about courting?"

He shrugged one shoulder. "I don't know. I just do." Turning to Sadie, he added, "Mamm, if you kiss Atle, that means you and him are really serious."

Cale rolled his eyes. "Couples courting do other stuff besides kiss, Jason. Don't be stupid."

"Well, of course I know they live together, too." He brightened. "And make babies! Mamm, are you going to have a baby with Atle?"

Viola gasped. Cale groaned.

And then all three stared at her.

"*Nee!*" she blurted. "I mean, I don't know. I mean, we shouldn't talk about this." Pressing her hands to her burning face, she said, "What I'm trying to say is that all that really matters right now is getting a Christmas gift for Atle."

"What about the rest of us?" Jason asked. "I want to give him a present, too. What do you think I should give him?"

"I can't answer that. But I will tell you that if each of you made something for Atle, it would make him happy indeed."

"I'll have to think about Atle after I get Hope a gift," Cale said. "There's no way I'm going to sit there while she's giving me a quilt she made and not give her anything in return."

Viola smiled at all of them. "See, everyone? That is why I brought up Hope's secret gift. Some things just shouldn't stay secrets."

Sadie reached over and covered Viola's hand with her own and smiled. "You are right. In this case, I'm glad you let Hope's cat out of the bag. All of us have some gifts to attend to."

"I hope none of them will take long," Viola warned. "After all, Christmas is just around the corner."

thirty-two

The news about Carson was dire. He had not only sustained several serious injuries, but he was also in a coma.

"There's no reason to wait here at the hospital, Miss Cousins. We can call you when he wakes up," the nurse said.

Just imagining Carson waking up alone made her heart hurt. "There won't be a need to call," Jane replied with iron in her voice. "I'm going to stay here until he wakes up."

—*Finding Love's Fortune*, page 422

As much as Cale liked working on his room, he liked working in Atle's workshop even more. The workshop took up most of his barn and was full of tools, generators, big sawhorses, tables, and lots of pegboards.

What was really fantastic were all the samples and projects Atle had displayed on shelves on the front wall. Atle had told him that some were kept for sentimental reasons—like the first toy train he ever built—while others were mistakes or small samples of what a bigger piece might look like.

Finally, in the very back, covered in old sheets and tarps, were about a dozen pieces of furniture that customers could come in and buy right out of the workshop.

When Atle went inside his house for a few minutes, Cale took some time to study everything more carefully. He still had no idea about what to give Hope, but he needed all the ideas he could get.

Cale was examining a box made out of cherrywood that had a flower carved on the lid when Atle returned.

"What are you looking at?" he asked. "Did something strike your fancy?"

"Actually, I'm trying to think of ideas about what to get Hope for Christmas. Viola told me Hope's been working on a present for me, a really special quilt. I've got to get her something back."

"Ah. Why do you look so worried?"

"Because I hadn't thought about it, and now I'm almost out of time. Plus, it needs to be special. There's no way I can just give Hope a box of candy or something if she's giving me a handmade quilt."

As he usually did, Atle pondered Cale's words for a few seconds before answering. "Hmm. *Jah*, I see your point. Well, now. Hmm. *Jah*, I could see how that is a problem." Walking to Cale's side, he took the box from him. "Are you thinking of making something like this?"

"Maybe. Or, maybe I could give this to Hope and then pay you back by working extra hours for free?"

"I'm afraid I can't let you give this one away."

"Is it sentimental?"

"*Jah*. I made it years ago."

"Oh."

"But it's not real hard, you know. Perhaps you could make a box for Hope here."

"Do you think so?"

"I don't see why not. These aren't too hard to make. Plus, we're almost done with your bed. I reckon we'll have time."

Giving Hope a box didn't sound very romantic. "Do you think girls like wooden boxes?"

Atle grinned. "I read in a book that girls like anything their beaus make for them. If that's the truth, then I think Hope will like it a lot."

"What are you making Mamm for Christmas?"

Atle's confident grin faded. "Why do you ask?"

"Well, you are Mamm's beau, right?"

"I am, indeed." He opened his mouth to say something more, then seemed to change his mind.

Studying Atle's face, Cale realized he wasn't the only one in a heap of trouble. "You don't have anything for her, do you?"

"I didn't say that." But his eyes looked guilty.

"You haven't said anything." Feeling triumphant, Cale grinned. "Atle, did you forget, too?"

His blue eyes narrowed. "What do you mean by 'too'?"

"Everyone in our house has forgotten about some Christmas gifts."

"Really?"

Atle was staring at him intently. "Oh, yeah," Cale added. "We had a whole discussion last night at supper, and now everyone is in a panic."

"Even your mother?"

Remembering how his *mamm* looked like she'd just swallowed a fly, Cale grinned. "Especially *mei mamm!*"

"I didn't think she forgot anything."

"You might be surprised about that."

After studying the box in his hands for another long moment, Atle said, "All right. I guess I should tell you the truth. I haven't made anything for your mother yet. I didn't forget, though . . . I've just been trying to think of the best thing to buy for her. Do you think she'd like a plant?"

"Ah, no."

"Really? She seemed to like the flowers I brought her."

"She did, but trust me on this. You can't go to the store and buy my mother a poinsettia and expect her to think it's special. Your Christmas gift needs to be something you made."

"I don't know . . ."

"You should make her a box, too."

He scratched the scruff on his jaw. "*Jah*, but then what would I put in it?"

"That's up to you. I can't think up the whole present."

"You're doing a pretty *gut* job of it so far."

"If Jason was here, he'd tell you the same thing."

"Jason?"

"*Jah*. Jason is like the wisest person around when it comes to courting. He was dispensing all kinds of good information last night."

Atle frowned. "I wish I would have known that. He could have saved me a lot of time. Well, come along, then. We're going to have a lot to do in order to get these Christmas boxes made and looking good—on top of finishing your room."

"I'm ready. What do we need to do first?"

"First off, we're going to need to find some wood. Come on."

Atle led Cale over to a stack of many types of wood in the corner that he hadn't even noticed before. Unlike some of the scrap piles, this one seemed to be organized a little more neatly.

"Take a look and decide which type of wood strikes your fancy." Atle bent down and picked up three pieces with patterns that Cale had never seen before. "You can't have this, though. I'll be making Sadie's Christmas box out of it."

That suited Cale fine. He didn't think Hope was going to care too much about what her gift was made of; she was just going to be disappointed if he didn't give her anything in return. Looking down at the pieces, he found a few that looked smooth and pretty. Picking them up, he asked, "Atle, can I have these for my project?"

"Oh, *jah*. That is maple. It's a good hardwood and shines up real pretty, too. That's a *gut* choice."

"Now what?"

Atle grinned. "Now, Cale, we begin."

❄ ❄ ❄ ❄

Later that night in Hope's living room, Cale couldn't help but be pleased with himself. He had measured, sanded, and stained his scraps of maple, and he could already tell they were going to make a fine box for his girl. Even better was that he now had something to smile about every time Hope asked him questions about Christmas, like she was doing at the moment.

"We have relatives coming in next week. Do you?"

"*Nee*, it will just be us," Cale said.

"That's kind of lonely, don't you think?"

"Not really. I'm used to it. Plus, I think Mamm will probably ask Atle over for Christmas dinner."

Her eyes widened. "They must be getting really serious."

"I think so. Of course, you know my *mamm*. She doesn't share a lot." Deciding to take the plunge, he said, "Will I get to see you on Christmas Eve or Christmas Day?"

"I hope so. I'm sure my parents will let me see you one of those days." She smiled at him.

He loved how Hope never tried to hide how much she liked him. He knew some of his buddies liked relationships to be full of surprises to keep them guessing, but he always thought that was a waste of time. "I'd like to come over on Christmas Eve if it's okay with your parents. I have a gift for you."

Her blue eyes widened. "You do?"

"Of course. I couldn't let the day go by without getting you something, Hope." Boy, he hoped Viola and Jason never told Hope how close he'd been to not having a gift for her.

Looking pleased, she said, "I have a gift for you, too. I mean, I will have a gift. I'm making it, but it's not done yet."

"My present isn't done yet, either."

"I guess that means we're going to be really busy until Christmas Eve." Her eyes widened. "We might not even have time to see each other."

"Of course we're going to have time. My gift won't take that long to finish."

She slowly smiled. "You sound really sure about us needing to see each other, Cale Mast."

"I'm not going to have it any other way." Realizing he was sounding pretty bossy, he added, "Well, what I'm trying to say is that it took a lot of nerve to ask your parents if I could come calling. I'm not going to put those sweaty palms to waste."

As he'd hoped, she giggled. Unable to help himself, he allowed his gaze to flicker across her lips and wondered what kissing her would be like. As if she knew what he was thinking, she licked her bottom lip and looked right into his eyes.

His heart started beating faster. Maybe he shouldn't wait to kiss Hope after all. After peeking at the kitchen doorway and seeing it empty, he reached for her hand and leaned closer. Hope's lips parted.

Was it time? Maybe. He could just give her a peck on the cheek.

He leaned closer. "Hope—"

She leaned closer, too. Their noses were almost touching. "Yes?"

"Hope, do you need more cookies?" Mrs. Overholt called out.

She jumped and scooted away. "*Nee*, Mamm. We're *gut*!"

"Are you sure?"

She pressed her palms to her cheeks. "*Jah*. I'm very sure!"

When Cale heard her mother's footsteps fade away, he exhaled in relief. He would be banned for life if Mrs. Overholt had caught him kissing Hope. "Your mother has really good timing," he whispered. "It's like she has a sixth sense or something."

"You have no idea," Hope said as she picked up the plate of cookies. "Eat a couple of cookies, Cale. And, um, drink some hot cider, too."

"I'm not too hungry."

"Cale, if you don't, my parents are going to have a whole lot of questions about what we've been doing instead. Trust me on this."

He picked up a sugar cookie in the shape of a snowman and took a big bite.

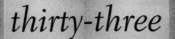

thirty-three

Four days had passed, but still Carson remained unconscious.

Jane was forced to leave when the Marks family arrived. Carson's mother had told the hospital staff that Jane was most definitely not part of their family.

—*Finding Love's Fortune*, page 440

Feeling as if her stomach had been filled with bumblebees, Sadie had spent much of her afternoon preparing for Atle's visit. She'd cleaned the living room even though she'd just cleaned it two days ago. She'd made a savory snack mix with cereal, peanuts, pretzels, and almonds because Atle had once commented how much he'd enjoyed it. Then, she had gone ahead and made a batch of frosted brownies because she now knew he had a hidden fondness for chocolate.

She'd washed her face, taken down her hair, and brushed it until it shone. Then, she pinned it back up and placed a crisp, freshly ironed *kapp* on top. She also put on her favorite deep blue dress, the color of fresh blueberries in July, which she had always thought brought out the color of her eyes.

All of her prepping and fussing was no doubt prideful and a bit silly, too. After all, she was no longer a fresh-faced young woman with her first beau. Even so, Sadie couldn't deny that it felt nice to concentrate on herself for a bit . . . and hoped Atle would notice that she cared enough about him to go to so much effort.

When he'd first walked inside, his usual serious expression lifted into a true smile. "You look lovely, Sadie, and your *haus* smells wonderful-*gut*."

"*Danke*," she'd murmured demurely as she took his coat. But inside? Well, she was practically dancing a jig, she was so pleased.

Almost an hour after they'd first sat down on the couch, Atle smiled at her and said, "Do you ever find it humorous that half the time when I come over here to sit on your couch, your boy is doing the same thing at the Overholt *haus*?"

"I think about it all the time," Sadie confided. "Sometimes I even half expect Charity Overholt to come over and ask to chaperone us."

He grimaced playfully. "I hope that never happens. Charity is a *gut* woman, but her watchful eyes and ears would put me on edge."

Imagining the sight, she chuckled. "You and me both, Atle. Can you imagine?"

"Unfortunately, I could. Cale has told me Charity has a habit of lurking in the kitchen doorway just in case they need anything."

"He's mentioned that to me, too, though once he said Charity lurks just to make sure they don't *try* anything."

The lines around Atle's eyes deepened with his smile. "I suppose that shouldn't surprise me, since we happen to have our own chaperones here. Where are they?"

"Up in their rooms." Remembering her discussion with Viola and Jason earlier that day, Sadie said, "I asked them to give us some privacy tonight."

He tensed. "Oh?"

"*Jah*. I started feeling like the two of us weren't getting much of a chance to talk to each other because they were wanting all your attention." She felt foolish complaining, but she couldn't help it. Now that she'd gotten her mind wrapped around dating again, she wanted to enjoy this special time with Atle.

"I'm impressed, Sadie. That had to have been quite the conversation."

"It wasn't too bad." Feeling embarrassed by his knowing look, she blurted, "You don't mind, do you? I mean, I don't expect anything to happen . . ."

Still looking thoroughly entertained, he grinned. "You don't?"

Oh, but this was horrible. "*Nee*. I mean, I think I just wanted a little peace and quiet."

Little by little, his teasing grin faded. In its place was something far more heated. "Really, Sadie? That's all you wanted?"

She felt her cheeks heat. Oh, but what was he doing to her? "Of course." When Atle's blue eyes still studied her, she shifted uncomfortably. "I mean, um, what else would I want?"

"I don't know . . . Maybe for me to hold your hand?" He reached for her and gently linked their fingers together.

Holding his hand was nice and all, but it certainly wasn't all that she'd been thinking about. No, what she wanted was to be in his arms. And, if she was being perfectly honest, she'd like a kiss, too. It had been so very long since she'd had a sweet kiss. Marcus had stopped kissing her years ago.

"Sadie, are you going to answer me?"

"*Nee*."

After blatantly glancing toward the stairs, Atle shifted. And next thing she knew, his arms were wrapped around her back, and she was leaning against him with her palms flat on his chest.

He nuzzled her neck, and his scratchy stubble brushed against her skin, igniting almost every nerve ending. "To be honest, I wasn't exactly thinking about hand-holding, either, Sadie," he whispered.

When he lifted his head and gently touched his lips to hers, she didn't feel a shred of hesitation. For what felt like months now, she'd found herself growing closer to him, trusting him more. And with that closeness and trust came the awakening of a desire she'd thought unattainable after so many years. She'd begun to imagine his kisses, how his lips would feel on hers, if he would ever feel the same things she did.

One kiss became two, which turned into something deeper. When Sadie felt his fingers lightly caress the bare skin of her neck, she sighed with pleasure.

Then, all too soon—far too soon—he lifted his head. Immediately, he searched her face. It was obvious he was looking for any sign that he'd scared her, done too much, and overstepped her boundaries.

She would've smiled if she thought she was capable of anything beyond staring at him in wonder.

"You all right?" he asked.

"Oh, yes," she murmured before she realized how inane that sounded. Why, she sounded like a veritable lovestruck girl instead of a widowed woman with no less than three children. "I mean, *jah*, it was just fine."

The corners of his lips twitched. "No offense, but I liked your first response better. I, too, was feeling a bit 'oh, yes' myself."

If he wanted honesty, then Sadie would give it to him. "You took my breath away, Atle. Truth be told, I didn't know if that was possible. I'm glad I was wrong."

He scooted a safe distance away but stayed close enough for her to feel the warmth of his body. And close enough for her to notice that he wasn't unaffected, either. There was a slight tremor in his hand as he ran his fingertips through the ends of his short hair.

"I've been wanting to kiss you for some time, Sadie. Years, really."

She didn't want to push, but her heart needed to hear the words. "Truly?"

Looking contemplative, he nodded. "I couldn't seem to help myself. Sometimes I even wondered if I should give up. Even as we became friends, I was afraid to wish for something more. Afraid to hope for this moment." Cupping her face and running his thumb along her cheek, he said, "It was worth every fear, every second thought. Without a doubt, it was worth the wait."

Tears pricked her eyes before she could stop them. "Atle, that was the sweetest—"

The back door slammed. "Mamm, where are ya?" Cale called out.

Sadie sighed. "Here, Cale. Atle is here, too."

"Oh, *gut*. Hiya, Atle," he said with a smile as Viola and Jason ran downstairs.

"Hi, Atle!" Jason called down.

Atle smiled at him. "Evening."

"Mamm, Jason and me figured if Cale was in here, we could be in here, too."

"Of course," Sadie said as she wiped one of her eyes. Taking a ragged breath in a hasty attempt to calm down, she patted the cushion on the other side of her. "Come sit down, and we'll all talk."

Only then did she notice that all three of her children were staring at her face in shock.

"What did you do to my *mamm*?" Viola demanded as she rushed over to Sadie's side. "Did you hit her?"

Atle froze. "Hit her? Of course I didn't hit your mother. Viola, I would never hurt her."

But either Viola didn't hear him or she was choosing to ignore his protests. Before Sadie could stop her, Viola reached out toward her face. "Mamm, where did he hurt you? Do you need ice?"

Sadie's insides crumbled as her children reverted back to the past. This was what they'd known. Her tears and bruises were what they'd grown up with. Pain for their memories and guilt for not discussing their father's abuse almost took her breath away.

"Atle didn't hurt me, Vi," she said. When the words still didn't register, Sadie reached for her daughter's hand and squeezed gently. "I promise you, Atle didn't do anything bad to me. He's very kind, remember?"

Jason shook his head as he hurried to his big brother's side. "Cale, make Atle go away."

Luckily, Cale had seemed to recover first. He threw an arm over Jason's shoulders and pulled him into a rough, brotherly hug. "*Nee*. It's okay," he murmured. "Mamm isn't hurt. Are you, Mamm?"

"I am fine, *kinner*." Looking over at Atle, who still seemed to be in a state of shock, she smiled. "I was crying because Atle had said something sweet to me. They were happy tears."

Atle got to his feet. His expression was solemn, but there was real pain in his eyes.

Was he about to leave?

If they had been alone, Sadie would have reached for him, but because they certainly weren't, she remained where she was, wondering what was going to happen next.

"I'm sorry," Cale said to him. "We shouldn't have gotten so angry. We shouldn't have thought . . ." His voice drifted off.

"*Nee*, Cale," Atle replied. "There is no need for that." He drew a deep breath. "Cale, Viola, Jason, I would never hurt a woman. I *especially* would never harm your mother."

"But what if you get angry?" Jason asked.

"If I get angry, I suppose I'll be angry. But that doesn't mean I would ever lay a hand on her. That is not who I am."

Looking a bit like a mini-Doberman, Jason stepped forward. "But what if—"

Atle shook his head. "There is no 'what if,' boy. I have admired your mother for a long time. I feel blessed that the Lord gave me a chance to court her, to show her how much I care for her." He swallowed. "I am blessed to get to know each of you, too. I've been alone a long time. Now that God has given me this chance to be your friend, I would never do anything to jeopardize it. I would never harm any of you. Ever."

Viola's eyes filled with tears. "I'm sorry, too. I don't know why I jumped to conclusions."

"It's all right, child," Atle murmured. "I'm glad you were ready to take care of your mother. That shows your love, ain't so?"

"I don't know." Viola looked confused.

Glancing at Sadie, Atle's blue eyes filled with compassion. "I think it would be best if I left now."

She didn't want him to leave, but she knew her children were rattled and they needed some time to decompress. "*Jah*. Maybe so." Walking to his side, she placed a palm on his bicep. She felt it tighten under her touch. "I'm sorry," she whispered.

He shook his head. "There's nothing to be sorry about, Sadie. Never apologize to me for your family's love."

Then, before she could say another word, Atle plucked his coat and hat from the hook by the door, then walked outside.

When the door closed softly behind him, Sadie felt almost as if part of her heart had left with him.

But she could ponder what happened with him another time. For now, there were three important people to take care of. Turning around, she faced them with a watery smile. "Let's go into the kitchen, children. I think it's time we sat down and had a good talk."

And with that, she turned and walked out of the room. They would follow in their own time. She just needed to give them a moment.

thirty-four

After being asked to leave the hospital, Jane went home and had a good cry. But then, to her amazement, she felt stronger than ever.

When Ed over in human resources called to say that Carson still hadn't found a secretary and there was no one to run his desk, she knew what she had to do. The next day she handed Dalton her letter of resignation. Carson needed her, and she needed to be close to him—even if it was just sorting his correspondence.

Whenever anyone stopped by to ask how Mr. Marks was doing, she said he was doing as well as could be expected. As the days passed, more and more people looked at her with a bit more respect.

—*Finding Love's Fortune,* page 446

"How mad do you think Mamm is at us?" Viola whispered after the three of them watched her walk out of the living room.

Cale had no idea. Their mother wasn't one to ever get very upset with them at all. He couldn't ever remember her raising her voice. But it had also been years since she'd announced that they all needed to have a talk. That had been the day their father had died.

Realizing that his younger siblings were still waiting on an answer, he shrugged. "I don't know. I guess we'll soon find out."

Jason frowned. "I was really mean to Atle. Even though he said he didn't mind, I'm sure he did." After casting a look toward the kitchen, he whispered, "I think Mamm is angry because she likes Atle a lot and we hurt his feelings."

"She likes us a lot, too," Cale said. "Don't start making up things to be upset about."

Jason still looked like his world was about to end. "I hope she doesn't take away Christmas."

"No one takes away Christmas, Jason," Viola said. "That's Jesus's birthday. It is what it is."

"I guess."

Hearing a chair scrape back in the kitchen, Cale said, "Come on. Mamm's waiting."

"*Jah*, we better go before she gets more irritated with us," Viola murmured.

Cale led the way through the living room. Belatedly, he noticed how festive it looked. Their mother had not only lit a fire in the fireplace, but she had also arranged some pine boughs, pine-scented candles, and pinecones on top of the mantel and put out a large bowl of cranberries and pomegranates on the coffee table. She'd gone to a lot of trouble for Atle's visit.

His heart sank. The three of them had managed to mess it up in less than ten minutes.

He'd half expected her to be tapping her foot like she sometimes did when they were running late for church. Instead, she was sitting at the end of the table eating a brownie. Four cups of hot chocolate with dollops of whipped cream and red sprinkles were in their places. In the center of the table was a plate of iced brownies.

"It's about time you three decided to join me. I feared your drinks were going to get cold."

"Wow," Jason said as he sat down. "We never get sprinkles unless it's a special occasion."

Cale met Viola's gaze as they sat down. Her blue eyes reflected what he was feeling: that neither of them had ever acted as goofy as Jason was right now.

"I guess this is a special occasion," Mamm said. "We're all going to have a grown-up talk." She looked around the table, meeting each of their eyes. "All four of us, together."

"All right, Mamm," Viola said in a subdued voice.

After taking a deep breath, she said, "Children, what happened this evening is my fault."

Cale shook his head. "*Nee*, Mamm."

"Dear, let me explain." Clearing her throat, she began again, "I don't like to talk about some of the things your father did because the memories still hurt. But that doesn't mean I don't remember or that I think you don't."

"I don't like to talk about it, either," Viola said. "We don't have to talk about it tonight, Mamm. I promise, next time I see Atle, I'll be nicer."

Jason nodded solemnly. "I'll be good, too."

Mamm frowned. "Viola, Jason . . . one more time, you didn't do anything wrong. The problem lies in the past. See, I think we all have a lot of memories, and sometimes our feelings about them get jumbled up in the present. At least, they do for me."

Seeing the pain in their mother's eyes made Cale feel even worse. "Mamm, it's okay."

She looked at him and smiled slightly. "You're right, dear. It is." After taking a sip of her drink, she continued, "Your father wasn't a bad person. I know he loved each of you, and he loved me as well. He . . . Well, he sometimes let a lot of his demons get the best of him."

"He yelled at us a lot," Jason said.

"He used to hurt you, Mamm," Viola said. "And me. And Cale, too."

Cale kept silent. As far as he was concerned, there was nothing his father did that he wanted to relive.

"He did. That is true." Their mother folded her hands in her lap. "I'm not going to lie to you and pretend that his actions pleased the Lord or any of us. But I have forgiven him."

"Really?" Cale asked before he could stop himself.

"Really. Our faith asks us to forgive, even when it is not easy."

"But he hurt you a lot, Mamm," Jason said.

"I know. There were many times when I wished he was different. And sometimes he *was* different. He was just like the man I'd fallen in love with." She smiled softly. "He liked to go on hikes with us, remember?"

"Once, when I tripped, he held me until I stopped crying," Jason said.

Their mother nodded. "I remember that. You were just a little boy when that happened. Your father felt terrible."

"He used to teach me how to identify all the trees and plants," Cale said. To his surprise, he realized he'd forgotten those moments.

"Daed liked all the animals, too. He said he could never bear to think about shooting any of the deer," Viola added. "Not even at Thanksgiving."

Mamm smiled. "You're right. He wasn't a hunter. Not at all."

"Or a fisherman," Jason said. "He told me once he liked to see fish in the stream instead of on the table."

"He butchered the hogs once a year because his father had

taught him to do it, but he hated every minute of it. Your *daed* would've been a happy vegetarian, for sure and for certain," Mamm said softly, smiling. With a sigh, she continued, "The reason I brought that up is because there's been more than one time when Atle has held out a hand to me and I've flinched. There's a part of my brain that still expects to be hurt."

"What did he do when you flinched?" Viola asked.

"He got sad, so I had to explain to him that I wasn't flinching intentionally . . . It was just that my body reacted like it used to."

"What did he say then?" Cale asked.

"That he hoped one day I would have so many other good memories that I wouldn't flinch anymore."

"But he wasn't surprised?" Viola asked.

"*Nee*, dear. I don't think anyone who was near us would be surprised at my reaction. I never spoke about all the injuries I received, but everyone knew. Preacher Andrew even tried to talk to your *daed* about his temper, though it didn't do much good."

Looking reflective, their mother continued, "That's why I don't want you to feel bad about how you reacted to me crying today. You all were used to seeing me get hurt and then lie about my injuries. I will always regret that." She paused, then added, "However, I will never be upset with any of you wanting to help me."

"What should we do next time we see Atle?" Jason asked. "Or do you think he's not going to want to come over again?"

"I can't speak for him, but I'm pretty sure Atle understands why you all reacted the way you did. That means you can do whatever you want."

"I hope he'll forgive me by Christmas."

Cale shook his head at Jason. "You always have Christmas on the brain."

Jason lifted his chin. "What's wrong with that? Christmas is just a couple of days away."

Viola rolled her eyes. "Jason was worried you were going to cancel Christmas, Mamm."

She chuckled. "Christmas is bigger than all of us, Jason. It's going to happen no matter what. Even if we didn't have a Christmas cake or a single present or we were alone and didn't have any food on the table. Jesus's birth was a miracle, ain't so?"

Jason nodded. "I hope we can still have cake, though."

"Me, too." She smiled tentatively. "And that our friend Atle will spend the day with us and not alone."

❊ ❊ ❊ ❊

Later that night, after they'd all hugged their mother and she told them to get some sleep, Cale sat in bed and forced himself to remember life with their father. He thought about the good times and the bad and prayed for his father, finally forgiving him.

Then, as he rolled to his side and gazed at the stars twinkling in the distance just like they shined for the wise men so long ago, Cale thought about his mother's words and how Christmas was coming no matter what. And that's when he realized how very wise she was. Days passed and time moved on. All that really mattered was how a person decided to begin each day. Forgiveness and acceptance were easier to bear than regret and shame.

As he closed his eyes, his body completely relaxed. Maybe for the first time in years.

thirty-five

Confined to the hospital bed, Carson had never felt so helpless.

"Mother, you had no right to kick Jane out of the hospital," he said the moment he learned what had transpired.

"I had no choice, Son. You were only supposed to have visits from loved ones. She is just your secretary."

"No, Mother. She is far more than that."

—*Finding Love's Fortune,* page 450

The quilting bee was tomorrow, and Hope still had one more block to complete. She would've finished it two days ago except for the fact that she'd ripped one of the squares, then managed to damage another piece when she was taking apart the seams. Then, of course, she discovered she was out of the exact color she needed, which meant she had to go to the fabric store.

So now she was walking into town with Anna instead of doing any of the dozen other things that needed to be done before hosting a group of women at the house the next morning.

"I should never have decided to give Cale that stupid quilt," she said. "It's going to be ugly, and I'm going to be completely embarrassed."

"You need to stop worrying so much," Anna said. "Everything is going to work out just fine."

"You keep saying that, but we both know that's not true."

"*Nee*, I know it *is* true. You don't believe it because you're a worrywart. Cale is going to like your quilt, Hope. I promise."

"I hope so."

"I know so. Look, here we are. Let's dash in, get your fabric, and then go to the diner and get some soup."

Realizing that the soup would probably go a long way toward making her feel better, Hope smiled at her sister. "*Danke*. Soup is a good idea. I'm actually starving."

Ten minutes later, when they walked into Vicki's Diner, they practically ran into Cale and his little brother, Jason. "What are you doing here?" she asked.

"I'm guessing the same thing as you are," Cale replied with a grin. "We're getting lunch."

"Want to join us?" Anna asked.

"*Jah*, can we all sit together?" Jason added.

"It's fine with me," Hope said.

Cale walked to the hostess stand. "Vicki, we need a table for four, please."

"You got it." She walked them through the crowded restaurant and seated them in a corner booth by the window.

"Jason, sit next to me," Anna said. "I want to hear about school."

"I guess that means you and I will have to sit together, Hope," Cale teased.

"I guess so," she murmured as he slid in by her side. When their knees touched, she scooted over a bit to give him more room.

"No need for that," he half whispered. "I'm good here."

And there came that tingly awareness again that she always felt whenever he was close. "Me, too," she said, before realizing she likely sounded a bit silly. But all Cale did was smile at her again.

"What are you girls doing in town today?" Cale asked after the server came and took everyone's orders.

"Oh, just a few errands for Christmas," Anna said. "What about you?"

"I promised Jason I'd take him out to lunch this week since he's on Christmas break now."

"That was nice of you."

"It's not like I had much of a choice, did I, Jason?"

"Nope. If I didn't keep reminding him, he'd be too busy working at Atle's."

"Atle Petersheim?" Anna asked.

"*Jah*. He's been allowing me to help him in his woodworking shop. I like it."

To Hope's relief, Anna merely smiled and didn't dredge up everything that had happened with their parents again.

"Guess what else we're gonna do?" Jason blurted. "We're going sledding!"

"Really? I haven't been sledding in ages," Hope said.

"Me neither," Anna added. "Where are you going?"

"Over to the hill near your house," Cale replied.

"It's my favorite hill," Jason added. "It's fast."

Hope smiled at Jason. "I'm jealous. It sounds like fun."

"Why don't you both join us?" Cale asked.

"What?" Immediately, thoughts of zipping down a hill with Cale's arms around her brought on a blush. "Oh, we couldn't."

"Are you sure?" Cale asked. "It is right near your *haus*."

Hope glanced at her sister, who was grinning at her like she could read her mind. "Anna?"

"I think we should go, Hope. It's almost Christmas. We deserve to have some fun."

"But we have all those errands . . ."

"We also have an invitation to go sledding on a fast hill," Anna said. "We could just go down a couple of times and then go home."

"What if Mamm and Daed find out?" Of course, she wasn't worried about them finding out they went sledding. It was that they might find out that she'd been spending time with Cale without asking permission first.

Anna shrugged. "I'm not going to tell them about it, but if they do find out, all we have to say is that we just happened to see Cale and Jason there."

Her sister was wily. She needed to take lessons! "All right."

Cale's expression warmed. "You'll come?"

There might be a dozen good reasons to say no, but there was also one very good reason to say yes. Smiling back at him, she nodded. "I'd love to." That was the truth, too.

"This is the best day ever," Jason announced.

Hope laughed, but she didn't disagree. This moment did feel special. Not only were she and Cale growing closer, but she was feeling closer to her sister, too. She might be sixteen, but in a way, she felt like she was growing up at last. She was discovering her voice, testing her backbone, and becoming more confident. She liked the changes, and it seemed the people she cared most about liked the changes, too.

Later, when she was flying down the hill with one of Cale's arms securely around her, she knew she had never been happier. She felt free and exhilarated and even a little bit giddy. When the sled popped over a log, she squealed like a young girl.

Cale laughed as he held her tighter. "Don't worry. I've got you, Hope."

"I know," she said. As she placed one of her mittened hands over his, she realized that she had him, too.

❄ ❄ ❄ ❄

Twenty-four hours later, Hope was stitching next to Viola Mast and watching in amazement at how fast her fingers could move. "How did you learn to sew so well? You're incredibly fast."

Viola grinned at her. "I don't know. I've just always liked to sew. My *mamm* said the Lord gave me lots of sewing skills because she's not too good at it."

Concentrating on keeping her stitches small and straight on the pattern she'd traced on the fabric the night before, Hope giggled. "Your mother is too modest."

"Cale is going to love this, you know," Viola whispered.

"You don't know how many times I've thought about not giving it to him. There's a lot of mistakes. Obviously."

Viola nodded. "There are, but he won't care. He thinks everything you do is *wunderbaar*."

Hope stitched again. "I feel the same way about him."

Mrs. Troyer, who was sewing the opposite end of the quilt, looked up and smiled at Hope. "This was a mighty fine idea, dear. December is always such a busy month, we never make time to chat with friends."

"I appreciate your help, Mrs. Troyer. Obviously, I couldn't have done all this work by myself."

"You shouldn't have to. After all, you've done the hardest part. Cale Mast is quite the catch."

All five of the women surrounding her giggled. Even her mother. "He is a good man."

"He's worked for you and Jeremiah for years now, hasn't he?"

"He did, though he's moved on. He's working for Atle Petersheim now."

"Rumor has it that Atle is courting Sadie Mast." As if she realized she'd spoken out of turn, Mrs. Troyer blinked. "Oh, I mean, your mother, Viola."

Viola looked a bit taken aback by the elderly woman's bluntness, but she answered in a sweet tone. "The rumor is true. Atle comes calling most every night. Cale is doing work for him, too."

"Atle made my dining room table," another woman from their church district announced. "If Cale is learning woodworking from Atle Petersheim, he'll have a bright future ahead of him. Mark my words about that."

Hope smiled. She knew Cale was struggling with decisions about his future, just as she was struggling with her own insecurities. But as far as she was concerned, none of those things mattered.

"Everything happens in its own time," her mother said. "There will be highs and lows and most likely an obstacle or two. But that is what makes life interesting."

Hope smiled to herself, thinking that her mother stated everything perfectly.

thirty-six

If Carson's leg wasn't broken in two places, he would've run over to Jane's apartment and asked her to forgive him for everything that he'd done wrong. Instead, he made do with calling her from the phone next to his bed.

—Finding Love's Fortune, page 454

It was the day before Christmas Eve. At last, Cale's new bedroom was completed. In order to make it feel a little more special, Atle had asked Cale to not help him for the last few days. Taking advantage of the privacy, Atle had installed baseboards and made a bench seat and some cubbies on one of the walls. He'd also moved in a bedside table to go with the bed frame that he and a few of his part-time workers had moved in yesterday.

All in all, Atle couldn't have been more pleased with how the room turned out. It was spare enough to not seem completely out of place in the back of a barn, but nice enough for anyone to enjoy a good night's sleep.

Sadie would allow Cale to see it all tomorrow—she'd made the decision after she learned that Hope was going to be giving him the quilt when the Overholts came over tomorrow to exchange gifts.

Now, though, it was just him and Sadie in the remodeled space. Supposedly they were doing a walk-through, but Atle couldn't bring himself to care about anything other than Sadie. He was so very pleased to have an excuse to spend some time alone with her.

It had been several days since their kiss, her tears, and the children's outburst. He'd seen all of the *kinner* since then. After a few awkward moments, they'd returned to their usual easygoing selves. He was grateful for that.

"So, what do you think?" Atle asked Sadie after she ran her hand along the top of the bedside table.

"I think everything is beautiful and perfect," she said. "I love the table and the extra touches. Cale is going to be so happy."

"I think he will be pleased, too. It's a fine room and a fitting place for your young man."

Atle and Cale had had many conversations about how this gift was almost more for Sadie than Cale. For some reason, Sadie had had a real need to provide Cale with these things. Atle would never regret the job, though. Because she'd reached out to him, he'd finally gotten up the nerve to actually try to court her. And it seemed that Cale had needed a new direction, too.

Looking up at him, Sadie smiled. "You've done so much for all of us, Atle. I don't know how to thank you. Are you sure I can't pay you for it?"

"We already discussed that. I don't want your money. This is a gift."

She still looked doubtful. "It's an expensive one."

"Sadie, I don't need the money. Plus, like I've said, I've enjoyed this project and the opportunity to work with Cale. You have nothing to thank me for."

She rested her hand on his forearm before quickly dropping it. "You know what I mean. You've made me so happy. I didn't know if another relationship was ever going to be possible for me. I'm glad you proved me wrong."

"I don't know if I proved you wrong as much as finally got up the courage to do something." He shook his head. "When I think of how nervous I was when I first asked Sarah Anne for help, it makes my head spin."

Sadie gave him a puzzled look. "What does Sarah Anne have to do with anything?"

What had he just said? His heart jumped firmly into the back of his throat. "Well, ah . . . she happened to give me some reference books on courting," he said slowly. His stomach churned, though he hadn't exactly lied. However, he reckoned it was the first time anyone had ever referred to *Finding Love's Fortune* as a reference book.

Her eyebrows rose. "You asked for reference books on courting?

I didn't know there was such a thing." Looking bemused, she murmured, "I'll have to ask Sarah Anne about them next time I'm in the bookmobile. I could probably use a refresher."

The conversation just kept getting worse and worse! Even though he knew she was joking, he couldn't seem to keep his mouth shut. "*Nee*, don't do that."

"Whyever not?"

It looked like he'd come upon the moment of truth. He could either continue to evade and deflect or admit what he'd done. There was really only one choice, but it definitely laid him bare. Taking a deep breath, he forged ahead. "Because the book I read wasn't exactly from the reference section."

Sadie scooted away a few inches and folded her arms around her middle. "Atle, I'm beginning to get a little worried about this conversation. If what you did is none of my business, please tell me. But if you're lying?" She paused as she took a deep breath. "If you're lying, then I'm afraid I won't be all right with that. I have to be able to trust you."

"You can trust me. I love you!"

Her eyes brightened with happiness, but she firmly tamped it down. Sitting on the edge of Cale's new bed, she looked at him square in the eye. "Atle Petersheim, if you love me, then you can tell me anything, right?"

Anything? "Right."

"Then tell me the truth about what you read."

"Fine. I checked out a novel from Sarah Anne, a romance called *Finding Love's Fortune*."

She blinked. "Say again?"

Atle shoved his hands in his pockets and half turned away. He didn't know if he'd ever had a more awkward conversation in his life. "I read a romance novel, okay?" When she simply gaped at him, he started talking so fast, his words were practically tumbling over each other. "I liked you for a long time, Sadie. But you've been married, and I had next to no experience courting. I didn't know how to win you over."

Realizing how embarrassing his words were for both of them, Atle turned away so he wouldn't have to view her amusement. "You know how I was brought up. *Mei* mother died when I was young, and my father was a solitary sort. Plus, I . . . Well, I'm shy by nature, I guess."

When she remained silent, he decided to admit the whole ugly truth so it was out in the open. "Sadie, the fact of the matter is that I didn't know what to do or say every time our paths crossed. Why, I could barely get up the nerve to talk to you, let alone get you to like me."

Feeling wrung out, he stopped his terrible tirade and waited for her to start laughing.

However, Sadie still remained silent. Half fearing that she was quietly walking out of the room, his palms started to sweat.

"Atle, are you ever going to turn around?"

Her voice sounded as sweet as always. At least she wasn't laughing. She didn't sound mad, either . . . not exactly. "I will," he said. "Just give me a moment."

After another pause, he heard the rustle of her dress as she stood up. He closed his eyes. Was she so appalled by his weakness that she was leaving the room? That would probably serve him right.

But then, to his amazement, he felt her hands lightly touch the backs of his arms and then, ever so slowly, slide around his chest. He stood motionless as he felt her touch through the worn fabric of his shirt and drew a sharp inhale when her slim fingers linked together, right over his heart. "Sadie?" he asked. It was almost all he could manage, too. Because he really had no words.

"I decided if you didn't want to come to me, then I would come to you."

Her voice was soft and loving. He'd heard that tone when she spoke to her children.

"Does this mean you don't hate me now?"

To his amazement, she leaned her head against his spine, right in between his shoulder blades. "Oh, Atle. Don't you understand? I don't hate you at all. I love you, too."

"Even though I had to read a romance novel to learn how a man should properly call on a woman?"

"I love you for a great many reasons, but most especially because you read a romance novel in order to come calling. How could I not? What woman wouldn't want a man who cared so much that he would go to any length to woo her properly?"

He pressed his palm over her linked hands. It was no doubt his imagination, but he reckoned she could probably feel his heart beating as fast as a galloping horse.

"Atle?" she whispered. "What are you thinking?"

"That I should probably kiss you."

"'Probably'?"

He turned, looked into her beautiful eyes, into the face that had starred in many a dream, and curved his arms around her, pulling her close. "I misspoke," he whispered. "I meant to say that I should definitely kiss you." Just as Sadie started to smile, he claimed her lips and pulled her closer.

Everything was perfect. He was no Romeo, but Sadie had just showed him that he didn't need to be. It turned out that he was enough after all.

Taking a breath, he traipsed kisses along her cheek and jaw, finally resting in the nape of her neck. This moment was worth waiting forty-two years for.

thirty-seven

Jane was not only thankful it was the weekend, but also that it was almost Christmas.

When her phone rang at home late one night, she elected not to answer it out of fear it might bear bad news about Carson.

So, Jane spent all of Saturday sitting on the couch and watching the snow falling throughout the city. She was starting to wish she had the nerve to put up a tree.

—*Finding Love's Fortune*, page 458

Atle had stayed far longer than either of them had anticipated, but Sadie knew she would never regret a moment of their time together. Not only had his kisses been amazingly wonderful, but their new closeness had also given her even more hope for the future.

For quite some time, she'd started to believe that she was frozen inside. That she'd been so hurt by marriage and disenchanted with the vows she and Marcus had taken, that she honestly hadn't known if she would ever be able to fall in love again.

She was glad she'd been wrong!

However, she also knew that what had really stolen her heart and finally banished the last of her doubts about falling in love again had been Atle's confession about the book. After all, many Amish men didn't even read fiction, let alone romance novels. Atle's willingness to go to such great lengths to court her said everything she needed to know about his love and devotion.

After finishing her morning prayers, she sat down at the kitchen table with a cup of coffee and waited for her sleepy children to join her. Sadie had assured them last night that they could stay up as late as they wanted, as long as they didn't forget to do their chores in the morning. When she'd collapsed on her bed at a quarter to midnight, she heard whispering in Viola's room down the hall and couldn't help but smile to herself. No, things weren't perfect in her house, but they were awfully good. Her children were happy and close to each other, and all four of them had adjusted to the many changes of late.

She'd fallen asleep giving thanks for their many blessings.

❄ ❄ ❄ ❄

When she heard the first footsteps approach just after eight in the morning, Sadie turned to greet Cale but saw Jason instead.

"Hiya, Mamm," he said sleepily.

"*Gut matin*, Jason." Reaching over to press her lips to his brow, she added, "Do you know what day it is?"

His sleepy expression brightened. "Uh-huh. It's Christmas Eve."

"You are right! That means we have a lot to do. The Overholts are coming over for lunch today, remember?"

Jason brightened. "Yep. Then tomorrow is Christmas, and Atle will be coming over."

"*Jah*, he'll be spending the day with us."

"And we'll get to open our presents to each other."

"We're going to be busy, child. That means you need to go out to the barn and tend to Bonnie and Gwen. No doubt Gwen is feeling like we've all forgotten about her."

"Me? But Cale usually does that."

"Cale isn't downstairs yet, so it's your job now."

"But—"

Tired of her son's complaining, she hardened her voice. "Jason Mast, Bonnie and Gwen are important members of our household. It's because of them that we are able to use our buggy. Now, you go out and clean their stall, feed and water them, and give them lots of attention, too."

He got up and started stuffing his feet into boots. "I'm going to be out there forever."

"You certainly will if you don't get busy. Now, do as I say, and don't forget to put on a coat."

"*Jah*, Mamm." He stuffed his arms into his coat and pulled on his hat.

"When you come inside, I will have a surprise for you."

He paused to turn to her. "Is it an early present?"

"Of sorts. Now, go on with ya. And don't you cut corners. You clean their stall like Cale has shown you. We'll all notice if you don't."

"I will." Looking slightly more driven, Jason grabbed hold of a pair of black knit gloves and headed out the door.

Chuckling to herself, Sadie got out the bacon and eggs and turned on the oven. She was making a quiche for the lunch but waffles for breakfast. Several days ago, Atle had given her a converted waffle iron that ran on batteries. She doubted she would use the contraption very much. Atle had warned her that the thing used a lot of battery power, but she was very much looking forward to seeing Jason's expression when she served him real waffles at long last.

After placing a pan of bacon in the oven to cook, she began cracking eggs and beating them in a bowl for the quiche. Just as she added a cup of cream to the eggs, her next child appeared. "Happy Christmas Eve, Cale."

He smiled. "*Danke*."

"Ready for *kaffi*?"

"Not yet. I need to go tend to Bonnie and Gwen."

"There's no need. Jason's out there."

"Is Viola helping him?"

"*Nee*, but your little brother can clean a stall and tend to the animals. He'll do fine."

Cale still looked doubtful. "It's going to take him all morning."

"It's good he's already out in the barn, then." Bringing over a cup of coffee, she murmured, "Have a seat, Son. We need to let Jason tend to them."

"I hope he remembers to check the straw for mice."

"I reckon if he doesn't, he'll remember the next time."

Holding the cup of coffee between his hands, her oldest stared at her. "You're sure being calm about Jason and his lazy ways."

"You reminded me the other day that it's time he did more around the house. I've realized you were right."

"Okay, but I'm still going to go out there later to make sure he did everything right."

"I would expect no less." She took the pan of bacon out of the oven and placed the strips on paper towels, then got out the lard to make a piecrust. "Are you excited about exchanging gifts with Hope today?"

"*Jah*. The box I made for her isn't perfect, but Atle said it turned out well."

"Did you think of anything to put in it?"

"*Jah*, but it's kind of a secret, though. I mean, it's between Hope and me."

"That's how it should be, I think."

"*Jah*, I thought the same thing."

When the door flew open, both she and Cale stared at a frightened-looking Jason.

"There was a mouse in the straw, and Gwen freaked out and kicked one of the slats in their stall! Then Bonnie looked upset, too."

Cale got to his feet. "Turn back around and keep them company. I'll go out and help you in a sec."

"*Danke*, Cale," Jason said as he hurried out the door.

Just as he pulled on his coat, Cale glanced Sadie's way again. "Mamm, you're right about Jason needing to learn . . . but maybe just a little bit at a time."

Sadie laughed as the door closed. From the looks of things, it seemed as if the day was going to be mighty busy, indeed.

"What's so funny?" Viola asked as she appeared in the kitchen already showered, dressed, and bright eyed.

"Your little brother. Come have some coffee, and I'll fill you in on his antics, dear."

"Okay. Oh, Mamm, guess what? It's Christmas Eve!"

After giving Viola a hug, she said, "It is indeed. I think it's going to be a wonderful day, too. After breakfast, you may help me set the table for the Overholts."

"Okay, and then don't forget I'm going to see my girlfriends later."

"I haven't forgotten."

Reaching for a mug, Viola smiled. "I can't wait for Cale to see Hope's quilt."

Remembering how much fun Viola had at the impromptu quilting bee, Sadie said, "Did the quilt turn out well?"

"As well as it could," she said.

Sadie thought that sounded cryptic, indeed.

thirty-eight

When the doorbell rang, Jane opened it curiously.

"A delivery for you, ma'am," the courier said.

Taking the crystal vase filled with two dozen red roses from him, she plucked out the card and read, *I'm so sorry, Jane. Please forgive me. —Carson*

"Don't forget this, miss," the courier added.

"Thank you," she said as she took a tin of home-made cookies inside. They were likely as inedible as his brownies, but she wouldn't tell him that. After all, not every woman had a millionaire suitor who also attempted to bake his way into her heart.

—*Finding Love's Fortune*, page 460

Hope, Anna, and their parents had arrived at one o'clock. Though they all asked if they could see his new room in the barn, Cale had told them it wasn't possible. He'd promised his mother and Atle he would abide by their wishes to not see the finished project until late Christmas Eve, and he was sticking to that promise. He hadn't even peeked when he was helping Jason in the barn that morning.

Though Mr. and Mrs. Overholt had nodded like they understood, Hope looked a little worried. She'd seemed quiet when they'd shared a meal, too, but Cale hoped that had been more to do with the fact that so many other people had been talking than because she was upset about anything.

It truly had been a rather boisterous meal, what with Jason sharing the story about the mouse.

Mr. and Mrs. Overholt had laughed and laughed about Jason's attempts to capture the pesky rodent. Mr. Overholt had even smiled at Cale when he'd said Jason's antics reminded him a bit of Cale's first days working on their farm. "Remember when Prudence used to ignore everything you did, Cale?"

"She still does," he said. "I don't know why that sheep never liked me."

"Charity and I think it's because she was jealous of your relationship with Hope," Mr. Overholt said.

"What?"

"I'm afraid it's true," Mrs. Overholt said. "She actually seems to be happier now."

Hope giggled. "Daed also got a new ram who is mighty handsome. Prudence now follows him around like a lost puppy."

"I almost wish I could see that," Cale joked.

When the meal was over and everyone was sipping their last cups of coffee, Cale's mother shared a look with Mrs. Overholt before turning to him. "Cale, why don't you take Hope into the living room by the fire and exchange your gifts? We'll stay here in the kitchen to give you some privacy."

"*Danke*, Mamm." He shared a smile with Hope. "Ready?"

She nodded. "I put your present by my cloak. I'll meet you there."

After running up to his room to get his own gift, which had been wrapped with Viola's help, Cale met Hope in the living room. She looked a little worried but had a smile for him.

"Here we are again," she teased. "You and me hoping for privacy while parents lurk in the kitchen."

"I was just thinking the same thing. Knit yourself some mittens or something, Hope. As soon as your parents allow it, I'm taking you outside for long walks. I don't care if it's ten degrees outside."

Smiling softly, she said, "I'll do that."

"Are you ready to exchange gifts?"

She nodded. "I am."

They'd just sat down on the couch when his mother popped her head in. "We're not doing anything, Mamm!" he called out.

"Oh, hush. I only wanted to tell you that I decided to take everyone out to the barn to see your new room."

He jerked his head to face her. "Are you serious?"

"Oh, *jah*. Charity and Jeremiah were interested in seeing Atle's and your handiwork. So when Anna suggested that we all go out there, I thought it was a *gut* idea. We'll be back soon, though," she warned.

"I understand."

He smiled at Hope as they heard everyone don coats and walk out the door. "I think, if we're lucky, we might get ten whole minutes of privacy."

She grinned at him. "That's ten more minutes than I thought we'd get." Taking a deep breath, she placed her present on his lap. "Here. I want to go first."

It was a big rectangular box with Santa Claus wrapping paper. "Santa Claus paper?"

"It's a joke in our house. I'll tell you about it another day. Open it up," she said impatiently.

He tore open the paper, then carefully opened the box, reminding himself to act surprised about her gift. But, when he pulled out the quilt, he didn't have to pretend anything at all. "Hope, this is beautiful."

"*Nee*, it's not. There's lots of mistakes, but I thought it could go on your new bed. I mean, if you want it to go there."

"I do." He ran a hand along one of the squares. "I can't believe you made this!"

"Well, I had a little bit of help at the end. We actually had a small quilting bee at the house a couple of days ago."

"I remember Viola said she was going to a bee, but she didn't say where she was going."

"I'm glad about that! I was so afraid she was going to let the cat out of the bag."

He unfolded another section, then looked at the back to see the pattern of the stitches. "Wait a minute . . . Are those hearts?"

Blushing, she nodded. "*Jah.* Anna traced the pattern on the back of the quilt. But, um, don't worry. No one will know that you have hearts stitched on the quilt when they first see it."

Cale had never wanted to have anything heart-shaped in his room—but that was before his girlfriend had put them there. "I love it," he said honestly.

Pure relief filled her expression. "Truly? I wasn't sure what to get you, but—"

Before he could stop himself, he pressed two fingers to her mouth to stop her from fretting anymore. Unfortunately, his fingertips tarried too long there. It was as if every one of his senses was cataloging how soft her lips felt. Embarrassed, he pulled his hand away. "Sorry. I just didn't want you to worry anymore."

Something new flickered in her eyes. "So you decided to cover my mouth with your fingers?"

"Well, it was either that or kiss you," he joked.

"Maybe I would have rather had a kiss."

He was a lot of things, but he'd never had a problem putting two and two together. "Are you sure?" he asked as he reached for her hand.

"I'm sure. I mean, I'm sure, if you would like to kiss me . . ."

He leaned forward, touched his free hand to her jaw, and carefully pressed his lips against hers. Hoping he was doing it right, he lifted his head, scanned her expression, and then kissed her again. This time, Hope leaned in slightly.

When they broke apart, he smiled at her. "At last, huh?"

Covering her mouth with a hand, she giggled. "At last, I've had my first kiss."

"It was mine, too," he confided. After they shared a smile, he thrust his present into her hands. "Here. We better hurry before everyone gets back."

Hope smiled at him as she untied the red bow that Viola had tied for him and then carefully peeled off the paper. "Oh, Cale!"

"It's a memory box. I made it."

Her eyes widened as she ran a hand over the smooth wood. "I didn't know you could make things like this."

"I didn't know, either, but Atle taught me." Excited now, he motioned to the lid. "Open it up. There's something inside it."

After she set the lid on the couch, she looked at the slip of paper folded inside. "What's this?"

"You have to open it to find out."

He watched as Hope slowly began to unfold the tiny square of paper, and his insides warmed the moment she realized what it was.

"You kept this all this time?"

"I had to. You wrote it to me." It was a note she'd written to him back when they were only ten or eleven. She'd handed it to him the day he'd shown up at school with a bunch of bruises on his arm from where his father had grabbed him for not sweeping the floor of the barn better. That sweet note from Hope had meant everything to him.

She smoothed the note on her lap. "'I will always like you, no matter what,'" she read.

Cale tensed, suddenly realizing that she might not even have remembered writing that note. He hoped she wouldn't joke about it.

"Hmm," she said as she folded the note back into a small square again. "I guess I was smarter back then than I realized."

"Does that mean you still like me?" he teased.

"Of course, Cale Mast. We might have gotten older, but some things never change. I will always like you, no matter what."

Just as he was contemplating practicing another kiss, the door flew open, and their families strode in.

"Did you like each other's gifts?" Mrs. Overholt asked.

"Oh, *jah*," Hope replied. "Cale made me a box out of maple, and it is absolutely perfect. One of the best gifts I've ever received in my life."

Cale held up his quilt. "Look what Hope gave me, Mamm. It's a quilt she made me for my new room."

After inspecting it carefully, his mother said, "It's a lovely quilt, Hope."

"*Danke*, Mrs. Mast," Hope said as everyone surrounded them and began talking at once.

Cale didn't get a chance to speak to Hope privately again until he helped her put on her cloak. "I loved my quilt, but it wasn't my favorite gift from you," he whispered.

"I love my wooden memory box, but it wasn't my favorite gift, either," she replied with a smile.

After they left, Cale couldn't help but think that maybe Viola had gotten everything wrong. Maybe he hadn't needed to run around and make something special for Hope. All he'd needed was one single kiss.

thirty-nine

Unable to stay away a moment longer, Jane tore out of her apartment and headed to Carson's mansion on the other side of town. She didn't care if it wasn't appropriate for her to visit him. She didn't care about anything but seeing Carson face-to-face.

—*Finding Love's Fortune*, page 468

Sadie had almost fallen asleep late that night when she heard a door open and close. When the sound of footsteps heading downstairs followed, she pulled on her robe and slippers and went to investigate. After all, it wasn't a secret who it was. Jason hadn't been himself from the moment Cale had told them good night and went to spend the night in his brand-new room.

Sadie was halfway down the stairs when she heard the front door rattle. "Jason, please wait!" she called out softly.

"It's not Jason. It's me," Viola said.

Her daughter was also wearing slippers and a robe. However, she was holding a thick quilt. "What are you doing up, Vi?"

Looking guilty, her daughter worked her bottom lip. "Nothing?"

Sadie folded her arms over her chest. "Please try that again."

"Fine. I'm going out to see Cale."

"Child, don't you think it's a little late to chat with him? It's after eleven."

"I know." Viola continued to stare at her like she was doing her best to be patient with her mother's pesky questions.

Maybe it was time she went at this from another direction. "Dear, does Cale know you're going out there to see him?"

She shrugged. "Probably. Jason's already there."

"He is?" Sudden visions of her youngest getting lost in the dark between the house and the barn flooded her. "Is something wrong? What happened? Why didn't you come get me?"

"Probably because we didn't need anything from you?" When Sadie was about to ask another set of questions, Viola said, "Mamm, settle down. Nothing's the matter. It's just strange with Cale being outside, you know?"

Finally it all clicked. "Oh. *Jah*, I imagine it is." She opened the door. "May I join you all? Or is this get-together only for *kinner*?"

Viola smiled in the dim light. "You may come, too, Mamm."

Pulling on her cloak, Sadie threw it over her shoulders and stepped out into the dark night with her daughter. Only a few stars were visible, due to the expected snow on Christmas Day. However, it still felt like Christmas Eve. Maybe it was simply the anticipation of the morning or the fact that Christmas was just mere minutes from arriving.

"I guess we should've brought a flashlight with us," Viola whispered. "It's really dark out."

"I was thinking the same thing. It's a shame all the stars aren't out tonight. I always like to look at the stars on Christmas Eve and think of the wise men."

"I don't think the three wise men needed the stars out, Mamm. I bet the angels kept guiding them to baby Jesus."

It was a lovely, whimsical image for sure. "I never thought about those angels leading the kings through the desert, but I guess they could've done that."

"I think so," Viola said. "I mean, all these years later, we still search for Jesus even without the stars to help."

Viola was absolutely right. Prayer, faith, and a hope in a better future had certainly guided her through many a journey.

When they opened the barn door, Bonnie whickered, and Gwen bleated a hello.

"Who's there?" Cale called out from the other side of his closed door.

"Who do you think?" Viola asked. "It's me. And Mamm, too."

"Mamm's here?" Pure alarm was in Cale's tone.

"I am," Sadie said. "It's dark in the barn. May we come in?"

The door opened, and Jason poked his head out. "Hiya," he said.

"Hello to you, too." Sadie felt like rolling her eyes. Only her youngest could act so blasé about sneaking out of the house without permission in the middle of the night.

Cale's new bedroom looked much like it had just a few hours earlier, except that it now looked like her son actually lived there. As always, his clothes from the day before were tossed on a chair, the digital alarm clock in the shape of a horse was on his bedside table, and an assortment of nails, screws, paper, and change were in a haphazard pile on his desk. Those little things brought Sadie a sense of satisfaction. Some things might change, but others seemed destined to stay the same.

When she turned her attention back to the children, she realized they were all staring at her with varying degrees of apprehension. "What is going on?" she asked.

Cale, the only one of them not wearing pajamas—he was in an old pair of sweatpants and a gray T-shirt—turned to his little brother. "Do you want to tell Mamm or should I?"

"I'll do it," Jason said. Sitting back down on the side of Cale's bed, he added, "Mamm, Cale being out here didn't feel right."

"I know it's strange, but you'll get used to it."

Jason sighed. "I know. But I didn't want to get used to it tonight."

"Did you know he was going to come out here, Cale?"

"Kind of. He was acting worried all day."

Jason lifted his chin. "I *wasna* being a baby, though."

"Of course not." Looking at Viola, who was now sitting on the other edge of Cale's bed, Sadie raised her eyebrows. "And you, dear?"

"I didn't want to be upstairs without both of them. At least not tonight."

"I see."

Her children exchanged guilty looks. "I'll walk them back, Mamm," Cale said. "I promise, we'll all get used to me being out here real soon."

There was such a resigned tone to his voice, she was caught up short. That had been their lot in life. Whether it was Marcus's fits of temper or Sadie starting to work or even her courtship with Atle, she'd asked her children to adjust and make do. And they did, usually without complaint.

Never had she imagined that Cale moving out to the barn would be yet one more thing for them to have to get used to. What had she done?

After pushing his clothes to one side, she sat down on Cale's chair. "Years ago, when you all were younger and your father was having more bad days than good, I used to sometimes dream about what I wanted for the future." She shrugged. "Now, looking back on those days, I realize I was being mighty selfish. I had three children I was proud of and a roof over my head and food on the table. All were things to be thankful for."

"Mamm, you don't have to talk about this," Cale said.

"*Nee*, I think I do." She cleared her throat. "What I'm trying to say is that I was so grateful for you all and I was glad to not be hungry, but I wasn't especially happy every day. Living with your father was not easy. One Christmas Eve, I looked up into the sky, saw the bright stars, and made a promise to myself that one day I would find happiness and do my best to make each of you happy, too." She drew a deep breath. "I think this is what I had in mind when I asked Atle to build you a room, Cale. I told myself it was a gift for you. That you were older and needed some privacy. But maybe I wasn't taking into account what you wanted. I should've asked you if you wanted to come out here or keep sharing a room with Jason."

"I like the room," Cale said quickly. "It is nice."

"It should be, since you helped build it." She smiled at him. "What I'm trying to say is that I should've talked to you about this room a lot more. I should have asked all of you if you were ready for more changes."

"Are you talking about Atle, too?" Cale asked.

"I suppose I am. I guess I'm thinking about a lot of things that are different than how they used to be."

To her surprise, Viola broke the silence. "Mamm, I remember a talk we had a couple of years ago. I was complaining about my body and how all my other girlfriends were getting taller and curvier, but I still looked like a twig."

Sadie smiled. "I remember that talk, too. You were mighty upset."

"Well, you told me that life was filled with changes. Some of them were asked for, and others were not. You reminded me that I can't control everything and that sometimes the best things happen unexpectedly. Do you remember telling me that?"

"I remember parts of that conversation." She remembered telling Viola to calm down . . . but not the lecture about unexpected gifts. "What made you think of that?"

"Because I think Atle is your unexpected gift, Mamm. And to tell you the truth, I think he might be an unexpected gift for all of us as well. We like him."

Jason nodded. "We like him a lot, and if you two get married one day, then we'll have Atle, too. And you'll be happy."

"What we're trying to tell you is that it's all going to be okay, Mamm," Cale said. "We are all going to be okay."

"I mean, if the wise men can travel all kinds of distances to find baby Jesus, we should be able to find our way through life, too. Don't you think?" Viola asked.

A lump filled Sadie's throat as she nodded. Gathering herself together, she looked at her three children. "So, um, what did you all plan to do at this slumber party?"

"Nothing. Just be together," Cale said.

Making a sudden decision, she got to her feet. "In that case, I'm going to leave you to it."

Viola got to her feet. "You don't have to leave, Mamm."

"*Nee*, I think I do. Good night, children."

Cale stood up and hugged her tight. "Merry Christmas."

She chuckled. "Ah, so it is. Merry Christmas! Now, don't stay up all night."

Jason and Viola rushed to her for hugs. "Merry Christmas!"

After pulling her cloak on, she smiled at her children and walked out the door before quietly making her way past Bonnie's stall. Both Gwen and Bonnie seemed fast asleep, or maybe it was rather that they didn't feel compelled to acknowledge her.

When she walked out into the dark night, Sadie pulled her cloak more securely around her. It would be the first night in her life that she was going to sleep by herself in a house.

"It's a shame there's no stars out," she murmured, looking up to the sky again.

But there was her surprise. A small portion of the clouds had parted, revealing a tiny patch of clear sky. The stars that shone down were enough to guide her way back to the house.

She realized then the truth of Viola's words. The wise men really hadn't needed much to guide them to Jesus, just a will, a hope, and a desire to listen to a beckoning angel.

If they could do all that, then she could be guided, too. Taking a fortifying breath, she allowed herself to be led along His chosen path.

forty

When Carson opened the door, he was balancing on crutches. He looked pale and haggard but just as handsome as he had been the first time Jane had seen him.

"You came," he said.

"I couldn't stay away," Jane said as she threw her arms around him. "It's almost Christmas. I couldn't celebrate it without you."

"Good," he said simply as he led her inside.

Jane smiled as she closed the door behind them.

—*Finding Love's Fortune*, page 480

The house was quiet. Christmas Day was almost over, and it had been a beautiful day. Atle had arrived soon after Sadie and the children had eaten breakfast. Then, after he had the honor of reading the story of Jesus's birth from the Book of Luke, he'd joined them in front of the fire to exchange gifts.

To the children's surprise, he'd brought each of them presents. Jason had received a puzzle, Viola a wrapped package of some of her favorite fabrics, and Cale a red metal box with several tools in it.

In return, Jason, Cale, and Viola had presented Atle with his present from them—a handmade calendar.

"It's because we're planning on spending all of next year with you, Atle," Jason said.

"I can't imagine a better gift," Atle replied. Then, with a small smile on his lips, he handed Sadie her gift. It was a gorgeous wooden box.

"Atle, this is like Cale's gift to Hope."

He smiled at Cale. "Well, we did make them together."

"Atle's is a whole lot fancier, though," Cale said. "Mamm, look at how the edges are beveled and he carved your initials in the top corner."

Holding the box up, Sadie admired the handiwork, as well as the six flowers that had been carved into the wood. "This is a work of art!" she exclaimed. "It's truly beautiful, Atle."

"What's inside?" Viola asked. "Did you put something in there for Mamm?"

"*Nee.* I thought perhaps your mother might like to start filling it up with some of her new favorite memories."

Knowing that she would carefully place a piece of the wrapping paper in the box that evening, Sadie smiled at Atle. "I'll enjoy that, Atle. *Danke*."

"It's your turn, Mamm," Viola prodded.

"*Jah*, it seems it is." Feeling shy, she stood up. "I got you something, too, Atle."

Atle looked surprised. "You didn't have to do that."

"I think I did. I heard it on good authority that courting couples give each other Christmas presents." She sat down next to him holding two wrapped presents on her lap. Suddenly, her good idea didn't seem all that good anymore. Maybe it was too silly. Or, Heaven forbid, maybe Atle would take it the wrong way.

He grinned at Cale before smiling at her. "I've heard that same thing."

"There are two presents. One is the 'real' one, and the other is more for fun." That was a lie, though. She'd been excited about both of the presents for him. Both meant something to her. The only problem was that she wasn't sure if they would mean the same things to Atle.

"Does it matter which I open first?"

She thought about it, then picked the one she thought might be best received and placed it in his hands. "This one."

"It's a big package."

Cale chuckled. "Just wait until you see inside, Atle."

He ripped off the paper, uncovered the cardboard box, examined it a bit, and then pulled the taped flaps open.

She could tell the exact second he realized what she'd put inside. His eyes widened, then filled with mirth. "Sadie, you got me a cookie jar?" he asked as he pulled out a bright red ceramic barn.

"I did." She smiled. "But I made sure not to get you an animal jar, since you don't like pulling off the head to get treats."

He looked embarrassed but also pleased. "It ain't natural," he said as Jason, Viola, and Cale laughed.

"It's a cookie jar, Atle," Viola teased. "You aren't supposed to think about taking the cow's head off."

"Well, for the record, I'm mighty pleased about the barn." His voice warmed. "*Danke*, Sadie. I like my gift very much."

Jason started giggling. "Atle, look inside!"

Seemingly delighted, he opened up the lid and grinned. "Sadie, you made me monster cookies."

"We all made them for you," Viola said.

Sadie smiled. "We agreed that we *canna* think of a single person who loves those cookies as much as you do."

"They are the perfect cookie."

"You say that every time you eat one," Cale teased.

"I imagine I'll keep doing that, too. Your *mamm* is a mighty fine baker."

"Now can he open the other gift?" Jason asked.

Sadie was tempted to ask her pesky children to go away and give them some privacy, but as she saw their shining eyes—and Atle's joy of being part of a family—she knew they all needed this time together. This special Christmas together.

"Here you go," she said lightly. "It's, um, I thought you might appreciate the thought behind it."

A line formed between his brows as he took the package and pulled off the wrapping. He stared at the book in shock. "Sadie, you got me the book?"

She grinned. "Sarah Anne helped me find a copy from a used bookstore."

Viola read the title. "*Finding Love's Fortune*?" She frowned. "What does that have to do with anything?"

"More than I ever imagined," Atle said. "*Danke*, Sadie. It's a perfect present." With care, he set the book on the coffee table before speaking again. "I have to admit this has been the nicest Christmas I can remember," he said.

"Me, too," Sadie said as she reached for his hands and squeezed tight. "Maybe even my favorite one so far."

acknowledgments

The writing of every book takes on a life of its own. A *Christmas Courtship* was the book I was most excited to write in the Berlin Bookmobile series—and it was also the most difficult for me to complete. I had grand plans for this book: two romances, a tight Christmas season timeline, and a made-up novel to inspire the characters. All of this sounded pretty good in my mind but created a lot of headaches when attempting to put it all together on the page.

First and foremost, I am grateful to my editor, Sara Quaranta, for her enthusiasm for the story, her sharp eye for detail, and her ability to organize timelines. She's been a kind and wonderful editor to work with, and I've been blessed for the experience. I'm also so grateful for Christine Masters and Lara Robbins for their edits and suggestions during the copyediting stage. The whole team at Gallery and Simon & Schuster championed this series, and I'm so thankful for the many ways that Anne Jaconette, Sydney Morris, and Lucy Nalen marketed and promoted the whole series. They also happen to be a very kind and thoughtful group of ladies. I felt very blessed to work with them.

I am also indebted to Cathy Cermele, who selected street teams, encouraged readers to review the books, and encouraged me in countless ways. Thank you, Cathy, for leading the Buggy Bunch!

Finally, I need to give a shout-out to my husband, Tom. This novel was the last book I had to write in 2020, and by the time I was facing the looming deadline, I was one very tired author! Tom encouraged me, took care of a hundred things so I didn't have to, and even persuaded me to get out of my office, stop stressing about Atle (lol, I really worried about Atle), and go for a walk. He's the reason I was still smiling on December 1.

reader questions

1. Christmas stories are probably my favorite types of books to write. I love incorporating Christmas traditions that have a message of faith. What are some of your favorite Christmas traditions?

2. I had a great time imagining the gifts each couple would give to each other. Do you ever make gifts for people you love? What are some gifts you have made in the past?

3. Atle's study of *Finding Love's Fortune* was a salute to the number of letters I've received from men who picked up one of my Westerns and ended up enjoying the romantic story line as well—much to their surprise! Can you think of a book you've read that you unexpectedly enjoyed more than you thought you would?

4. Trust and faith are central themes in this novel. Many characters had to overcome painful memories in their pasts in order to find happiness. Do you think it's possible for a person to ever completely put aside a traumatic experience and move forward?

5. The building of Cale's bedroom symbolized the characters' growth throughout the novel. What do you think will happen to that space as Cale grows older?

6. "Fear not: for, behold, I bring you good tidings of great joy" is a favorite scripture verse of mine. Do you have a favorite Christmas verse?

7. I found the following Amish saying to fit the story well. What does it mean to you? "The smallest deed is better than the greatest intention."

8. What are you looking forward to most this Christmas?